A HOUSE TO KILL FOR

Books by the Same Author

Trilogy
Mistaken Obsession
White Roses for My Love
Mistaken Angel

The Passport Mystery: Introducing Gray and Armstrong Private Investigations
Files of the Missing (book 2 of the Gray and Armstrong series)
Innocent (book 3 of the Gray and Armstrong series)
Jeopardy (book 4 of the Gray and Armstrong series)

A HOUSE TO KILL FOR

Book 5—Gray and Armstrong Private Investigations

Eve Grafton

Library of Congress Control Number: 2019915935
ISBN: Hardcover 978-1-7960-0624-7
Softcover 978-1-7960-0623-0
eBook 978-1-7960-0622-3

Print information available on the last page.

Rev. date: 10/11/2019

To order additional copies of this book, contact:
Xlibris
1-800-455-039
www.Xlibris.com.au
Orders@Xlibris.com.au
800278

The fifth book in the series of Gray and Armstrong Private Investigations, with Alicia and her grandmother and staff Ken and Kate

CHAPTER ONE

When the bookshop and house were burnt down, it sent the investigation team into depression, but as the Christmas period was fast approaching, Alicia took charge and booked the flight to visit Australia for a month holiday, organising James's parents also to meet them there. James's sister and her husband would welcome them all, and it should help lighten James's mood to have all his family around him for the first time in some years.

Percy was going to Australia also, hoping to catch up with his son, Simon, whom he had not seen in four years. Simon had left home all those years ago and had been travelling the world looking for excitement. He seemed to have stayed in Australia longer than anywhere else, but then it was a big country.

Granny asked to be excluded from their journeying, blaming insurance inspections and forms to fill out, and the council had plans for the area where her bookshop and house had been for over a century. She did not want to miss a beat if decisions were made, and a month seemed too long to leave it behind, floundering.

The only request she made was they give her leave to move out of the lovely apartment that Derek Choudhury had loaned them, and she asked if she could stay in the office for the period the others were away. As she could no longer drive a car, because of her right arm being partially incapacitated—she could not turn the wheel when driving—she wanted to be in an area where she could catch a coach to visit her good friend Rob Gooding, whose health was failing, and also be at hand when there were forms to fill in.

The office was so centrally situated next to a shopping mall and had a small area with a bed and a bathroom. They were small, but so was she, she explained. The kitchen area was adequate for one person, and she would have access to the computer and phones and act as a guard while the office was officially closed. She would not feel cut off from civilisation, as she would alone in the large apartment, away from the town and unable to drive. There was no complication with having too many clothes or belongings; they all disappeared in the fires of the house and bookshop, so she would manage the smaller spaces.

At the Monday staff meeting, after some consideration, this was all agreed. Alicia was at first uncertain that her grandmother could cope alone, then her Granny said, 'I was alone for many years, Alicia, while you were working on the airlines. I am sure I can manage for a month.'

Kate and Ken would be going to the Isle of Wight for a month with Kate's children, so they would be unavailable if Granny needed help. James came up with the name of Aaron Dunstan to help Granny if she needed it. Alicia immediately brightened. 'Oh good, he owes us big time. I will ring him now and put it to him.'

She rang his number and was answered immediately, and when asked to keep an eye on Granny, Aaron remarked, 'Nothing would give me more pleasure. After what your granny did for us, looking after Jody whilst Sandra was in hospital, we will watch over her like hawks.'

Granny laughed and exclaimed, 'I am a bit older than Jody and do not need much supervision, although I would welcome a call now and then to say hello. Thank you, Aaron.'

So it was decided. Granny could visit with Aaron and Sandra and their little girl, Jody, for Christmas lunch, and she could fill the rest of her time wandering the shops when she wanted to be amongst other people. For something to do, she needed a new wardrobe of clothes, to replace those burnt up in the fire of her house. None of this needed for her to catch a bus or drive a car. To visit Rob Gooding in his nursing home in Winchester, the coach station was an easy walk from the office, so Alicia was satisfied that Granny would manage for a month.

The team were waiting for a call from Divit Edwards in Africa; they had not heard from the party that Derek had collected to go to Africa with Divit to help him out, although they had been gone for two weeks already. James kept saying to himself, 'No news is good news.' He could not help himself from worrying that all was going well with the young man. The group consisted of Derek and another financial whiz who had lived in Africa most of his life, as had also the others chosen, a lawyer and an assistant and two bodyguards, that they had asked the London police force to assist with.

All except Derek spoke Shona, the native language to assist if any incidences of a racial matter came up. Each member of the group was well versed in the local conditions and customs.

At last a call came from Derek saying all was well. Divit had asked the government that he be allowed to take the name Douglas Oliveri, his grandfather's name, as he felt it was held in high esteem in various African countries, and the change would facilitate in any agreements that came up in the future. This was being organised by the lawyer. The accountants had been busy going over financial matters, and all seemed in order. The economy was slowly gaining from the terrible slump in the past few years. Now they only needed the changeover of the signatory from Jason Bowering to Divit's name to go through, which included banking procedures. They were making enquiries into changing the British banking held in the UK to be changed over to Divit's name also, as the locals had news that Jason Bowering had died while visiting in the UK.

The biggest news of all was that the will made by Douglas Oliveri stated that he left all his businesses and goods including several houses to his grandsons, Jason and Edward. Divit and Derek agreed that this was why Jason Senior needed to kill the boys in order to gain full control. Jason Bowering had been acting as his stepsons' guardian, but it was obviously not enough to satisfy his greed. As Edward had died, everything should go to Jason (now Divit as we know him), so matters were simplified at the bank with the news of Jason Senior's death and had only to be released to Divit for the changeover to take place.

The team were ecstatic with this news; they had been on tenterhooks since Derek and Divit and the group flew out of the country, wondering how things were being managed and whether Divit would be well-received. It seemed there were still a number of respected people who remembered that Douglas Oliveri had been a valued member of their community and country, and they accepted his grandson to take his place.

James felt settled now; he had worried about the group and whether Jason Bowering had hurt the name of Douglas Oliveri in his project of taking over the wealthy man's life work. He could go to Australia now to meet up with his family and relax.

The burning of the bookshop and house that had belonged to Granny had really set James back. He felt it was his fault for inviting Divit to move in to their apartment with them, to keep him safe. Yes, he had been kept safe, but no one had envisaged having the SUV ramming the doors of the bookshop and exploding, killing the occupants of the vehicle and leaving a furnace behind them.

There was one good luck story to come out of this. One of the firemen had rescued the paintings from the walls of the living room of the house before the walls collapsed. They were paintings done by Alicia's mother before she died. Alicia treasured the paintings, especially the one of herself as a four-year-old sitting in a wicker chair in a garden of flowers. She loved that painting and cried when the firemen presented it to her several days after the fire.

They all had to go shopping for clothes and necessary items before they had enough to pack their suitcases. Percy remarked, 'I wore some of my clothes for twenty years, so I got the wear out of them, and they never really went out of fashion. Men are lucky like that, but it was time for a makeover, and I will let James help me choose the new wardrobe. We are lucky the summer sales had not finished yet. We will get quite a few bargains.'

It would be summertime in Australia, and they were all pleased to leave the cold for a month and looked forward to sunshine and surf. They were ready to close the office for business and put a sign on the door, announcing, 'This office is closed for a month, and the staff will all be back in February. Leave a message on the phone, and an answer will follow up when the office is ready for business again.'

They cleaned the Choudhury apartment that Derek had loaned them, thanking Mr Choudhury when they returned the keys and before going to the airport, where they would leave the car in a long-term car park. They dropped Granny off at the office, which was to be her home until something else came up. They would worry about where they were all going to live when they arrived back. The idea was to clear their minds and have a holiday.

CHAPTER TWO

Granny waited until the car was out of sight before entering the office again. She had waited for this moment. It had been in her mind since glancing at the photo album found at Bowering House, which James had brought back and pushed into a drawer after glancing through it. She had been in the office that day and also had glanced at the album, and what she saw in it, nobody else noticed. They had all been too busy with the case when she saw it. She wanted to confirm what she had seen, perhaps because it had been a momentary glance that it was not who she thought she had recognised.

Five minutes later, she found the album and sat down at the boardroom table with it in front of her, holding a magnifying glass she had seen James using in the past, hesitating to open the album. She had been shocked when she had seen it previously, but she hid her concern from the others, who were too busy to notice her reaction anyway at the time.

Finding the page where a group were gathered for a wedding photo, she found the couple she was looking for. Standing at the side of the group was a young couple. The woman looked like she was family, a sister of the groom. The young man standing with her had dark hair, and he stood out in the group of fair-haired people. It was difficult in the black-and-white photograph to make out eye colouring.

Granny looked at the photo for a long time, but she could not escape it; this couple were her grandparents. She was related to the Haskells.

What a revelation she had found! She was a member of this family. The photograph was dated June 1914. She remembered her mother was born in March of 1914. It was the year World War I started, so it made it easy to remember. She was probably upstairs in the nursery at the time this photo had been taken.

Her own parents had met before World War II and had a daughter in 1942, the consequence of a leave her father had taken before going back to be killed soon after. She, Valerie, had grown up not knowing much of her family history. Her mother was always too busy looking after her and going to work to have time for history chats, and somehow, it never came up.

Valerie went through the album from the front again, this time taking more note of individuals. They were a handsome family, not weaselly, as James had described Ian Haskell when he met him. They had the gentry look, proud and assured, so were not common folk.

The following pages showed how they had grown up. The girls looked a little like ballerinas; they were so slight and dainty. The boys also were slim and looked as if they would be at home in the schoolroom. She eventually got back to the group wedding photo and looked again at the bride. She also was small and dainty but had a wild look about her, as if she wanted to run away. Her hand was held by the slim Haskell bridegroom, looking dreamily at his bride.

The longer Valerie looked at the bride, the more she could see that the girl looked frightened more than anything. Was it because she was entering into a big family alone? Was she frightened of her groom? Or perhaps the whole deal even? There did not appear to be any of her own relatives present in the photo, or perhaps it was that single man standing at the back. He had darker hair, possibly red although it looked dark in the photo, but he also had freckles. That was not common in the group. She looked at the bride again and, under the veil and tiara she wore, could just discern wisps of the same hair, so he was her relative, perhaps a father, but more likely a brother.

It appeared as if she was a reluctant bride. It would not have been the first time that happened; many brides did not get a choice of groom in days gone by. The wedding photo was the last in the album, although there were many empty pages after it. Valerie wondered, *Why? What went wrong in the Haskell family?*

She went back to the drawer where the album had lain and pulled out a large envelope with single unmounted photos filling it. She spread the photos out over the boardroom table and started sorting them out. Children to one side, those with parents and children to another, and groups to another. There were no more pictures of her grandparents or her mother that she recognised. Something had happened in the family that stopped the orderly pasting of these family photographs. A picture of identical twin boys caught her eye; they had the slimness and the fairness of the family. Valerie looked at the back of the photo dated 1925. Perhaps these were the sons of the bride in the earlier group photo. She looked for other photos of the twins and put them in a pile so she could look closer at them as they grew.

The last photo of the twin boys was of them standing next to a small aircraft. She remembered the name as Tiger Moth. They had been a popular aeroplane in the early days of flying. The boys were decked out in goggles around their neck, flying helmets, warm-looking jackets, three-fourth pants, and long socks tucked into long black boots. She thought they looked very swish. She laughed at her own description; it was never used nowadays, but this sounded right for the two young men about to fly. There was no date on the photo, only a comment: 'Duncan and Adrian ready to fly off.' She gauged the boys were about eighteen or nineteen. They were still so young and looked like they were in fancy-dress clothes.

She thought about recent happenings and said to herself, 'They were using the aircraft to fly back and forth even way back then, before the Second World War.'

There were no other photographs of the twins after that particular one, which seemed strange to Valerie. When was the house abandoned? What happened to the twins? She turned to the other photos and thought she recognised one of the boys, about five or six, going off to school for the first time. She looked at the back of the photo, and it said, 'Clement, aged six, going to boarding school.' Stirrings of memory started; she knew this boy. *A bit older than myself, but I remember him. He was so kind to me because I had no father, and neither did he. Both our fathers were killed during the war. His father had been a pilot and was shot down over the Channel. Was his father one of the twins? My father had been killed also during the war. If I can remember that, why can't I remember more about him?*

Valerie suddenly felt very hungry and looked at her watch. She had been looking at the photos for hours and had no lunch, and now it was dinner time. She left the photos spread out, saying to herself, 'I will get back to these tomorrow. I will find a cafe somewhere in the mall to have a snack, and then I think bed will call to me.'

As she closed the album, a newspaper clipping fell out of the last pages. It was the local newspaper by the look of it, with a photograph of the bridal party, saying, 'The honourable Lady Margaret Forrester makes her home in this area, marrying local farmer Hugh Haskell. Lady Margaret, or Meg as she prefers to be called, is quoted as saying she prefers the green fields of Bowering House to the smoke and grime of Glasgow.'

'Ah, that is why there are so many Scottish names in the family. I was wondering about that.'

After having a snack in a coffee shop, the only eatery that seemed to be open at that time of night, Valerie returned to the office and went to bed; it was a daybed in case of anyone feeling unwell during the day. It was not uncomfortable, or perhaps she was very tired after a long day, and she slept well.

CHAPTER THREE

She woke up in the morning feeling fresh to start a new day on her own. She started up her tablet to look at her emails, and there was one from Alicia at Dubai airport, saying, 'We have had a comfortable trip so far. We slept all the way and should arrive feeling ready to go.'

Her mind turned to the photos on the boardroom table, and she once more sat down and went through them. This time she was able to recognise her grandmother as she was growing up. A petite young girl and woman, with long blonde curls over her shoulders and sometimes coiled on top of her head, which made her appear taller. There were no other faces that looked familiar to her, so her family did not visit each other after they left home. Was there a falling out? Strangely, there were no other wedding photos, of her grandparents, for instance. Had someone destroyed them all, or were they in another album? Her own mother was a direct descendant of the family, and yet Valerie had never heard of the name until James had brought it up in his investigations.

Thinking it over, she wondered if there were other newspaper reports of the family over the years. She would ask Aaron Dunstan how to go about finding them. Suddenly she remembered James saying the stepmother of Jason Bowering had abandoned her husband in a nursing home somewhere. Valerie knew most of the nursing homes around the city; she had visited many of them in search for her friend Rob Gooding's, placement. It was several years ago, but surely they would have stayed the same. A phone call around might find the man whose name was assuredly Haskell.

Convinced she was on to something, Valerie took up her tablet and entered *nursing homes* in the search area and instantly came up with a list. She mentally went over the list, and the decision to start at the top and work down was made quickly. There were so many of them, more than when she had looked for her friend Rob Gooding.

Asking for a patient named Mr Haskell was declined by many until she reached what she had thought of as residential care rather than a nursing home, and someone said, 'Yes, he is available. I will put you through.' Valerie was amazed at the easiness of it and said to herself, 'Now I feel like a detective.'

When the person on the phone said, 'Clement Haskell speaking', she punched the air as she had seen James do many times. 'My name is Valerie Newton, and I am looking for long-lost relatives. I was told you were in care, so I have taken the chance of contacting you. Would I be allowed to visit today or tomorrow or any other time that suits you?'

'By all means. I do not get many visitors nowadays. I will welcome a visit today. I find my voice goes croaky if I do not use it, so I can give the staff a rest from me.'

Valerie had a quick shower and got dressed and looked up the number of bus she was going to need to get to the residential care home. Luckily, the bus went from the next street over, so it was easy for her. She took the album with her in a shopping bag, pleased that although it was a cool day, it did not look like rain, so she was not handicapped by an umbrella and an overcoat.

She arrived at the destination she had asked the driver to point out to her. Walking into a beautiful reception area, where the receptionist pointed her to Mr Haskell's suite. She thought to herself, *Suite?*

Walking down the carpeted hallway, she could not help noting the difference between Rob Gooding's care home and this one. This was obviously for the well-to-do, not the average person. Coming to 5A, she knocked at the door, and Clement Haskell invited her in with a smile, saying, 'I remember you, a tiny little girl who looked after me so tenderly when I had nowhere else to go.'

'You are the same Clement I remembered!' she exclaimed. 'We have grown old, of course, but you are recognisable. My memory has not failed me.'

Clement Haskell smiled. She noticed the light-blue eyes, although the hair was now white. He said, 'I think it was the times, we all felt rather desperate. Your street had been bombed once, and my school had looked for places, preferably relatives, for their students to go if they could not go home, because the school was in the flight path of the planes flying over to drop their bombs on the shipping in the port. Your house had a huge, deep bomb shelter in the back garden, and I remembered the fear we felt when the planes went over the house. I only stayed a few months because I was given transport to go back to Bowering House at the end of the school year, and I never came back.'

Valerie shivered. 'I remember missing you terribly. I was so young, but I never had a brother, and you quickly had become that brother figure to me. I had a photograph of us together, and I kept it for years on my bedside table. I took it with me when we were evacuated. I suppose that is how I remember you. Shortly after you left, we were all sent inland somewhere to get away from the bombing, and that was lucky because a few weeks after we left, the whole street was gone. After the war, we had our houses rebuilt for us, and we moved back to where you had visited. How did you manage at Bowering House? Were you bombed?'

'No, we were well off the flight path of the night bombers, and we blacked the windows out, so we were in darkness from the air. By that time, the house had been taken over by the government as a hospital for those wounded in the war, to recover from their multiple wounds. Granny Meg and I had to move to the attic to make room for them, and we lived there for the duration of the war. It was not really a total attic. It had been used in the early days as servants' quarters. We used half of it, and the nurses were quartered in the other half. My grandmother taught me my school lessons, as we were too far from a school, and we had no petrol even if we could have gone.

'Things grew quite miserable at times. We felt as if we were rats locked up. Granny Meg was going downhill. The reason she had come to Bowering House many years before was that she was asthmatic and thrived in the fresh air of the farm and house. We went for walks, but she was growing old and ill and could no longer stride out like she used to, and the walks grew shorter and shorter.

'As the rest of the house was used by the army patients and staff, we were confined to the attic area, and it was gloomy in winter. Granny Meg's asthma came back, and I was worried. She looked very ill. I begged for the nurses to come and look at her, and some did and were very kind, offering inhalers for her breathing. But I think she was staying alive because of me. I had nowhere else to go and no one to claim as my own.'

'What happened next, Clem?' she asked.

'Near the end of the war, I was almost a teenager, and Granny Meg was dying. It was plain to see. She was too young to die, and I tried my best to see that she was comfortable and warm, but I think she had given up. The staff made room for her downstairs in what had been our work office when the farm was up and running, so she received tender care from the doctors and nurses, and I sat by her side for the few days she had left. One morning, she did not open her eyes. She had died through the night.

'The army team at the hospital were very sympathetic and, because nobody came to claim me and I had no place to go, decided for me what I should do next. They took me under their wing, and I became a shadow of the doctor as he did his rounds. I virtually became his assistant. He taught me so much. I was young and interested and soaked up the knowledge. There was no end of patients. Some would become able to go home, and we would receive more the same day, so the beds never grew cold. I became quite proficient in bandaging and taking temperatures and even diagnosing what was wrong.

'It was some time after the war had ended that the hospital wound down, and the patients gradually left us. It was suggested by the staff that I take up a medical career as a doctor. I was overwhelmed when one doctor promised to pay my fees at medical school, and I was sent off to study. With my patron's help, I graduated a full-fledged doctor.'

'What happened to Bowering House after the war, Clement?' she asked.

'By the time the army had finished with it, it had become very rundown. It was old-fashioned, and no one in the family wanted to move back to it. Being so far from the town, which we had always thought of as an advantage, had become a hassle. At the time, it was hard to get fuel. The farm had not been worked since my grandfather had died, and to be honest, it had become a dead-end place by then. Just a dilapidated house a long way from town.

It was sold for a very small sum, but even the new owners found it too hard and did not stay. It needed too much work on it to bring it up to the modern-day standards, and of course, by then it was no longer a farm. As it was a very large house, it would have been very expensive to renovate.'

'Have you been to see it since Jason purchased it, Clement?'

He looked hard at her and said, 'You know about that, Valerie?'

She looked hard back at him and said, 'Your wife and eldest son died burning my bookshop and house down. Did you know that, Clem?'

He looked at her with horror; several expressions passed over his face.

'It was your bookshop and house, Valerie? No, I did not know that. I was advised when the accident happened, but I did not realise it was your shop and home.'

'Accident, Clement? You are kidding yourself surely? That was no accident. You do not line up your large vehicle and charge at the door for an accident. Sure, they did not mean to kill themselves, but Jason was set on killing his stepson and perhaps my granddaughter and her husband as well, who were looking after Jason Junior, in the apartment above the bookshop. Just how much do you know about these things and about your son's doings?'

'Obviously not enough, because I did not know all that.' He was looking uncomfortable, so she changed the subject.

'Tell me about you family, Clem. Did you bring them up, or were you an absent father?'

Once again, he smiled at her. 'That is a good description of me, Valerie. I was away a lot. I chose a country practice as I felt awkward at being a doctor at first. I was still so young. Being a country doctor meant I spent a lot of time visiting people at farms away from the villages, because they were unable to travel when they were sick. Back in those days, the doctors went to see the patients rather than having big clinics in towns where the patients came to you. That changed gradually over time, but when bringing up a family, it meant you did not see much of them. Even

Sunday is not sacred for doctors when someone is ill. My wife was my nurse in my clinic, so she was also busy, and the children ran wild for a time.

'Jason was always a studious boy, and we did not have too many worries about him. The twins were a different matter. Ian was quite out of hand, answering back and going his own way, no matter what we asked of him. Fiona was his only friend, and they did a lot together. I think she kept him from going too wild. The day I caught him setting fire to the cat's tail, I walloped him, hoping to curtail his nasty tendencies, but I failed there.

'Fiona was not like him at all, although they were twins. She had a much gentler nature and liked to read, but Ian would not let her do her own thing generally. I do not know where his dangerous moods came from. They were not something I recognised in the rest of the family, although from what Granny Meg used to tell me, my father and his twin brother were both a little wild.'

'What about Faye? She appears to be several years younger than the others,' asked an interested Valerie.

'My wife died of breast cancer when the twins were about fifteen. I could not manage them alone and run my busy practice, so I remarried, another nurse, quite a few years younger than me, and Faye was born. I quickly tired of Barbara. She was a woman who was never satisfied and got on my nerves whenever she was around. She was not a companion as Jenny had been. Jenny and I had a good relationship, and I was completely devastated when she was told she had a terminal cancer.

'Barbara showed no discipline over the older children, by then in their teens, and so I left her. She took that badly and would never leave me in peace, always wanting money and more money. That is why I am holed up here in residential care. I have been here at least ten years, but it was the only thing I could do to get away from the woman. She was a silly woman and had a silly child, and

I paid and paid and paid to get them out of my hair, but they kept coming back for more.'

'How did she get mixed up with Jason to renovate Bowering House? Had she always been friendly with your son?'

'I suggested to Jason when he talked about buying back the old house, to get Barbara to help him renovate it. It was the one thing she was good at, especially when there was money to spend. She had style. I have to give her that. I think it was that I married her for until I realised day-to-day conversation was not her thing. Our marriage did not last long, but it was hard trying to convince her that I had given up. It was all too hard in the end, and so I came here in this residential care to get away from her.'

'Have you seen the house since it was renovated, Clem?'

'Yes, once. Jason came and picked me up and took me for a drive, and we ended up there. I was greatly surprised because I did not know how far they had got with the renovation. It looked just as it did when I grew up as a small child there. I have to admit I shed a few tears about it, because it was so lovely, and I could imagine Granny Meg wandering around there in her stately way.'

'What happened to all the money, Clem? I have an album of photographs here that shows the family was very well-off. What happened to cause the decline?'

'When Grandfather died, it was realised that they had been living on borrowed money for some time. Grandfather had become a gentleman farmer, more the gentleman than the farmer it seemed. The farm had deteriorated slowly for some time, and when it was analysed, it was realised that Grandfather had been sick for a very long time. He had been gassed in the trenches on the Somme, and he was demobbed after the war. But he never really got over the gassing, and his lungs were damaged. He was unable to keep up with things, and there had been nobody willing to take up the reins.

'The wars had caused a lack of staff, and Grandfather had been unable to do everything himself when he became too ill to keep the farm going. It began to run down drastically. I was very young when his final decline started when he heard that both of the twins had been killed overseas. Granny Meg sent me to boarding school early so as not to be under her feet, I suppose, while she nursed Grandfather until his death.

'Their only children, the twins Duncan and Adrian, were more interested in flying than farming. They spent a big part of their time in Paris, just a stone's throw over the Channel from us. My mother was a Frenchwoman I never saw. One day my father, Duncan, returned from France with me as a small baby in the passenger seat of the Tiger Moth for my grandmother Meg to bring up. My mother was a dancing girl in the Folies, I believe, and did not want a child to hamper her career, so my father paid her to have the baby, me, and ferried me back to Bowering House. He joined the air force when the Second World War began and died after being shot down over the Channel, quite early in the war.After Adrian died too as far as I knew, the family had died out except for me. We never had visits from any other family members. You were the only one I ever met. I do not remember my father at all. He had given up the farm for the good life in town, leaving me with Granny Meg, and then he joined the air force very early on, possibly even before the war began.

'Adrian was just as bad. He was never at home. Our cellar was always stocked with wines and cheeses from France smuggled in, and he also joined the air force. Once the actual war began, he was shot down and became a prisoner for a while and was shot trying to escape from the prison camp.

'I suppose the wildness in Ian can be explained by them. The money we lived on after that came from Grandmother Meg's inheritance, but after the county rates and taxes were paid and fines were paid for the boys' smuggling and aeroplane and so on, the inheritance died with Grandmother Meg, and nothing was left.'

Valerie sat taking the story in whilst Clement went on. Looking at her watch, she said, 'I have been here for hours, Clem. I should go. May I come back another day?'

'I have enjoyed the memories, Valerie. Not all good ones, alas, but part of my history I do not often get a chance to go over. Stay for lunch. I ring the bell, and a lass will appear with a menu to choose what you want. I am enjoying your company, Valerie. Sit down again. I have not asked about your history.'

'Thanks, Clem. It is lunch time, and by the time I get back to town, it will be late, so lunch would be welcomed.'

They had a delicious salmon mornay for lunch, and Clem suddenly looked tired. He explained, 'I usually have a nap after lunch, and the staff encourage it. I am sorry, Valerie.'

She smiled. 'I could do with a nap too, Clem. One seems to need it as we grow older. I will leave now and come back another day. I will ring before I come to make sure you are still here.'

'There is only one other place I would be, my girl. I am not ready for that yet.' He laughed as he said it.

CHAPTER FOUR

As soon as Granny arrived back at the office, she sat down and wrote up everything that Clem had told her of his family. She needed to plan her next questions. It was obvious to her that he was in touch with his children, even those in jail. He had also known about the bookshop and house burning down. He was not locked away as he suggested to her.

He seemed up to date with all his family doings, she thought. What if Clement was the one behind all the family's wrongs, and there were many? The first when Ian Haskell tied up his young druggie wife and his cousin and set alight to the house. Sure, he described his son as a young scoundrel. But what if he had been encouraged by his father to 'get rid of that girl. She is nothing but trouble'? Not necessarily to kill her but to get her out of the family, and Ian had done it his way. He was not a conventional boy and had probably grown up the same way.

Jason seemed to keep in touch with his father. Was he influenced also when he complained of being the lackey of a wealthy man? Did his father say again to 'get rid of him, and then you would be in charge of all that money'?

A suggestion that had got Jason to take advantage of the turmoil in the country they lived in to kill Douglas Oliveri and his wife and, after them, his own wife, saying the locals had been drugged up and did the nasty deeds. Just by chance, it was two groups of the same family, but he would be under suspicion if the boys had been killed too and therefore had to work out a different fate for them.

Bringing them to the UK would defer the moment until he worked that one out. He finally decided, or his father had, that his sisters could do the job. But they had not counted on Fiona's gentle nature. She was not made of the same mettle as her brothers and had failed to kill the boy we now call Divit, although her 'silly' sister, as Clem had described her, killed the younger boy.

To her, it all sounded true, but how was she going to prove it? Perhaps she could visit the girls in jail to convince them to tell their story. Valerie had never visited a jail and was not sure how to go about it. She considered all the people she knew that could help her.

Granny did not want to connect Aaron Dunstan to her story. He had a wife and a daughter to consider, and who knew what would come out of it all? Next on her list was Alex Overington, the lawyer connected to James and Percy's business. She thought for a while and decided he was not a tough enough contender. What about DI Paul Morris? He would know the way to visit the girls in jail. He did not have to visit the girls himself—she would do that—but he could take her there and go through the motions with her to get to see them. Yes, she would give him a call and see what he says after she described her visit to Clement.

She looked at the clock. Yes, there was time to call him. He would just be thinking now of going home. She would invite him to dinner in the Italian restaurant that was her favourite to tell him her story and suggestions to see what came out of it. She looked up his number in James's index and made the call and was answered by a friendly voice asking how she was getting on alone.

She smiled to herself. *I think I have got this right. He is the one to help me.*

'Hello, Paul, I am doing great, thank you. I have a small problem though that I would like to tell you about. It is quite a long story, but I think you would be interested. Can I invite you to dinner tonight or sometime soon to relate it to you to see what you think of it?'

Paul sounded amused; it was not too often he was invited out to a restaurant by an elderly lady. 'Can you give me an idea of what you have there, Mrs Newton?'

'Remember the photo album you and your team brought back from Bowering House, Paul? I looked at it again yesterday, and I am convinced I am related to the Haskell family. Does that get your interest?'

'Wow, Mrs Newton, so they are not all baddies in the family. I am interested in the story! Do you want me to pick you up, as I believe you are unable to drive nowadays?'

'I would appreciate that, Paul. I have booked us into the Italian restaurant where we always get friendly staff and a good meal. What time suits you, Paul?'

'I will be right over, Mrs Newton. You have my interest. Perhaps we can have a quiet chat in the bar before we eat.'

'I look forward to seeing your smiling face, Paul. Thank you for not brushing me off as a time-waster.'

'I would never do that, Mrs Newton. James has the greatest admiration for your prowess in helping to solve problems. He willingly gives you credit for a lot of his clues in his cases.'

'I am sorry to say, Paul, that I did not admit my relationship to the Haskell family to James and Alicia. James was so depressed after the fires of the bookshop and house and blamed himself, and it was not his fault at all, but he could not see it. I did not want to add another burden on his shoulders, and I think the time away will bring him back refreshed. That will be time enough to confess all.'

'Give me fifteen minutes, Mrs Newton. I will be right there.'

Valerie put the photo album and the papers she had written after her visit to Clement at the residential home and also her phone in her bag. She had taken some photos of the suite and reception area and of Clement whilst he was studying the menu. She had dressed before ringing Paul, so she was ready to go. He arrived as he said he would—in fifteen minutes. She liked a man who kept good time.

They locked up the office together, and he escorted her to his vehicle, just as James would have done.

When they arrived at the restaurant ten minutes later, they sat in the small bar area at a table for two, and Valerie brought out the photo album and showed Paul her grandparents as guests in the wedding photo. She said, 'I do not know all these other people, so I do not know which were my grandmother's siblings. They all seem to look similiar. I have wondered if the groom is a brother. They seem to look alike.

I grew up with only my mother. My father was killed during the war. I have not had any relationship with others of my family except for Clement Haskell, when he boarded with us during the bombing early in the war. He was only with us for a few months. He was a child then, but I did love him. I was a small child at the time, and he was so kind to me. He eventually went back to Bowering House and stayed there until he was old enough to study as a medical doctor.

'One of those twins in the smaller photograph was his father, who died after being shot down during the war. Both of the twins died during the war. They were still very young to die. What I am showing you is, the photograph in the album were Clement's grandparents at their wedding. The twins were the only family from that couple being married, and Clement Haskell was brought up by his grandmother. His grandfather had died when the boy was quite young.

'That was the end for Bowering House. It had been taken over by the army for a hospital for convalescence of wounded soldiers, and Grandmother Meg died just before the end of the war. Clement was left at the house as an orphan without any money and was taken under the wing of one of the doctors who could see his potential.

'I think Clement has come out of that story as someone thinking he deserved better. He had been at the house through its glory days, but with all the deaths of responsible moneyed people, there was nothing left for him—no family, no money. I think as he struggled over the years to bring up his family whilst he was a country doctor, his fate got to him, leaving him angry with his life. His wife died quite early, leaving him with a clinic to run and teenagers to help along. He remarried but found quickly that he had made a mistake in his second wife.

'He still had his children, but Ian had turned out badly. Ian killed his wife and cousin, as you know, and got away with it. I am sure Clement knew the ins and outs of it. The children still clung to him for advice.

'I believe that Clement, in a throwaway announcement, said, "You have a warehouse full of cocaine worth a million dollars, and you do nothing about it." That started Ian planning the customs house heist.

'I truly believe that Gerald is the loser in all Ian's doings. He was in love with Fiona, and where Fiona was, there was also Ian pushing him to join him in the pursuit of the cocaine. He grudgingly helped Ian, but he was reluctant. He loved his wife and family, and he had a good job and was happy until Ian interfered.

'We come to Fiona. Clement described her as a gentle, loving daughter who liked to read, when Ian, her twin, would allow it. She followed in whatever Ian wanted her to do all her life.

'Faye was the daughter of Clement's second wife, Barbara, and his description of her was "a silly woman with a silly daughter".

'Jason's story is the best yet. He was the wonder boy who excelled at school and studied mining engineering and went out to Africa to make his fortune. He was not making it fast enough, even though he founded a diamond mine. The owner of the land was assuredly Douglas Oliveri, but Jason wanted what he thought of as his due. He had found the mine, he counted it as his property, and Oliveri took him up on this. Jason was on his payroll, and the work had been done in Oliveri's time and on his land.

'Jason asked his father what he should do, and Clement advised, "Do away with the Oliveri family. There is so much tumult going on in that country at the moment. No one will believe you have anything to do with it if you can drug up some locals to do it for you." So he took his father's advice. He probably got the right drugs from his father. As a doctor, he would have known which ones to use for maximum effect.

'What to do with the two boys? He does not care for them but must show that he does and cannot afford another massacre attempt. It would raise suspicions about him, too much too soon, so he brought them here and abandoned them, thinking they would grow weaker in time without money to buy food, and he would get Fiona to kill them.

'He had not planned on Gerald paying the boys for selling his cocaine and then Fiona's softer nature. She did not want to kill anybody but was pushed into it by her brother, so she took her younger half-sister with her as backup.

'The sister, Faye, was up for any thrill. I believe, by her manner, that she was on cocaine herself. I could be wrong. I have only had second-hand information about her. I have not seen her myself, but the descriptions Alicia gave me of her sounds like someone on drugs.

'So there you have it, my relatives, the Haskells. I think it has all been brought about by Clement being abandoned by the Haskell relatives when he needed someone when his grandmother died and the loss of the only home he knew. He wanted it returned to his family in the style he knew about, because he had been brought up there.

'What he has not realised is, most of the families at the end of the war were battling to survive themselves. There were many who had lost someone they loved often the bread winner of the family. Food, and clothing and fuel were strictly rationed, and this went on for a long time. For most it was a fight for survival and jobs.

'I feel sorry for Clement. I loved him like a brother while he stayed with us, but then he went away. I think I believed that everybody goes away sooner or later. It is the story of my life. I did not get to know my father because he died during the war. My mother, husband, son, and daughter-in-law died within three years of each other, leaving me with Alicia, a small child at the time, so I know about loss.'

She stopped speaking and looked at Paul Morris, who appeared to be enthralled by her story.

Paul said, 'Summing it up, you believe Clement Haskell—the father of Ian, Fiona, Faye and Jason—is the person pulling the strings behind all the crimes?'

'Yes, Paul, I do. Don't you think it is too hard to believe that each one was operating on their own? There was someone behind the scenes operating and pulling the strings. He did not do the jobs himself. He is in his eighties now, I think, so he would not be agile enough to do the deeds. But he did not have to. He organised his children to do it for him and for themselves to rebuild the farming community that was his home as a child. I believe he wants to die there with his memories.

'After he has gone, his boys would farm the land like his antecedents had and make a good, clean life for themselves. I don't know about the others, but it seems Jason shared his dream. All Jason needed was a lot of money, and he thought he had found it, even though he had to wipe out a whole family to get it. Meanwhile, Clement sits in his luxurious suite in the residential care apartment and dreams and schemes.'

'It is a good story, Mrs Newton, but do you have any proof?' asked Paul.

'Ahh, that is where you come in, Paul. I want to visit the jail and interview the two women, Fiona and Faye. Separately, of course. I think Fiona will be fed up with the deal she got and may be ready to talk, and from all I have heard, Faye does not stop talking, so I might be able to find out about her father from her. I am hoping you could arrange the jail visits for me. I have never visited a jail and have no idea how to go about it. I realise you are a busy man, but if you could make a few phone calls to arrange it for me, I will be greatly thankful to you.'

Paul thought about it and said, 'Will you be placing yourself in any danger, Mrs Newton? It seems to me that Clement has not yet attained his goal and seems to be taken over with his thoughts on it. To me it sounds like a compulsion to return to his childhood dream. He cannot have too many more years ahead of him. Is it worth pursuing him? He may die before he comes to justice, and meanwhile, you will be within his firing line. He will not give up yet. He needs to keep going while he can. I would not like to see you as his stooge because he has gone through the rest of his family. Can he wait until one or two of them are released? What is his health like? Does he seem to be slowing down?'

'Actually, Paul, he looks very good. Still an upright figure and still has the mental capacity to corrupt his children. He has not admitted to me that he has been the man in charge, but I do not doubt it. I also believe he is merciless in his quest. Asking for murders to be done is no small thing after all. It occurred to me while I was sitting in his suite that he is the spider in the centre of a web, and anything that comes in contact with him is in danger. That includes myself. I was terribly cross that he may have orchestrated the attack on my bookshop and, consequently, my home. I still feel angry about that and want to bring him down, even if he is a family member. The rest of my family, whatever is left of them, are good people, and I hate to have to admit a relationship with the Haskell family and what they have become.'

'Having met the majority of them, I have to agree with you, Mrs Newton, but it is only the one branch of the family tree that has gone wrong. Do not align them with yourself.'

'I have a feeling that the rest of the family begrudged Lady Meg her position in the household. She was a foreigner to them, and perhaps she played on the "lady" title. She would have had an accent, a burr, that would be difficult for some to understand. I cannot recall any time she was mentioned by my mother, so she was not a loved member to be cherished as some elderly people are. When she became ill, nobody responded to her, leaving Clement to take the burden and he was still a child. In a way, I feel and understand the grief that he still carries. Though his deeds in the last few years go beyond having any sympathy for him now.'

Paul said, 'I too can understand how he suffered, but as you say, the times were tough for everyone, and he is acting as if he was the only one badly done by. That is no excuse for the lives he has ruined in his quest to have his past back.'

'Will you help me, Paul, to visit the two women in the jail?'

'I have been thinking it through as you were speaking, Mrs Newton, and do not agree that you visit them. I think it is better if you do not see Clement again. Leave it to James and Percy when they come home or even Alicia to visit the girls. Why do you think James is always partnered when on a case? Things can get very dangerous out there, and I believe this is one of those jobs. This is not a case where you can call for backup in a crisis. You are not a member of the partnership, even if James calls upon your knowledge from time to time. I am sorry, but the description of this man you have given me, I would describe as one of the dangerous ones. He is not going away, so wait for James to arrive home to finish what you have started.'

Valerie sat looking at him with tears in her eyes. 'I was hoping we could do something before James returned. Yes, Clement is dangerous and has a distorted vision of himself, but he will not stop now. He must be stopped.'

Paul looked away from her tears; they made him feel sorry, but he was not going to give in. It was too dangerous for her.

'I tell you what, Mrs Newton. I will go and see the police chief and talk it over with him. He may allow us to listen into Clement's phone calls. He may also not allow him to have visitation rights to the prison. We will get a warrant to monitor who has been to see him in his care unit in the past year or two. I think that would show up how many times his family has visited him and the times when they have come. We might be able to read something into those visits. Other than that, there is no proof at all.'

'I suppose I will have to go along with that. Will you let me know what is allowed?' she asked.

'Of course, I will be in touch. One thing I have realised is that Jason Bowering knew that Divit was in the bookshop apartment and that James and Alicia were there too. Knowing this, I do believe you are in danger. Someone must have told him about the apartment upstairs as that was the target. They would not have left James and Alicia alive as witnesses.

'Today you made Clement aware that you knew all this, so watch yourself, Mrs Newton. I do not want to scare you, but you have to have the truth as I see it, so you can take precautions. We do not know if this man has any other followers to do his work for him, but you will have to operate carefully, in case he does have others.'

'I can see your point of view, Paul, but I am pleased I went to see him. He is a cousin after all. But what I read between the lines truly shocked me. I hope I am wrong about him, but the more I think of his conversation, the more I think he is guilty of corrupting his children to gain back his boyhood memories. Life is not like that. We all have cherished memories of our childhood. What would happen to the world if we all acted like Clement?'

'Your heart was in the right place, Mrs Newton, when you went to see him, but do not go back. He is a monster. Do not trust him at all or fall into feeling sorry for him. Think of the lives that have been taken without a backward thought. You do not want to be his next victim. Do not eat with him again. If he has drugs available to him, I think that you may find yourself drugged in some way, and having a drink or lunch would be the way he would do it, as he is unable to move around freely because of his age.'

'Wow, I had not thought of that, but drugs have featured in most of the deaths, haven't they? How easy it would be for him to give me a delayed-effect drug so he does not appear guilty of giving it to me.'

'Time to go home, Mrs Newton. I will phone you each day to see how you are and if there have been any new developments. James would never forgive me if I did not follow up on your story, so I will see the police chief in the morning. I will let you know what he thinks.'

'Thanks for believing in me, Paul. I hope you had nothing else planned for this evening.'

'I believe in you because James is always saying how clever you are. The only thing I would have been doing tonight is sitting in front of the television trying to find something worth watching. This has been much more interesting.'

As he drove her to the office and walked her to the door, he said, 'By the way, did you tell Clement where you were domiciled now?'

'I was careful not to. As soon as he said he was sorry about my home burning because of an accident, I started to be more careful of what I told him and left him to do all the talking. My suspicions started at that moment and never went away.'

'That was a good move. We cannot be sure if he will try anything against you, though I do not believe he would think you are living in an office.'

'Thanks, Paul, I will hear from you tomorrow. Thanks for coming to dinner. I enjoyed the company.'

CHAPTER FIVE

The next morning, Paul rang about ten o'clock and told her, 'I have been to see the police chief, and he too thought it a real possibility that you are right about Clement, mainly because of the whole family being caught up in his web, especially Jason Bowering, as he called himself. He agreed that you let sleeping dogs lie for the time being, and they would monitor Clement's phone calls and have him closed off from jail visits. That was all they could do at the moment, as so far it had all been conjecture and no proof available.'

Valerie thanked Paul and said, 'Okay, Paul, I will not visit for the time being unless something comes up that necessitates it, and I will let you know if I do go.'

She could imagine Paul shrugging his shoulders and saying to himself, 'Well, I tried.'

Her brain would not let it all go, but she had promised Paul. She went back to looking at the photo album and could see in the photos before Hugh's wedding to Meg that everybody looked happy and busy. She wondered if the coming of Granny Meg had upset the applecart somewhat. She thought about it for a few minutes and decided to look into the history of the woman.

She googled the Forrester Industries in Glasgow and found it was a huge conglomerate, still going today. Presumably they had done very well during the wars, so why had Meg's inheritance stopped with her passing away? Why was it not continued to her heirs? Sure, the twin sons had gone, but there was still Clement. Perhaps it was because Duncan had not married his French dancing lady. Would that have been why? She would have to ask Alex, the lawyer, that question.

Scrolling through the businesspeople and family members, she noticed that most of the people were robust-looking characters, not like Meg at all, who, by the photo in the album, was quite small. Perhaps her asthma had something to do with that; a grimy, smoky atmosphere, would bring the asthma on. Clement had described her as stately. Would that have been only because she carried herself well? Or was his memory of her tainted by age? Also, most of these people shown were older, so perhaps they had put on weight as they aged. She chided herself for jumping to conclusions with only a few people on the web pages to look at.

Her phone rang, and she saw the name of the care home that Rob Gooding was based at. 'Hello, Valerie Newton speaking.'

'Hello, Mrs Newton, we are ringing to advise that Rob is looking very ill this morning. You wanted us to advise you if that happened. If you decide to come to see him, we have assigned a room for you to stay for a few days or however long you think is necessary. There is no payment required for this. Rob himself paid in advance some time ago in case it was necessary, because you had advised us of your interest.'

'Thank you, I will come straight away. I will be there by lunchtime. Is that all right?'

'Certainly, Mrs Newton, we look forward to your company.'

Valerie rang Paul Morris and told him where she was going to be and said she would advise him when she returned. She also rang Aaron Dunstan to say she would be away for a few days, perhaps longer if needed. At least she did not have to pack a heavy bag to carry; she had not had time yet to do that necessary shopping.

Luckily, the coach for that time of day was waiting when she arrived at the coach station. She was afraid she may have had to wait for some time. The kindly driver helped her on board, recognising her from when she had her arm in a sling and came to visit Rob. She was able to manage much better now, but it was always nice to have someone to help. The driver also knew where she usually went and dropped her off outside of the nursing home when they reached Winchester.

The staff were very pleased to see her; she had been visiting her friend Rob Gooding for many years and had become friendly with the staff. Rob was a favourite patient, always with a smile and a cheery chat, no matter how he suffered from his advanced painful arthritis.

Valerie was shown to a room adjacent to Rob's and told it was hers as long as she needed it. She put her bag down and washed her hands in the small en suite bathroom and went to see Rob across the passageway. He appeared to be sleeping, so she sat down next to him in the comfortable chair and dozed off herself, only awakening when she heard her name.

Rob was turned on his side and was looking at her and was saying, 'Hello, dear friend, how nice it is to see you.'

'I have come to stay for a while with you, Rob, to keep you company. The girls tell me you have not been well, and they have called in the troops to cheer you up, so I will stay for a while. Alicia and James and Percy have all gone for a holiday to Australia so they can catch up with their families, and I opted to have my holiday here with you. You are my family.'

'That is a lovely thing to say, Valerie. I appreciate nice comments nowadays. The girls try to jolly me up when they have time, but no one can say it like you do. No, I have been off colour since I heard about the bookshop and house. It stopped my dreams of returning, although I always knew it was only a dream, but locked up here unable to move around much, one does have to dream now and then.'

Valerie was startled to hear him say that. 'I asked the staff not to tell you about the burning of the bookshop and house, Rob. Who told you?'

'None of the staff, my dear. I was doing my daily walk and visited another chap living long term here, and he had a newspaper. I picked it up, and the front page told me the story. The shock of it made me ill, I am afraid, and I seem to be going downhill ever since.'

'I am so sorry, Rob. I knew you had that dream, and that is why I asked the staff not to tell you. I too have been shocked but have to keep up my chin and pretend, because James was blaming himself and was growing depressed with his life, and I could not have that.

'James is wonderful at his job. Unfortunately, it brings out these crazies who want to get at him. He loved living at the apartment above the shop. It was so close to his office and saved a lot of travelling time for both him and Alicia. They were close by if I needed help, which has been often in the past two years. It has been wonderful for all of us.

'Percy too has been living with us in the last year or so, supposedly as an extra precaution against these crazies, another hand on deck sort of thing. However, when someone decides to go the whole hog to get at whoever they have decided to get at, there is not much anyone can do about it. It was very lucky that we had decided to go out for dinner that particular evening, so no one was home. We leave a light on inside the apartment and the house and a radio going to make sure a burglar does not think the house is empty, but we were not counting on visitors who wanted to kill those in the apartment, so they thought we were home. It worked against us that time.

'It was bad luck for them that they did not assess the target first. James had installed heavy-duty doors when he arrived, only because we were not too sure someone was targeting me to make me fall when I broke my arm and elbow. Even if they had targeted the window, that would not have got them in, as that was heavy-duty glass I had put in when I did the renovation of the bookshop. It would possibly have cracked, but that is all.'

'It seems the world is going crazy. Using a vehicle to break into a shop sounds weird to me, but reading the papers, it seems to be an everyday occurrence nowadays.' Rob said

'It was unfortunate that we lost the bookshop and house, but looking on the bright side, the perpetrators only killed themselves. We are all still alive and kicking and wondering where we are going next. We have not had time to work that one out yet'

'You have made me feel a little better, Valerie, putting it like that. I had not thought of that angle. I was distressed about the fire, but I was worried about you, and I am so glad that you and your menagerie of family are safe. I am so happy at seeing you safe and well and here to visit me. I know that is a selfish way to look at things, but I am happy to see you, my girl.'

'My thoughts are daily with you, Rob. You are mentioned in my prayers at night, and my mind often wanders to how you are each day. You are not alone in the world. We survived, and Alicia and James also send their love to you, even if they are half a world away.'

'I feel almost completely revived now you are here. If you pass me my robe at the bottom of the bed, I will get up and escort you to lunch,' he said cheerily.

'That is the fastest revival I have ever seen,' said a voice from the doorway. They turned and saw Sharon, Alicia's friend, standing there, and she said, 'Hello, Mrs Newton, I have just come on duty. Do not believe that man will escort you to lunch. I am here to do that, and he will be in a wheelchair beside you, to create the illusion of an escort.'

They all laughed. Sharon was amazed at the sight of Rob looking so happy. The staff had thought he was on his last days. They would hate to lose him; he was their favourite patient.

The entire dining room population called with cheery remarks to Rob as they went in; he was so popular. It was obvious that the others had noticed how he had retired hurt after reading about the fire in the bookshop, where he had spent almost his entire adult life until coming into care. Valerie had been his next-door neighbour for most of her life, and Rob had settled the bookshop on to her and Alicia, when he could not manage anymore because of his arthritis.

Valerie was glad she had come early enough to cheer him up and bring him back from the brink of death. She would have hated the burning of the shop to have caused the end of his life. It would have caused more depression for James, who had taken the fires badly, blaming himself for taking Divit in to live with them in the apartment above the shop.

Rob Gooding had lived and worked in the bookshop as long as Valerie could remember, but because his arthritis had got so bad, he eventually gave the business and apartment to Valerie and Alicia and retired to the nursing home. Alicia and James had lived in the apartment since leaving London to care for Valerie when she broke her arm.

Valerie stayed for three days at the nursing home, sitting with Rob most of the time, chatting of earlier times. It was getting closer to Christmas, and she had promised to go and visit Aaron and Sandra and Jody for the day. She still had to buy presents for the day to put under the tree, so needed to go back to the office to go shopping. Rob was back to his usual happy self, so felt it was okay to leave him and said she would be back as soon as she had sorted out some other problems.

When she arrived back to the office, she made a phone call to Aaron to confirm her date for Christmas Day. After that conversation, she asked him how she could research old newspapers from Glasgow.

Aaron sounded intrigued, 'What are you researching Glasgow's newspapers for, Mrs Newton? That is an unusual request.'

'Yes, Aaron, I have never been to Glasgow, but isn't there a way I can do it by computer now? I want to find out more about the Forrester family of Forrester Industries based in Glasgow. One of my relatives was a Lady Margaret Forrester from that family. She joined our family by marriage in 1914, just before the start of the First World War. It seems a strange alignment, and so I decided to see if there was anything about her to make her move to the south coast of England. Will that be a difficult job, Aaron?'

'I have not tried the Scottish newspapers, Mrs Newton, but it is quite easy to get into the English ones. So perhaps I can try the Scots one out, and we can have a discussion about it over Christmas lunch. Bring your tablet, and I will show you how to do it.'

'Thanks, Aaron, I knew your journalist interest would be awakened. It is probably nothing at all, but I wondered why she married so far afield of her hometown. It seems a strange thing to do, and how did she meet a southerner so far from her home? These questions keep going over and over in my head. The bookshop always kept my head busy, but with that gone, it seems I have gone off in another direction to find something else to keep my mind occupied.'

Aaron laughed. 'I can imagine the loss of the bookshop has left a big vacancy. It is a great shame, but knowing you, I am sure you will find something else to do. I cannot see you just sitting around like most women of your age.'

'No, Aaron, my mother never taught me to crochet and knit, which occupies so many older people. Bingo is not my thing. Perhaps I should take up playing bridge. I have heard you get fanatical with that card game, and it takes over your mind and life.'

'Well, we will try the newspaper snooping first. That becomes interesting, looking back at happenings in times past. After that, I can teach you how to play bridge if you are still interested. Sandra and I used to play it in the days before having Jody. It does take you over a little, I have to agree.'

'I will look forward to seeing you on Christmas Day, Aaron. I am enjoying my time being free at the moment. The bookshop held me captive for so long. I am enjoying each day with a freedom for different things to do.'

The next thing she did was to phone DI Paul Morris to ask him if anything had come up with Clement Haskell. Paul replied that Clement had tried to visit the jail to see Fiona and had not been allowed, and he had got angry at the staff, but they had stood firm. Also, his phone calls had been blocked to Fiona as well, and he had put in a complaint. The Haskell girls had not been allowed phone calls to their father from the jail, so there had been no communication between them. It was early days yet, but Paul said he would keep her up to date as things happened.

Valerie decided that there was nothing else she could do at the moment, so she went shopping. Her first free day for just shopping in years. The bookshop had held her bound for so long without a free day. There was no reason to hurry back to sit by herself. She had not had freedom like this for a very long time and relished it.

She went into the shopping centre along from the office, deciding to buy herself two or three dresses. The ones she bought in a hurry after her home burnt down were cheap ones to tide her over, and she decided now to dress up a little for her Christmas lunch with her friends.

As she walked through the centre, she felt as if someone was looking at her, but ignored the feeling and went into the dress shop showing a better type of dress. She looked out of the window into the mall and saw Clement walking to a seat near the shop. He must have been whom she could feel. She ignored him and went about the business of choosing clothes until satisfied that she had found the right things.

When she came out of the shop, Clement was still seated nearby, and she went over to him and said, 'Are you stalking me, Clement?'

He looked up at her and smiled. 'Certainly not, Valerie. I am here to ask you to have a cup of tea with me in the tea shop over there,' he said, pointing with his walking stick.

She thought for a few seconds and said, 'I do not have much time. I must find a present for my friend's little daughter. I am very fond of the child and look forward to spending time with her and her parents tomorrow for a Christmas treat. I am spending the day with them.'

'Sit with me for ten minutes, Valerie, and I will not delay you. I had hoped you would spend Christmas with me. I am feeling in the doldrums at present with all of my children unavailable to me.'

'I am sorry, Clem. This is a long-standing arrangement, and I have no wish to change it. As I said, I am very fond of the child and would not intentionally disappoint her. We have been looking forward to me spending at least the day with them and possibly staying on a little longer. I have returned from visiting with my friend in Winchester for the occasion.'

'I have been trying to see you, so you have been in Winchester?' said Clem with a glint in his eyes.

'Yes, I have been staying there with friends for the last week. I do not like being questioned like this, Clem. You have no rights to know where I am and who my friends are. Unlike you, I have lived in this city almost my whole life, and I have many friends. They look out for me. I realise you may be lonely, but you have the staff at the residential home to care for you.'

'Where are you living, Valerie, now your home has gone? I wanted to ask you to come to the residential care home.'

'No, thank you, Clem. As I said, my friends are taking care of me, and I do not need assistance.'

'I feel obliged to offer you a home seeing as my family have caused your loss. If you reconsider, please give me a call, Valerie. I would like to help you out.'

'If your family had not been so set on getting into my bookshop and setting fire to it and my home next door, there would have not been any thought of residential care. I have my granddaughter and her husband to take care of me, and I will not be entering into any other care group unless I become ill. From where I am standing at the moment, that alternative appears to be way off in the future.'

Clem appeared agitated that he was being rebuffed and said with a sound of a sulk in his voice, 'I wanted only to renew our acquaintance, Valerie. I am now alone in the world, and meeting you after all these years put hope in my heart and mind that we could continue as friends.'

'Thank you for the consideration, Clem. However, I have a life of my own to continue as I want, and I am not giving up my life to residential care yet. I am growing older, I realise that. But I am healthy in body, and my mind is still very clear. I do not have use for care for now and possibly never, if I am lucky.'

'Would you consider having a holiday with me some time somewhere? I do not want to lose you now we have found each other again after such a long time.' Clem was almost appealing to her to continue their supposed friendship.

Valerie said to placate him, 'I will think it over, Clem, but now I must rush off to finish my shopping. I am running late.'

She could see he was disappointed, but she felt frightened that he had found her so easily. How long had he spent sitting in the shopping mall waiting for her to appear? She supposed it was obvious if she lived in this area for so long that she would shop in the closest mall where it was familiar to her. She felt her heart pounding faster than usual and turned into the closest store to stand until her heart rate returned to normal.

She spent some time choosing gifts and wandered back down the mall, but Clement must have gone. She scrutinised all the obvious places he could be hiding, laughing at herself for feeling frightened of finding him still waiting for her.

She stood a while at the exit, looking in both directions, but he was not there, so she stepped out and made her way to the office, stopping and looking around herself before opening the door. Once inside, she still looked out of the window to see if he appeared and soon decided that with all these people doing their last-minute Christmas shopping, nobody would notice her. However, she did not turn the lights on in the front office, closing the door between before lighting the spaces she was in.

She decided to ring Paul Morris and bring him up to date, saying to herself, 'I know it is Christmas Eve, so I will not keep him long.'

Paul answered immediately and asked her where she was. She reported her return from Winchester and told of Clement in the shopping mall waiting for her and mentioned his request for a holiday. Before Paul had a chance to say anything, Valerie said, 'I intend to take a break and travel to Glasgow and do some investigating into the Forrester and Haskell families, and

I thought it would be a good idea to invite Clement along to see what comes of it. What do you think?'

Paul sounded alarmed. 'Are you sure you know what you are doing, Mrs Newton? This is the enemy you will be courting. Who knows what will come out when you are on a long journey? I do not think it will be a good idea.'

'Wait, Paul, you did not let me finish. I plan to have a driver take us to Glasgow in a luxury vehicle. I will sit in the back with Clement and sound him out—acting curious, but not accusingly. I have not chosen the driver yet and wondered if you have any suggestions?'

'I would volunteer, Mrs Newton, but I am tied up on a new case for the next few weeks, unless you want to wait until I am available. I could recommend Tony Walton. Do you remember him from your market day convictions? He is a handy man to have around, and I know James would approve of him looking after you. He is on leave for the next month and may enjoy a drive to Glasgow and back. I will ask him for you. He is due into the office shortly, and I will ring you back.'

'Thank you, Paul, at least you have not ruled it out, which I thought you would. James always said it is better to hold your enemies close to find out their thoughts. I am not sure I think of Clement as an enemy, but it does intrigue me how he has ended up. I thought if we could come to an agreement to find his family roots together, he may stop thinking of me as his enemy.

'Tony seems just the shot as a helper in the situation. I shall pay him and all the expenses, of course. I should be well off once the insurance company and the council house pay me for the loss of the house and bookshop. This trip could also fill my mind for a while. With the loss of the bookshop, I am now unemployed for the first time in many years, and I need the mental stimulation.'

'How long do you think you will be away, Mrs Newton? I need to give Tony an idea what he is up for in time away.'

'Although I have not looked at any maps yet, I propose a week at least. Two days to travel to Glasgow with an overnight somewhere in between so as not to overtire everybody. Two or perhaps three days in Glasgow and then again two days to return home should do it.'

'That sounds reasonable. I will ring you as soon as I speak to Tony. You are going to the Dunston house for Christmas Day, aren't you? Why not ask Aaron to go with you too, as a journalist and extra backup. I am sure he would be interested.'

'I would like to, but Aaron is the carer of his wife and daughter. As you know, Sandra is permanently in a wheelchair now.' Valerie thought about it and said, 'Aaron could say it is a job and should apply for help for Sandra. I will ask him and see what he says. Once again it is a good excuse to have him along as a journalist.'

'Keep thinking, Mrs Newton. You are doing well. I will catch you later when Tony comes in.'

Granny was happy that Paul had not tried to talk her out of it, and when Tony rang to ask her about the trip, he said he had a month leave starting from today and was willing to go along with her, as his plans for what he was going to do with a month of freedom had not yet been organised as he had been working hard for the last few months. He welcomed the time off. Having a drive to Glasgow sounded like a good idea. He had never been that far north, and it sounded like a holiday for him to see a bit of the country.

Valerie was so happy that the plan was going ahead and said she would ring him back on Boxing Day to finalise the details.

CHAPTER SIX

Christmas Day the following morning was a crisp, clear sky with a touch of frost early on, but it was clearing as the day moved towards ten o'clock. Valerie packed up her presents for a walk to the Dunston home, glad she had chosen small gifts that were not too heavy. She added the Haskell photo album to her bag and set off.

As she neared the units where they lived, she could see a small figure sitting on the steps wrapped up for the cold. As she drew closer, it showed her it was Jody waiting for her. As soon as she turned the bend, Jody came running towards her, saying, 'Hello, my darling Granny, I am so happy to see you.'

Jody had been placed in Valerie's care for six months while her mother was in hospital, and they had enjoyed their time together. Jody would be turning seven shortly and had lost her two front teeth, but her smile was still wide.

With such a greeting, Granny knew it was going to be a wonderful day with the family, and they walked on to see Sandra sitting by the window waiting to see her. Aaron also came to the door and kissed her cheek, saying, 'Welcome and Happy Christmas.' When she entered with Jody holding on to her hand, she saw a beautifully decorated dining room and sitting room decked out in the Christmas theme, and standing nearby waiting to be introduced was a motherly woman with shining eyes and a big smile.

Sandra introduced them, saying, 'Eileen Jensen is my cousin, newly discovered, or I would have called on her earlier. She is employed as a carer to give relief to families such as us, and when she came to the door, I could not believe I had forgotten about her until now. She moved away from our district when we were in our early teens and had come back here to a new job, and would you believe, I am her first call-out.'

'I am so pleased to meet you, Eileen,' said Granny. 'How long is your respite job to be?'

'I am allowed two weeks at each patient's home, and it can be extended if necessary. But I can see Sandra is coping well with her wheelchair with the help of Aaron and Jody, and she will not need me longer than that.'

'I have a proposal for Aaron if he is interested, and you are a sight for sore eyes because until now, I had thought it impossible,' said a delighted Valerie.

Aaron said, 'Come sit down, Valerie, and tell us of your proposal. You have me interested, and I have news for you too I am sure you will be interested in.'

'You go first, Aaron. What news?' said Granny as she sat down.

'Well, you got me interested when you asked how to check on old news stories, particularly you mentioned Forrester Industries. Because Lady Margaret Forrester was mentioned in the local newspaper, I started there first, starting from the date the wedding picture was published. The first thing I came up with was the report on men who had enlisted in the First World War. Hugh Haskell was amongst them in 1917. His entry to the army would have been set aside at first, because his farm activities were of essential services for food for the country. There was a story about the twins Duncan and Adrian Haskell learning to fly. Aircraft stories came up quite a lot in the years between the wars as they were the newest things out.

'The next story I found was more to the point. Remember I was looking for Forrester stories rather than Haskell, and there was a post–Second World War series of this particular one by that source. I have printed it out for you to see.

'Quote: "If anyone could contact us on the whereabouts of Clement Hugh Haskell, aged fifteen, we will pay a reward of £50." Later this amount went up to £100. That was a lot of money in those days,' said Aaron.

'So it means the Forresters were trying to locate Clem after the war!' Valerie exclaimed.

'Yes, there were at least half a dozen of these ads placed over the next two years. These were in the local newspaper three months apart,' explained Aaron.

'Clem was sent to medical school, but he did not tell me where. Obviously not locally or someone would have answered those ads. The money alone would have been a motive by itself. I see there is a telephone number mentioned. Have you tried it to see if it is still on line?'

'No, Mrs Newton, I thought you would like to try that yourself. I didn't know how to answer any questions that would be asked. Would you like to try it out now?'

'Very much so, Aaron, right now?'

'They will be sitting down to their Christmas meal. It seems likely all the family would be present, so someone might have answers for you. We can wait if you prefer.'

'No, you are right. It is good timing. Families gather on this day, so someone may know something about the advertisement. It is a long shot with so many years gone by, but as you say, someone might know something to answer our questions.' She took out her phone and dialled the number on the advertisement.

The phone rang for some time, then it was answered by a woman's voice.

'Hello, Helen Forrester speaking.'

'Hello, Helen, my name is Valerie Newton. I have recently discovered some Haskell names in my family tree and have discovered your families interest in knowing the whereabouts of Clement Hugh Haskell, from advertisements printed in our local newspaper here on the south coast of the country after World War II. Clem is my cousin, and I have recently renewed our acquaintance after many years. Is there anyone there with you who could enlighten me if you still have an interest in this subject? I must add that I was surprised the telephone answered to this number after all these years.'

Helen answered, 'I am the youngest member of the family here, and I do not recall anyone by that name, but if you wait for a few minutes, I will ask my grandparents. They are of an age to remember that far back.'

Valerie was quite excited they had struck the right family so easily. 'Yes, please, Helen, I will wait. Thank you.'

Several minutes went past, and another voice answered the phone. 'Hello, my name is John Forrester. My granddaughter tells me you are a member of the Haskell family and related to Clement, is that correct?'

'Yes, Mr Forrester, that is correct. My grandmother was the sister of Hugh Haskell, the grandfather of Clement, who was the grandson of Lady Margaret Forrester Haskell of Bowering House in Greenfields on the southern coast of England.'

Valerie could hear the sigh he gave before he spoke. 'It was my parents who looked for Clement after the war. So many had become displaced after the war, and when we found out my Aunt Meg had died during the war and Clement was alone with no parents or grandparents to guide him, my family wanted to step in and help him. Nobody ever answered our advertising, and we had a detective working on the case for some time. But there was such a mix-up with the population, a lot of it displaced. It was not an easy job. We hunted for two years without a word about Clem coming up.'

'Mr Forrester, I am in the position of being able to produce Clement in the next week or so. Would you be interested in meeting with him to tell him a little of your aunt Meg and satisfy his soul? He was very close to Granny Meg, I am told, and nursed her when she became ill during the last months of the war. As he was still a very young boy and he was left without family to help him, it must have been very hard for him. I personally was not aware of his circumstances at the time because I was born at the beginning of 1942, too young to know anything, and then our house was destroyed by the bombing.

'For a while, my mother and I also disappeared, as we were evacuated to York to be safer from the bombing, so nobody I am aware of could have helped. Perhaps you may learn more about him if we come to Glasgow in the next few days to visit with you. Would that be convenient to you?'

'Certainly, you have chosen the only week that we have closed the factory. We give all but essential staff leave for the week over Christmas. We have a large house, and you would be welcome to stay with us. All our family have houses of their own nowadays, so the house has many empty rooms, and we have the staff to help out. How many will you have in your party, Mrs Newton?'

'You are very generous, Mr Forrester. Please call me Valerie if you would. We are related down the years somewhere. I will have my driver and a journalist friend who is helping me in the search for family members, so there is four of us. Are you sure you want us all to stay with you? I could arrange some hotels for us.'

'No, No, Valerie. If you are here, we can hear the whole story of Clement's disappearance. It caused my parents a lot of concern at the time. I would like to make it up to Clem if I can.'

'Thank you, John. We will arrive within the next few days. I will have to confirm that with you as I have not spoken to Clem about it yet because I did not want to disappoint him if he was not welcome.'

'You will all be very welcome, Valerie. I for one look forward to meeting both you and Clem. We will see you soon.'

Valerie closed up her phone and turned to Aaron. 'Well, nothing ventured, nothing gained, and we have just won the jackpot. Will you come with me too, Aaron? I have not talked to Clem yet, but I do not see a problem with him. I have teed up a driver, who is a policeman and will be our backup in case we have any difficulties. He is a friend of James and Alicia. What do you say?'

'I will have to talk it over with Sandra and Jody, but I do not see any problem with me going along with you, and then you will have two backups. Eileen has arrived in the nick of time. She will be a great asset to have in our background. It frees me up to do jobs in the future, and she is a really nice person as well as being family.'

'I will pay you for the week, Aaron, so you can add that to your pleading. It will be just like going to work, and there may be a story in it all after we return. I cannot promise. It mainly depends on what comes out of this week. Will you be ready to leave tomorrow?'

'Let me check with Sandra first, Mrs Newton, and I will let you know today.'

Sandra's voice came from the other end of the room. 'I heard all that, Aaron. Of course, you must go. We owe Mrs Newton so much, and it will give Eileen and Jody and myself time to catch up with the past years of silence. Do you agree, Eileen?'

'It seems to me that Aaron could use some time away as he has been caught up so long here without a break,' Eileen confirmed.

Valerie said to them both, 'Thank you, Sandra and Eileen. It will give you a break also to catch up. Now let me ring Clement to see if our main guest is willing to accompany us.'

She dialled Clement's residential care home and was put through to Clem without a problem.

'Hello, Clem. You mentioned a holiday yesterday when we spoke. Can you be packed and ready to go by tomorrow morning?'

The phone went quiet for a moment while Clem thought about it, then he said, 'What have you got planned, cousin? This seems a sudden decision.'

Valerie laughed and said, 'Remember when I saw you at first, I said I was looking for long-lost family members? I have found some in Glasgow and have just now come off the phone having been invited to stay by the Forrester family. Are you interested? The only thing is, they will want us to go this week as the factory is closed for this one week, and they are very busy the rest of the year. I have agreed to go, leaving tomorrow by car, staying overnight somewhere along the way, and then going on to Glasgow, which is your Granny Meg's country. We will only stay two or three days with the family and return by car again, staying somewhere overnight, so you will only be away one week.

'I am going, and I have two friends also going to share the driving. I will supply the car so you will be comfortable even though it is a long drive. What do you say, Clem?'

There was silence for a few minutes as if he was checking over things for faults. Then he said, 'What time do you pick me up?'

'I have to organise that, Clem. I will ring you back later in the day with the details. It will be a holiday, Clem. You asked for it, and I have delivered. I was going by myself and decided this could be the perfect holiday for you when you mentioned it. I will ring back about four o'clock.'

'You have been busy, Valerie. I can see that. Do you need help with finances?'

'Not at this stage, Clem. I will ask if it becomes necessary later.'

After completing the call, she turned to Aaron and, with a laugh, said, 'That was easier than I thought it would be. Our only problem now is finding the luxury car I promised.'

Aaron was up with that. 'No problem, Mrs Newton. I have friends in the business. I often have to hire a car to transport important people. Give me a minute.' He looked through a system of business cards and came up with the one he wanted and rang them, saying as he did so, 'These are the only people open on Christmas Day that I know of, except for the airport's hire cars.'

After a few minutes on the phone, he asked for her credit card details and handed her the phone. It was all arranged, and Aaron would pick the car up at four o'clock.

Valerie immediately rang Tony Walton and got his address so they could pick him up at eight o'clock next morning. She rang Clement and left a message that the car would pick him up at nine o'clock. Next, she rang the office coffee shop that the staff used and ordered a picnic lunch for the next day for them to deliver to the office at eight thirty in the morning. After all that, she looked at Jody and said, 'Now it is your turn, Jody. What shall we do? Do you have a game to play?'

Jody said, 'I have monopoly, but Mummy said it takes too long.'

'Yes, it does, Jody, but do not worry. I brought a few gifts with me. Perhaps we will find an interesting game amongst them. Would you open them for me, please?

Jody gave her big grin and hugged Granny, 'Thank you, Granny. I knew I could rely on you.'

Everyone laughed. The day had become happy for them all.

CHAPTER SEVEN

The timing went as promised next morning. Whilst Clement was finishing off his packing, Valerie advised the two men that Clement used a walking stick, and she wanted it to remain in the boot of the car as a precaution. She had noticed when in the shopping mall sitting with Clement that it was the type of stick that had a removable drink phial on top of it. Until they could find out what it held, she wanted the stick to be put out of Clement's reach.

The men looked curious but agreed to hide it at the bottom of the suitcases when they were packing them in.

When Valerie introduced the men to each other, Clement looked at Tony and said to Valerie, 'Is it necessary to have a policeman in our group, Valerie?'

She turned to him with a cold look and said, 'Tony was to be my driver before I invited you to join us, Clement. Yours was a last-minute addition to a trip already organised, and besides being a policeman, Tony is a friend of our family and has been held in high esteem by us for some time as he is a truly helpful person to have around.

'Also, in case you are going to ask about Aaron, he is the journalist helping with the chasing up of newspaper stories for me and found the newspaper story about the Forrester family looking for you after the war. I have a copy of that story and will show you once we get started. Are you unhappy with my choice? If you want to withdraw from the journey, now is the time to do it.'

Clement looked shocked at her attack. 'I am sorry, Valerie. I did not mean to sound as if I distrusted you. I guess I have been locked away so long I have lost the ability to sound polite.'

'While we are on the subject, Clement, I have agreed to pay for Aaron's time to write a story for me about what we will find out on this visit to the Forrester family. It is not necessarily for publication, but it is about my history as well as yours, and I requested him to join me. Two minds are better than one for taking things in, and I believe a real story will show up for us. It is good to have a family story to refer to. I have been brought up not knowing anything about my family.

'It seems the wars were the cause of much of the devastation of our family, and I am anxious to find out the reason. I have also brought with me the photo album to show to you to see if you remember anything about any of the family members. The only ones I remember are my grandparents, and the rest are strangers to me. I find myself being very curious at how that happened.'

Tony smiled at Valerie. 'Time to get this show on the road. All aboard who are going aboard.' He held the back door of the vehicle open, and Valerie got in, followed by Clement. Tony took the driver's seat, and Aaron the front passenger seat.

Aaron drew the privacy panel closed so that it would be thought that those in the back seat were unheard in the front. Valerie knew that the conversations could be heard, but Clement did not. Aaron and Valerie had discussed it as a safety precaution during the drive to pick up Tony. He had yet to tell Tony about it, which he thought would become obvious as soon as they started up. As Valerie had said, 'She had no secrets to hide, but we might learn a little about what secrets Clement may be prepared to share.'

She breathed a sigh of relief; she had thought Clement might have decided not to go but thought his curiosity would be aroused enough when she mentioned the Forrester family looking for him after the war. It was a winning point for her, which he had not known of, despite his long life wondering why he was left behind. It occurred to her to wonder why he had never tried to contact the Forrester family himself.

There was a quiet few minutes while Tony concentrated on the correct route to get on to the M6 motorway. When they finally made it and were cruising along in the quiet machine, Clement spoke up, 'What is it you found about the Forrester family trying to find me after the war?'

Valerie picked up the bag from the seat between them and, opening it, pulled out the copy of the newspaper pages dated 1946, 1947, and 1948 and handed it to Clement. She watched as he read the article and saw the tears come to his eyes and the look of wonder at knowing they had tried to trace him.

Valerie turned to face him and said, 'This article was repeated for two or three years in our local paper. How was it that no one answered the advertisement? There must have been other Haskell family who knew about you. How is it possible there was no talk about you amongst them?'

Clement looked sad. 'Granny Meg had made herself unpopular with the rest of the family. I do not know the reason. She would never discuss it with me, but I do know that your mother was the only one to answer the request from the school to take me in when the bombing started. I was sent to school at six years of age because granny was nursing my grandfather who was very ill. I remember that he was gassed during the war in France and had terrible nightmares. Granny explained to me that it was better for me to go to school so she had time to look after him.'

Valerie felt some sympathy for him. 'At age six, I suppose you do not always know the ins and outs of things that grown-ups do and say. It seems strange to me that my grandmother who was living in town at that time and in a safer area than us did not volunteer to have you. Her house was not bombed, but ours was, so you would have been safer with her. These questions have been bombarding me since I went to visit you at the residential care house. What was the reason why you were not taken care of or at least contacted after the war?

'The reason my own mother never saw the advertisement was that soon after you went home to Greenfields, my mother and I were evacuated to the York area, which was considered safer for us. My mother became a housekeeper and companion to a dear old lady, and we stayed with her for quite a while until she died. And then we returned south to stay with Grandmother until our house was rebuilt. We were away six or seven years or so altogether. That answers why we did not see the advertisement looking for you, but there must have been other family members surely. The wartime experiences or something else seemed to have broken the family apart, because I can never remember a time when we went to visit any aunts or uncles or cousins even. It seemed there was only Mother and Grandmother in my life whilst I was growing up.'

Clement was thoughtful, thinking back to his early years. 'I was at school from the age of six, going back to Greenfields for periods of break at the school, but I never recalled seeing other members of the family visiting. Grandfather had died during my first year at school, and my grandmother always said to me that I was better off at school than staying at home with just her in the house. The Bartle family had moved out. They were the housekeeper/handyman/farmer family who had been with our family since before Granny was married. They had grown too old to manage anything any more, and I remember Granny saying she pensioned them off.'

'Do you agree with me then that something occurred to break up the family members?' Valerie asked.

'Yes, but what?' he said.

'I do not know yet, but I want to get to the bottom of it all. My curiosity is aroused,' she said.

'I cannot see that the Forrester family would know anything about any fallout within the family. I do not recall any time they came to visit us,' Clement sadly said.

'What I was counting on is, in that era, computers were not invented to go to the general public, so the means of communicating was letter writing. I believe if your Granny Meg was isolated in a country area away from her own family, she would write to someone in her past to help assuage her own loneliness. She was so far from her family roots she must have had a sister or friend or even a nanny she would communicate with. Her entire history could be contained in those letters, and if they were kept by that someone, we could find out the truth of what was going on.

'In my own youth, I remember a pen friend I wrote consistently to over a few years. It was something all my friends did too. There were no mobile phones, in fact, not so many phones at all. We had to run to a phone box to call anyone. There was no television to keep us amused. We went once a week to the movies, we had dances, and occasionally we went to live shows. We used to sit around the radio in the early evenings to listen to serials for amusement.To communicate even then, we wrote letters to our friends just across town.'

Clem smiled at her. 'Ever the believer, eh? I can understand your curiosity, Valerie.'

'Yes, Clem, that is me. I am curious. Anyway, we will discuss this with John Forrester. He may have some insight into things with your Granny Meg. After all, no one else seems to have.'

They could feel the car slowing down and looked out the window to see a sheet of rain coming down. Tony was looking for a safe parking spot until the rain abated. A few moments later, he pulled into a signed area with 'Do not drink and drive' and other signage.

Aaron opened the privacy panel and asked if they wanted a cup of coffee and a snack while they waited for the rainstorm to pass.

'What a good idea, Aaron,' said Valerie, picking up the basket from the floor and passing things around. They had expected some cause to stop out of the weather at some time along the route and had come prepared.

'After this snack, I may have a snooze,' said Valerie. 'How is our timing working out, Tony?'

'We are doing well, Mrs Newton. In fact, there are not so many cars on the road despite a holiday today. I think the advertised rain storm has put some off, and we have made good time. We will be in the Lake area as you wanted before it gets dark.'

'Lake area?' said Clem. 'I had my first medical surgery there so many years ago. It was a very happy few years with Jenny.'

Valerie answered, 'My husband and I honeymooned there so many years ago. You may have been the local doctor, and we did not know. We only spent a few days there and travelled to the Roman fort following Hadrian's Wall and returned home via York to show my new husband where I spent part of the war. This is a trip down memory lane for me too, so long ago, but such remembered happiness.'

'How long were you married, Valerie?' he asked.

'Twenty-five years only. We happily celebrated our silver wedding anniversary, then I had three bad years after that. First, my mother died, then my husband. Two years later, my only son and his wife were killed in a motor accident. That left me to bring up my granddaughter, Alicia, who was only five when her parents died.'

'That is so sad, Valerie. I am sorry. I did not know anything about it.'

'You see, Clement, you were not done so hard by after all. Why did you not look us up at some time? You knew where we lived.'

'I did actually call at your house once, but there was no one home.'

'You should have left a note. I was possibly only next door in the bookshop.'

'Ah, the bookshop, I did not know it was yours, Valerie. I did look it up in the business registery and saw it was registered to a Robert something or other, not in your name at all.'

'How old was the register you looked at?' She did not elaborate any more on it.

The heavy rain abated. They moved back on to the motorway, and Tony said, 'We can make the stopover for the night in two hours. Is everyone comfortable?'

Valerie turned to Clement and said, 'Are you okay with that?'

'Yes, it will not be dark in two hours, and I for one will appreciate to see the town and have a wander around to get my legs working. Perhaps see if my old surgery office is still in a working condition. I believe that it would be updated by now.'

'I have made a booking for the bed-and-breakfast house where we spent our honeymoon. I remember it was lovely and hope it is still up to standard. I am sure by the pictures I saw on my tablet that it has had a makeover recently, and I was pleased to find out that it had rooms for us all.'

'You have a tablet, Valerie? You are really up to date for an old girl. I have found in my residential care home that the older men and women have ignored the computer and have been left behind in today's technology.'

'I am up to date, Clement. I have had my granddaughter and her very up-to-date husband living with me. They have encouraged me to learn, and nowadays, I can bring up all sorts of information very quickly. For instance, I know that you are the major shareholder in your residential building.'

'How clever of you, Valerie. I did not realise that information would be available to the public,' said Clem, looking startled.

'Our lives are laid bare nowadays, Clement.'

'Yes, it is disturbing, isn't it?' He sat looking inwards, perhaps wondering what else was available on the net for all to see.

They both dozed off for some of the way, and Valerie suddenly woke up to find Clement gazing at her, and she asked, 'Am I that interesting, Clement?'

'To me you are, Valerie. I was wondering how much on the inside is still Haskell. Your grandmother married out of the name and had one child, a girl who became your mother. And you were married, so the name was changed again. That is three times removed, and you have had nothing to do with my side of the family. The only connection to you and me is my grandfather Hugh Haskell. Does the Haskell representation keep continuing in you? Granny Meg, for instance, is not related to you. That I can see.'

'That is all true, Clement. I do not look anything like the Haskell family. There has been too much dilution since Hugh. I must look like my father or my grandfather perhaps. I will never know as all photographs of family and happy times went up in smoke when my house was set fire to.'

He looked sad and said, 'That was an almighty terrible decision that cost me my son's life. I have been mourning Jason since it happened. I had believed in him. He was a lovely boy and a young man, and now he is no more.'

'From his own mistakes, Clement. What started him into going wrong? From all accounts, he was accountable for some terrible murders. He did not do the murdering himself but arranged it all, I have been told.

'What were you expecting from Jason, Clement? Was he going to set up Bowering House for you to return to live happily ever after? From stolen money? Were you going along with that? Were you included in the conversation about getting into the bookshop, which was set on fire by your so-called lovely son and your wife? The fire spread to my home, all to murder our guest and my granddaughter and her husband!'

He went very quiet and seemed to have gone back to sleep, and Valerie said to herself, 'I was told by Paul Morris not to wake the giant. Clement now knows I am aware of everything. I had better go back to sleep myself and be more careful in the future. I should sit back a little and let him convict himself. He is almost there.'

* * *

As the car reached the Lake District, both Valerie and Clement woke up to look at the view of the passing countryside through a streaked wet window. It looked as if it had been raining all the way. But there was faint sunlight ahead; the rain might have been left behind.

As they approached the first township, Aaron slid the panel open to say, 'Which way do you want to go, Mrs Newton?'

'We should check in at our B & B first to make sure they have kept the rooms for us. It will give us time to wash and freshen up. We can then go for a drive to find somewhere to eat our evening meal. The receptionist at these places can usually suggest somewhere good close by. Once we have got that far, we can go for a walk. I am sure you all need to stretch your legs a bit after the long drive. We can do more of the tourist thing in the morning after we check out. We have plenty of time free before we arrive in Glasgow. I had suggested to John Forrester that we might arrive between three and four in the afternoon.'

'That sounds good, Mrs Newton. It is only ten minutes away for us now to the B & B,' said Aaron.

* * *

The house where the bed-and-breakfast house was situated was only a few steps from Clement's surgery, which remained intact and busy, despite the years it had been used, now with a new add-on at the back of the building. He asked for a tour of the old building, and the receptionist indulged him when told of the memories it invoked. Valerie hugged him, saying she could imagine him as a young man starting work here.

'I came up here alone to my first real job. I had spent many years at the medical college, and hospital duty was part of that as well. And I had the certificates to prove it. I was only twenty-one years old, much younger than the normal graduate, but Jonty thought I was ready. Jonty had been my constant companion in those years since leaving Bowering House. We leant on each other.

'Jonty Shepheard was the head doctor at the house during the war, and Granny Meg had made an agreement with him that I would look after him if he would look after me. Jonty had Parkinson's disease, for which there was no cure. He had been a top surgeon before the war and had almost retired from his career because of the symptoms when the war broke out, and he was brought back to the medical fold to supervise at Bowering House.

'At the age of thirty-seven, you could imagine he would have felt wanted again instead of withering away at home as the disease ceased his career. His trembling hands stopped his special surgical skills. His brain was unaffected in those days, and he was a jovial chap, not one to cry over spilt milk. Granny arranged for him to help me into a medical career, and I would look after him. He did not have a wife and family to look after him. I agreed because we were both on our own.

'This we did until I graduated. He helped me to study, and I helped look after him when I had the time. Jonty was a South African who had come to England to study and stayed on as a successful surgeon until his hands trembled so much he could no longer hold a scalpel. He was close to retirement because of his illness, and then the war intervened. The country needed every doctor they could get, and so he was back into action at Bowering House. Not in surgery, he had to leave that to someone else, but he was brilliant in the overall care unit and management.

I was not aware of all this until after Granny Meg died. I had often seen her talking to Jonty but thought it was just a general conversation. I found out after she had gone what she had arranged for me. I had wondered why Jonty took so much interest in teaching me on the daily rounds of the rooms. In the end, it worked out the best for me. No one else came forward for me, and Jonty and I got on well with each other, so we helped each other out.

'Granny had set up an account for Jonty for my expenses, knowing that once the war was over, Jonty would not be able to return to his surgical career, so he would be looking for a lower-paid job to keep him going. As it turned out, the medical school took him on as a teacher for several hours a week, and Jonty and I were able to prepare his lessons together to help him out.'

'What happened to Jonty after you left to start your own career?' asked Valerie.

'Jonty decided he wanted to leave the world. His condition was failing daily, and he was unable to do much any more, without help. It had grown so hard for him. I wanted him to come with me, and I could continue to look after him, but sadly, he decided to do it his way. One morning, I went to give him his breakfast, and he was dead in his bed.

'He left a note saying he had enjoyed our time together, and I was ready now to stand on my own two feet without him as a handicap. I must say I was shocked when I found him. The local parson helped me to see Jonty's decision was for him to make, and he was tired of life as it was for him. They'd had long conversations together whilst I was studying, so he knew Jonty had not made the decision lightly.'

'How did you choose where you opened your practice, Clem?'

'That was Jonty's doing. He knew of a doctor, Francis Morton, about to retire up here in the Lake District and asked him to take me on and continue the practice, which he would oversee for six months. It worked out so well for me, I even took over Morton's receptionist/nurse Jenny, who was his niece, and we were married within a year. We were very happy together. That was a good time in my life. Jason was born after we were married three years, and I relished being a father. He was five when the twins were born, and things became a little harder to manage.

'We took on my wife's nephew Zack when her sister died of breast cancer, and he lived with us until he died. He came to us shortly after the twins turned three. He was still a baby, only eighteen months old. It was very difficult for Jenny at that time with three almost babies to care for. Especially as the babies grew into boys, Ian and Zack seemed to hate each other. You must know how that ended up.' He looked enquiringly at her. 'I think Ian was jealous of him from the time he arrived with us, usurping his position as baby in the family, I suppose.'

'Yes, I heard the story and wondered about it.'

'You seem to know far more about these things than I do, Valerie.'

She did not answer his enquiry, looking out of the window as they passed through another village and saying, 'We seemed to have moved away from the Lake District. We must be close to the border with Scotland.'

A few minutes later, Aaron slid the panel open and said, 'We are about to cross the border. Do you have any specific arrangements, Mrs Newton, for our arrival at the Forrester house?'

'I told them we would arrive between three and four, so it sounds as if we will be on time to find the house. Does anybody want to stop and polish themselves up? We can stop somewhere and have lunch and visit their bathrooms.'

'That is a good idea, Valerie. I for one should like to use the bathroom before we have to greet people,' said Clem.

'Okay. I will look out for a small restaurant any time from now,' said Tony.

When Clement asked for his walking stick at the restaurant stop, Tony showed him the stick was at the bottom of the suitcases and said, 'I will dig it out and bring it in with me if you can manage for the short walk.'

Valerie stepped forward and said, 'Hold on to me, Clem. You will be fine. It is only a short distance.' She took his arm and moved away from the vehicle.

She saw Tony take out the small jar she had given him earlier and was able to manoeuvre Clement forward, and Aaron walked behind, blocking any view of the car with its boot open.

Duly eaten and washed up, they set off again towards Glasgow. This time, Clem had his walking stick beside him.

As the city came into view, Valerie could feel Clem beside her clench up and said to him, 'They are only family Clem, like you and me.'

'As Granny Meg would have said, you are very canny, Valerie. Yes, I am nervous. Besides you—and you have been missing from my life for most of it—I have had no family before, and I am not sure how I should greet them.'

'I do not think you need to be worried about another cousin. John Forrester sounded very friendly to me, and I think he will lead the way.'

'It is amazing how selfish we can be. I had not thought of you as family poor, Valerie.'

'I have only had my granddaughter for the past twenty-five years, Clem, although she has brought a wonderful young man into our family with her husband, James. I think of him as my grandson now, not an in-law at all. We get on together as if he has always been with us.'

'Where are they now, Valerie?'

'Holidaying in Australia. They will be back shortly. They are enjoying the sunshine.'

'Why didn't you go with them?'

'I had a few jobs to do, like meet with the insurance people for the bookshop and house and all our possessions. Perhaps I will go with them next time they have a holiday, but I would not be here with you now if they were home, Clement. They are very busy people, and I try to keep up with them. James did ask Tony and Aaron to watch over me, so I am not alone. But being alone is not a new thing for me, and I do not mind my own company.'

'I know what you mean. I have never been a great socialiser. When we were in the country towns, we were expected to show up at all the events, but in the city, I find that most people mind their own business and leave you to mind your own. It can get a little lonely at times.'

'I am curious how your entire family got on the wrong side of the law. Usually, perhaps one person in a family goes wrong, but the whole lot of yours are incarcerated, Clement. How is that?'

Clement looked shocked. 'You do not believe I have had anything to do with it, Valerie?'

'I am still speculating, Clem. It is a mystery to me that all of your children and your wife, Barbara, have done terrible things. For instance, to ram my bookshop for getting entry is not what I would consider the polite way to come calling. I have been left with nothing but the clothes I stood up in, and I have been very angry about that.

'My way of earning a living and everything I held dear have vanished in the flames. In fact, if we had not chosen to eat out that evening, I would say that the whole of my family would have been killed. I simmer when I think of that, Clem. This trip for me is a way to clear my mind that you were not part of it all and to find out for my own satisfaction that there is something in Granny Meg's past that is the cause of it all, which leaves me out of the DNA for the criminal link.'

'Let me get this clear, Valerie. You think our DNA through Granny Meg has a criminal link?' he said with a scowl on his face.

'How else can we take it, Clem? You are the father of the group of killers. I have not heard of anyone else in the family who has gone to jail. Therefore, there is something wrong somewhere, or is it all a coincidence?'

He sat quietly for some minutes, thinking over her accusations, then said (and she did not interrupt his thoughts), 'You are right with your questioning Granny Meg, I suppose, Valerie. She is the only one you do not share DNA with. I have never thought of it that way. To me she was wonderful, although I do know that not many other people liked her. She was very abrupt and did not believe in wasting her time with gossip. I knew she put a lot of people off, and that is probably why we had no contact with the rest of the family. As a child, you do not see around corners. You just accept what is in front of you. She was very loving towards me, and I returned that love. I missed her terribly when she was gone from me. She was more a mother to me than a grandmother. She was all I had ever known.'

'I am sorry, Clem, that I have upset you, but you had to know how I was thinking before we get to Glasgow. Do not worry. I will not mention your family other than Meg, and I will be discreet about her.'

Aaron interrupted their conversation by opening the panel between them and said, 'We are only about half an hour away from the city outskirts, and I believe we are closer to the house this side of the city. Do you want to stop at a lay-by to tidy yourselves and go to the bathroom?'

'Yes, please, Aaron. We want to appear civilised when we get there.'said Clem.

'Thank you,' agreed Valerie.

CHAPTER EIGHT

Tony tuned the address into the navigation panel to make it easier to find, and within half an hour, they were looking at a beautiful, large double-storey, red-brick home, within a lovely garden. There were iron grille decorative gates to the property that had been opened for them and a long tree-lined driveway curving around to the lovely house. They stopped in the driveway at the front of the house, and a man came out to greet them and helped carry the luggage into the house through the front door. John Forrester and his wife, Nancy, came to greet them and showed them upstairs, with their man carrying the luggage, and they were shown into individual rooms and invited back downstairs to have a cup of tea.

Valerie was very impressed with the house. It was a Victorian-style home with modern conveniences, kept in a beautiful condition. It had obviously been renovated and brought up to date at some time and was really a beautiful home.

Nancy announced they would have some refreshments, and then she would show them around the house so they would be orientated quickly.

She said, 'While we are having our cup of tea, my husband has gone to fetch his aunt who will be staying overnight with us. Jessica is Meg's younger sister and is quite aged, but her memory has not gone. If anything, her older memories are clearer to her. John thought it would be helpful having her here overnight to answer any questions you may have. She is a dear old lady, not like Meg at all, if you believe what she has to say about it. She can make Meg out as a scary person at times.'

Clem and Valerie looked at each other, and Clem shrugged his shoulders and said, 'It seems we are going to get some clarity at last.'

Nancy heard him and looked his way. 'I believe you lived your early life with Meg, Clement, so I guess you know what I mean.'

'It was a very long time ago, Nancy. Meg died when I was twelve years old. But no, Granny Meg was loving to me always. I had no reason to be scared of her. She was just Granny Meg.'

'I am sorry, Clement. I did not mean to be hurtful to you. Of course, you would have seen a different Meg to the rest of the family. I meant no prior knowledge of my own. I did not enter the family until many years after Meg had left here and have only heard of her occasionally at family meetings when people are reminiscing about the old days. I would say you are about my husband's age, so all he would know of Meg would be second-hand as well. That is why we have asked Aunt Jessie for the next couple of days. She loves talking over old times, so she will be happy to let you into all the family secrets.'

'Thank you, Nancy, we appreciate your hospitality to us all to your lovely home. Has this always been the family house?'

'Yes, Clem. I came to it at our marriage, but the family had lived here for a long time before that. I think they moved here away from the city smogs about the time Meg was a child and suffered asthma attacks on a daily basis, poor child. It was thought the fresh air away from all the factories would benefit her. It is a lovely location and a real family home, so they stayed on over the next almost one hundred years. I am happy about that because I love everything about the house and the location.'

Valerie joined in, 'It is certainly a lovely house and beautifully kept.'

'Thank you, Valerie, for those nice words. I understand from John that you are related to us through Hugh Haskell?'

'Yes, he was my grandmother's brother. Unfortunately, the two world wars got in the way of much of the family keeping in touch. The men went to war, and those that returned, like Hugh Haskell, were seriously affected by their wounds. During the Second World War, our family was depleted when Meg's twin sons and my father were lost in action, so there are not many of us left. We had lost touch with Clement before his granny died. We were evacuated to York for our safety, as we were in the bombing zone for shipping, and we stayed several years.

'When we returned, no one knew where he had gone. I was still a child, but between having our house rebuilt after it disappeared in a raid and finding a job, my mother was not able to question what happened to Clement. It was a chance meeting that brought Clem and I together recently when I decided to do a family history. I looked him up, and here we are.'

'What of Tony and Aaron, where do they fit in?' Nancy asked.

'Both are friends of my granddaughter and her husband and are my helpers in this foray into finding my family roots. Tony is my driver and helping hand, pledged to my grandson-in-law to keep me safe. Aaron also is a family friend and has the journalistic skills which found your family's newspaper searches for Clement after the war. He is going to write up the history for me to pass on to my family members in time.' Valerie smiled sweetly at them all.

As they moved from the table to have their tour of the house, Clem said quietly, 'You are good at this sort of thing, Valerie.'

'I spent many years in the bookshop practising my people management skills, Clem. They have come in handy many times.'

The tour of the house was interesting, with its conservatory, beautiful gardens, and renovated interior and furnishings all well maintained.

Clement said, 'It must have been hard for Meg to leave her home here. It is such a wonderful house and garden. She always liked the outdoors and maintained the vegetable garden patch at Bowering House. It always produced lovely, fresh vegetables for our table. She loved being in the garden, and another hobby was walking. No matter the weather, she took long walks almost every day while she could. The only days excluded were the foggy ones. They brought on her asthma. We were not far from the sea, so it did get foggy early on a lot of days with the change of seasons.'

Nancy sounded interested. 'So her asthma stayed with her all her life?'

'Yes, I would say so. There were intervals when it was a sunny weather when she was perfectly well and not bothered with her inhaler. In her middle age, between her twenties and her forties, she was asthma-free, but it came back with a vengeance. First, when grandfather died and then when the war started and her sons were killed. I think the stress brought it on. There was just the two of us for some years until she died from pneumonia. I blamed myself for it because she was worried what would become of me, a lad of not yet teenage years.'

Just then, there was a flurry in the house, and John Forrester and his aunt Jessica came in to the conservatory where the group were sitting.

Jessie was certainly aged, having the curved back many old people seem to have. Her hair was coloured a beige shade so that it lightened her features; otherwise, Clem thought she looked as much as Meg would have had in her old age. She carried a walking stick but left it by the door to come and greet the others.

Nancy got up to welcome Jessie and said, 'You have arrived just in time. We were talking about Meg. Clement has given us the opinion that stress brought on Meg's asthma attacks. Through her middle years, when life was good, she did not suffer them. But they came back when Hugh died and her sons died during the war, and she was worried about Clement's future.'

After greeting the other guests, Jessie said, 'That was my opinion too at the time. Her letters were erratic, and I wondered at the time if she had the other thing come back as well.'

Clement looked startled and said, 'What other thing, Aunt Jessie? She never spoke about anything else to me, although there were some days she stayed in bed and would not talk to anybody, even me. It was as if she was hiding away from the world.'

'How long did those spells last, Clement?' asked his cousin John.

'Sometimes three or four days. Sometimes longer. They were happening longer each time as time went by. Then Jonty, the head doctor, went up to see her when I was seen wandering around lost and gave her some medicine to help her. After that, she was not as sick so often and joined in the nurses and doctors' dinners, which she would not do before Jonty spoke to her. She was always a little antisocial.'

'She never changed then,' said Jessie. 'She was diagnosed with schizophrenia when she was fifteen by our own doctor. She was very moody and refused to talk to people for days. We never knew who she was going to be when she woke up. She had multiple personalities, and our parents asked the doctor to examine her. I remember our mother was devastated at the diagnosis. She blamed herself because it was in her family, and she had passed it on to Meg. The rest of us did not have it, so we were lucky. Meg was even then a solitary person, and as my brother put it, 'she mooched around'. She did some scary things. Nothing too bad I think now, but back then, she was many years older than me, I thought she was scary.

'When I think about it now, I believe she was an opium addict. Back in those days, the medicine for daily use was laudanum. Nowadays, we know it has opium as its base, but back then, it was given to anyone who could not sleep, Meg for one, and those who had coughing spells, Meg again. And she was asthmatic to top it all off. When I read newspapers today, I often think of Meg. She had an addiction of which she was unaware. Everyone was dosing her up with a drug and wondered why she was so erratic in her nature. Those doses would have been small to begin with, but as she grew up, the doses would have been drastically increased. Poor Meg, she never had a chance.'

Clement looked as if he was floored when Jessie stopped talking, and he said, 'I was studying medicine since I was fifteen. My friend Jonty put my age to eighteen so that I could enrol in medical school. He told the authorities my birth certificate was lost in the bombing. Somehow, they never came back to me for confirmation of this. They trusted Jonty, who had been training me since I was twelve.

It never dawned on me that Granny Meg was a drug addict. She hid it well, and children accept their parents and grandparents for what they are, without question. With all my knowledge of medical conditions, I never once questioned her. I accepted the asthma as her problem. I can see now you are right, and it pains me to have overlooked the thought for most of my life. I had wondered about schizophrenia when I have had a patient with the symptoms, but as she never mentioned it to me, I have ignored it, thinking it was only her way of dealing with life. Nothing to worry about it. But doubled up with the opium, it explains lots of things. Now I can see.'

Jessie said, 'My mother took the blame for the diagnosis as she said it ran in her family, but mostly through the male line. She had not known of a woman having the condition. No one else I know has it, thank goodness. My brother and I missed out on it too. It seems Meg was unlucky.'

Valerie took care not to look at Clement, but she wondered about his son Ian. The very scary Ian who thought it was logical to kill people he no longer needed. Even his eldest son, Jason, was cold-blooded in his consideration of getting his own way. There was something to explore there.

'What were the personalities? Do you still remember any of them, Aunt Jessie?' asked Valerie.

'They were diverse. One I remember was Aunt Philida, a maiden aunt who disapproved of children, especially little girls. And as I was the only little girl in the house, her remarks were mainly centered on me. I was scared of the disapproving Aunt Philida. Another one was Ah Nee, a Chinese girl, who chased the cat saying it would be a nice snack, but she never caught it. The cat was also scared of Meg and would not come near her. They were her favourite personalities, but there were many more that came and went.'

'It sounds like sibling teasing to me with a big imagination let loose, Aunt Jesse,' remarked Valerie.

'Yes, I have brought myself to believe it now, but when you are eight or nine years old, it can cause nightmares, and it kept me awake at night many times. I never complained because I did not want her to know I was scared. In hindsight, it was just as well, or I would have been dosed with laudanum to help me sleep, we would have both been drug addicts.' Jessie laughed. 'Meg did make things better for me after she left home. I was the only one she wrote to, and I looked forward to her letters.'

Valerie and Clement looked at each other and leant forward, and Clement said, 'Did you keep Meg's letters, Aunt Jessie?'

'I did at the beginning, but by the time World War II started, they came less and less until they dried up. I supposed that the delivery was difficult. Not all the mail got through in those times. I did not worry at the time. I had moved house and threw the letters away.

'I had recently married and had a small son to bring up, so I was busy elsewhere. It was only after the war and we still did not get letters that we began to wonder what was happening with her. Our father sent a private detective to look her up, and he found Bowering House was locked up and deserted. He discovered from the local clergy that Meg had died, but the clergyman knew nothing of your circumstances, Clement.

'Meg had not been a churchgoer, and it was an army captain that had made the arrangements for Meg's funeral. We looked in the records and saw that Meg's death had been recorded by a doctor, but as usual, we could not read his name. I have found that with most doctors.'

Valerie said, 'We hoped you had saved your letters to give us an insight of her life in those years at Bowering House.'

'I am sorry,' said Jessie. 'It all seemed such a long time ago, and I have never thought anyone else would want to read the letters. I do remember when father and an investigator gained entry to Bowering House. They found a box of papers and a number of journals in the attic that Meg had left. Someone had cleaned the house after the army hospital crew moved out and put anything of Meg's tidily in the attic. The person who discovered these papers brought the box back intact for our father to look at it and go through it and read the journals.

'I confess he would not allow me to go through the box or look at the journals. He was greatly grieved for Meg, his eldest daughter. Mother died about the same time, and he mourned her. When Meg was included in the tally, it nearly broke him. Poor man.'

She turned to John, 'Can you remember that box of papers, John? Would it still be in the attic?

'I am sorry, Jessie, I do not remember the box of papers. I think you are mixing me up with my father, but we can go and see if we can find it. Perhaps Aaron and Tony can help me. I think it would be too hard for the rest of you to climb the stairs. I am not sure if I can manage them. I like to ride up in elevators nowadays.'

He looked at Valerie, and she nodded. Tony and Aaron stood up and enquired, 'Now?'

John laughed. 'No time like the present. We will do it now so that we do not forget about it later.'

Valerie turned to Aunt Jessie and asked, 'I have been wondering about the provenance of Bowering House and how the Haskell family came into possession of it. I have also been wondering about the circumstances of Meg marrying into the Haskell family so far from her home in Scotland.'

'That is easy,' said Aunt Jessie. 'Hugh Haskell was a second cousin to Meg, whose family came from a village outside of Glasgow. They were farmers, well-to-do, and their youngest son Adrian, Hugh's father, like Meg, was plagued with asthma. They searched for a place for him to farm in the south of England, away from the sea fogs and winds that come off the ice-cold sea here in this area and chose Greenfields village because it was very like their home, without the cold and snow. Meg told me later that they still had fogs from the sea, but they were warmer than the Scots ones. This was Hugh's father Adrian, and he was still remembered by our father. He visited them and proposed Hugh and Meg to marry. Everybody thought it was a good idea, and I have often wondered whether Hugh was told of Meg's problems other than the asthma and if they were given a chance to say yes themselves to the marriage idea. I doubt it,' she said dryly. 'Hugh's parents retired to Torquay to a care home after Meg and Hugh married. I often wondered if living with Meg brought on that decision. We found it difficult living with Meg and she was my sister.'

'Ah,' said Valerie, 'so those are my ancestors. Were they all fair-haired and blue-eyed?'

'I think so. I have not met up with them for many years. You do not have the blue eyes like Clement.'

'No, but my grandmother did. She was very much like her brother Hugh Haskell. My colouring has been diluted by time, I suppose.'

Jessie thought for a moment and said, 'They were a lovely family, both in looks and nature, and I am sure my father thought he was doing the right thing by marrying Meg into the Haskell family. We never heard a complaint from Hugh, but then we never heard from him at all, come to think about it. I do not think now that it was his nature to complain. I did not have much to do with him as I was still a child, but he came to visit when the arrangement for their wedding was announced. He was a fair-haired, handsome young man, a little diffident in his manner. I think he was shy and did not talk about himself that I can remember. Most of his conversations was about his farm and his house. It was a long time ago, and my impressions of those days are dim, but I thought he was a nice young man. I never saw him after that visit.'

'I have a family photograph album here, Aunt Jessie. Would you like to go through it? It may bring things back to you,' said Valerie.

'I would love to go through it, Valerie. However, I am getting a little tired now. Do you mind if I put it off until the morning? I am much better after a good night's sleep and seem to fade as the day goes on.'

'I know what you mean, Aunt Jessie. I usually have a nap after lunch also to help carry me through the rest of the day. I have been living with my granddaughter and her husband, and I need that nap to keep up with them. They never seem to stop,' Valerie explained. 'I will bring out the album and other photos tomorrow.'

Clem broke in to say, 'You haven't shown me those photos yet, Valerie.'

'Sorry, Clem, I have been carrying them around with me for the moment to come when you could look. Tomorrow I will lay the photos out for you all to see.'

Just then, John Forrester and Aaron came back with Tony carrying a box in his hands, which he laid down on a table in the centre of the conservatory. 'There are some journals in here,' John said, gesturing at the box.

Nancy came back to them and said, 'Dinner will be ready in fifteen minutes. Do you want to wash your hands and come to the table? Mrs Arther, the cook, will be serving in twenty minutes. We can go over things more tomorrow. Aunt Jessie will be resting after dinner. This has been a long afternoon for her.'

'Very wise, Nancy, I agree to that. I am tired too after the trip and the conversations. I would be happy with an early night and get up fresh for another chat,' said Valerie.

They all got up to go to their rooms, leaving the box on the table as they went out.

* * *

The next morning, they got up, and feeling fresh after a pleasant evening and a good sleep, they met for breakfast in the dining room at eight o'clock as Nancy had requested by saying, 'It is our religious breakfast time so we can start the day off right.'

After breakfast, they all made for the conservatory, eager to see what they could find. Aaron was the first to notice that the journals were missing. He had put one on top of the box to hold down the loose papers whilst in the attic, and it was gone. He looked through the box and said, 'The other two are missing also.'

Everybody looked at each other, but no one confessed to taking them.

Valerie was the first to say, 'I did not touch them.'

Clement also said, 'I would not touch them in someone else's home. Granny Meg brought me up better than that.'

Aaron and Tony looked helpless, both saying there were three journals when they delivered the box to the conservatory.

John and Nancy looked at each other, and John left the room and returned later with Aunt Jessie and the three journals.

Aunt Jessie said, 'I should have them, John. I was her sister. They should have been given to me when they came here, and Father would not give them to me.'

'I am sorry, Aunt Jessie. Clement is Meg's heir, and they shall go to him. He got little else from the family, at least we can give him his grandmother's journals. He has not asked for anything else, and this is the least we can do.'

Nancy hugged the old woman who was acting like a naughty child and stamping her feet. 'You had the letters from Meg, Jessie, and you threw them away and never shared them with the rest of the family. You have had your chance, and now it is Clement's turn to have something of Meg's. He is her only grandchild still living. You must see the sense of that.'

'Meg would have wanted me to have them. She only wrote to me, not anyone else in the family. They should be mine,' Jessie continued crankily.

'She broke her father's heart by not writing to him, and you would not allow him to see your letters. I am sure you were meant to share them, and then you selfishly threw them away so none of us could see them. Your father was heartbroken when you did that.' This was from John, who looked very cross with his aunt.

Nancy said, 'Would you like it if we did not honour your grandson by leaving him out of the family inheritance, Aunt Jessie?'

Jessie looked up and frowned deeply, looking piteously at her nephew. 'You would not do that, John, would you?'

'No, Jessie, we would not, but this is the point. You are denying Clement his inheritance of Meg's belongings. He is her son's child. You must understand that, and this box and everything in it belongs to him now.'

Jessie broke into sobs, tears running down her face, but still would not give up. 'Meg was my sister.'

Nancy took the journals from Jessie's arms and handed them to Clement. 'I am sorry about this, Clement. She is so old that she sometimes plays the dementia card to get what she wants. She will get over it after a while. We will just put them out of sight for a while. Why don't you put them in your room? She will forget about them.'

She helped Clement out of his chair, and he took the books upstairs, returning shortly after.

Jessie, by this time, was chatting to Valerie about the aspidistra in the corner of the room, saying how old it was. Her father had planted it many years ago, and it was still doing well. It seemed as if there had been no argument about the journals.

Clement sat down next to her, and she turned to chat with him, asking him where he lived and describing her residential care home when he told her that he lived in one too. They were back to square one. John turned to Clement and said, 'May I have a quiet word with you in my study, Clem? I do not want Aunt Jessie starting up again. This is private between us.'

'Certainly, John,' said Clement, getting up from his chair. As he moved out of the room, he said, 'This is a lovely place you have here. It is so quiet with no street sounds and just the sound of the breeze and birds twittering.'

They were gone for some time, and Valerie suggested to Aaron and Tony to take the car and have a drive around the city and coastline. She had looked at pictures when the first thoughts had come up about driving to Scotland, so now suggested to the two young men to take themselves a tourist drive. Neither of them had been to Scotland previously, and there were so many things to be seen.

Valerie said, 'I can fill you in later if anything of interest comes up. Meanwhile, have a good time.'

They went off with alacrity. It was a nice day, soft breezes and light sunlight without a sign of rain.

The three women chatted about their families, and Jessie asked if Valerie had been to Bowering House.

'No, I haven't. My grandmother was brought up there, but there have been two wars in between, and the families had lost touch. Now I understand that it has been empty for many years and had run down a lot.' She did not go over the fact that Jason, Clement's son, had brought much of it back to its earlier beauty.

'Meg always wrote that it was a splendid house and that the farm was very fertile until Hugh got too sick to work it,' Jesse said.

'So I believe,' said Valerie. 'However, because it has been unattended for many years, it is not a good proposition unless you have a lot of money to bring it back to a workable farm. It is not so isolated today as it was in the past. Modern motorcars have brought it into a circle where it may be liveable again. In Meg's days, it would have been insufferably isolated, especially when there was petrol rationing for so many years.'

Nancy said, 'This house was isolated too when the family originally moved here, but they did not mind. It was refreshing to have the peace and quiet after the noise and grime of the city. The city has caught up with us in recent years, but our land is big enough that we still have the peace and quiet to enjoy. Nowadays, there are shops nearby, which is an asset. When I first came to the house, it was like a country retreat with only small shops close for things like bread and butter and cheese and eggs. No clothes, we had to go to the city for them and anything else.'

John Forrester and Clement came back to the conservatory to join them, and Nancy said, 'You are just in time for coffee. I have asked Mrs Archer to serve it here. It is such a nice day. It is lovely to have the garden atmosphere to enjoy. We shall be locked up inside for many months to come.'

Valerie looked at Clem, who was looking stunned and a little unsteady, and she wondered what news John Forrester had given him to make him appear like that.

She did not ask; it was not her business after all. It was Clem who was the relative, not her. Although it did not stop her from wondering.

She said to the Forresters, 'We may start our way back to the south tomorrow after breakfast. We are returning via Hadrian's Wall, Carlisle, and then York. Neither Aaron nor Tony have been up this far previously, and we do not want to rush it. Is that okay with you, Clement?'

He did not comment, and she could see he was not listening and was lost in his thoughts. She smiled and said to Nancy and John, 'Do you want Clement to stay a little longer?'

'It is up to Clem. We are happy to have him. Leave it for a while, and we will come back to it later,' said John.

'I will show you the photographs that I have collected. You will find some of them interesting,' said Valerie, getting to her feet to collect them from her bag and handing the album to John and the collection in the envelope to Nancy.

Looking through them, Nancy commented, 'They are interesting, but there are none of Meg.'

'I noticed that as well,' said Valerie 'and presumed she was the photographer of the twins and Clement. The only photo of her is the wedding photo. It looks as if she dodged the cameras after that.'

John commented when he got to the wedding photograph, 'That is my father in the background, Meg's older brother. It looks as if no one else from here went down south for the wedding. How unusual. I would have thought her mother and father would have gone with her to celebrate the wedding.'

Valerie nodded. 'That thought also occurred to me. Also, from the look on Meg's face, she is an unwilling bride. Would that be a correct statement? Aunt Jessie, do you remember the wedding photo of Meg and Hugh?' The group turned to Jessie, holding out the album for her to see the photograph.

Valerie could see that Jessie had got over her tantrum and smiled at her. 'Why didn't you go to the wedding, Aunt Jessie?'

'I had the measles and was quite ill, so Mother said it was best if I stayed at home with her. Father was too busy at the factory to go. It was just before the First World War, and he was busy with the government orders, so my brother Duncan went with Meg to give her away at the church altar.'

Valerie asked, 'Can you remember if Meg was excited or happy to be marrying Hugh?'

'When I asked her, she turned into Aunt Philida and told me little girls should mind their own business, so I was too scared to ask her any more questions. Hugh was very handsome, even though he did not talk very much because he was shy, so I thought she should have been happy. I would have been, but I was too young for Hugh to be my beau, Mother explained to me.

'Meg was very hard to understand. I remember Mother sighing a lot about her, and the house was so quiet when she left it.' Jessie looked glum, as if she remembered the hard times Meg had given her and the disappointment of missing her sister's wedding—a big moment in anyone's life.

Clem had come to life when Valerie pulled out the photographs and had been looking at the ones of the twins as they grew up.

'Where did you get these photos, Valerie, and why did you not show them to me before now?' he asked.

'They came from Bowering House earlier on, and the moment to show them to you never came up. You are welcome to keep them, Clem. I would just like to keep the ones of my grandmother when she was a child. I think my granddaughter would like to see them.'

'Thank you, Valerie. I would like to have the ones of my father and his twin brother. I have had none to date of the early family. They are very interesting to me.'

Clem turned to John and asked, 'Do you have any photographs of Granny Meg when she was growing up that you can show us, John?'

John in turn turned to his Aunt Jessie and asked, 'I do not remember seeing any of Meg. Have you any, Aunt Jessie?'

She shook her head and said, 'Meg was always camera-shy, although I think Mother and Father insisted she have some photographs taken at a studio before she left for her wedding. Have you seen them, Nancy?'

Nancy looked mystified. 'I cannot recall seeing a photograph of her. She must have destroyed them before she left. How odd.'

It seemed Aunt Jesse had been putting on an act to get her own way earlier; she seemed normal now. It was lucky Clem had been advised to put the journals in his room. She had better warn him to hide them in his suitcase before too long to stop Aunt Jessie going, foraging for them.

Valerie put the question again to Clem whether he was willing to leave the following morning or whether he wanted to stay on for a few more days.

'If you want to go tomorrow, Valerie, I will be happy to go with you. I have enjoyed the visit but do not want to outstay our welcome. Do you plan to leave after breakfast?'

'I agree, we do not want to overstay,' said Valerie. 'We have been made very welcome, but like you, I think it better to come back another day. We did make a quick decision to come and have been made very welcome, but I have to return as I have a few things I must do. You could stay if you want and come back south by train.'

'No, I will drive back with you. I enjoy your company,' decided Clem.

'In that case, we will leave after breakfast. Perhaps we could have a quick drive around where Aaron and Tony went today. They have not returned yet, so they are having a good look around and will know which places to revisit for us.'

Clem said, 'I think I will have a short nap. I feel so overwhelmed with everything. I will see you at dinner. Nancy said it will be at seven o'clock.'

'Okay, Clem, hide those journals, lock them in your bag. I will put these other papers from the box in the bag with the photo album for you to look at another time, when there are not so many distractions for you. There may be nothing but household accounts, but you may find something amongst them to catch your interest. I will have to replace the photo album from where

I found it, but before I do, I will take some of them to be printed for you to keep.'

He looked at her strangely. 'Where did you find them, Valerie?'

Valerie looked around to see if she would be overheard. 'They were picked up by a police raid on Bowering House, and I happened to see it at the time and recognised my grandmother. I have to replace them in the records. I did not ask if I could borrow them.'

'So you are on my side then?' he asked.

She looked astonished and said to him, 'It depends on what side you are talking about. I only borrowed the album and photographs to bring on this trip to show the Forresters. From what I know now, I presume they had not received photos from Meg or of her family. She did not write to her parents, only to her young sister.

'I have no intention of keeping the album or photos. They may be needed for an inquest on Jason and Barbara. Because of the circumstances of their deaths, the inquest was delayed until my family returns to UK from their holiday in Australia. They were very stressed about the fire of the buildings and the loss of all they owned and were advised to take time off for a month to recover. They will be back shortly, for the ongoing case.'

Clement looked baffled. 'What do you mean the ongoing case?'

'It is not over yet, Clem. DNA had to be taken to prove who the couple were in the vehicle. An enquiry will be held on the circumstances of the case and why it happened. It is not going to be a happy period for you, Clem, while that is going on.

'It has been a terrible time for my family to come to terms with the burnt-out bookshop and apartment dwelling and of my house and all our goods, such as clothing, furnishings, and such things that we loved. Of course, the books in the shop were worth a large sum on their own. Someone has to be made liable. It is not going to be quick. You may want to come to Scotland for an extensive stay while the law takes care of it.'

'Is this what this trip is about, Valerie?'

'No, Clem, you made me feel sorry for you all alone, and I thought you needed a boost. This was the one thing I thought I could do to help you.'

'Well, you could not have done better. This trip has been an eye-opener for me. It is strange that things can be overlooked during your life. I overlooked Granny Meg's health in my own misery. I never contemplated the Scottish heritage. After all, I had never seen them in my life previously, and Granny Meg never mentioned a family, although I have taken note that she named the twins, my father, after her brother John's father and the other twin after Hugh's father.

'It was always Granny Meg and me against the world. I thought she had no one in her background. She never spoke of them. As I said about her, she was antisocial, so I rarely saw anyone else. And she was not a great talker about her history. I have learnt more about her in the two days here than I did in the twelve years we lived together. I have much to think over. Do not ignore me, Valerie, after we arrive home. You are my mainstay now in the time I have left on this earth.'

Valerie was shocked. She had not meant to be put in this position. What of the thoughts she had previously about the spider in the web?

She needed to probe further into his life to prove her theory; she could not ignore him now and wonder for the rest of her life what he was capable of.

'I would like to read Meg's journals and study them, Clem. May I do that? I am a quick reader. After all, I ran a bookshop and read almost everything that I sold. I would like to have a personal viewpoint. No one else seems to have understood her at all.'

'Perhaps we can share them, Valerie. You may be able to point out some things that I was never aware of. She was a complicated person from all the accounts we have learnt here. I was only a child, and I think children miss a lot about the adults who care for them. They take them for granted because they are always there.'

Just then, Nancy came back into the conservatory and said, 'Dinner will be ready in twenty minutes. We want to make this a special meal to farewell you. Your young men have just arrived back from their trip and are now washing up in preparation for dinner.'

'Thank you, Nancy. We appreciate the trouble you have gone to make us comfortable. We learnt so much about Meg that no one else could have told us, and it explains so much. We have had a lovely stay with you and John and Aunt Jessie,' said Valerie.

'We too have enjoyed your company, Valerie. We do not often meet relatives we have not met before, and it has helped us to understand Meg a little better as well as meeting Clement, who has always been the missing cousin for John, who has often wondered where he ended up. I know that John's father always worried about him.'

Clem laughed. 'The bad penny, eh? It always turns up.'

'More the missing link, Clem. You were still such a young boy when you disappeared from sight. Now we know that Meg arranged your disappearance, and we will never know why she did not contact her family to look out for you. It is a mystery we will not ever know now.'

CHAPTER NINE

The next morning, the group set off from the house after breakfast as arranged, circling the city to allow Aaron and Tony to show them the sights before heading to the border and going south towards Hadrian's Wall, which the Romans had built thousands of years ago in history to stop the Scots from raiding. They stayed in Carlisle overnight and set off the next morning towards York, where they stayed another night, and then drove toward home, well pleased with themselves and their touring.

Before arriving back to Clement's residential care home, he handed Valerie the journals and said, 'Seeing as you are such a quick reader, you go through the papers in your bag and read the journals first, and perhaps you can go over them with me later. I find I get very tired eyes nowadays, so it would take me much longer to go through them, and you deserve to read them just as much as me. I will look forward to finding the real Granny Meg, which must come out of the journals. It seemed everyone had their own version of Meg, and it has left me with a lot to try and recall about her.

'The fact that the opium-based laudanum was probably instilled in her from early childhood will be a strong factor for her personality. I need to do some research about that while it is fresh in my mind to see if it affected the rest of us in line. It may have been why Ian and Jason turned out like they did, and yet it seems to me to be too much distance to jump to them. There is still work to be done to find out, so I will be busy chasing that up.'

'That is good, Clem. I was going to try that theory out myself but do not know where to start. If you do that, we can meet in the middle with it later,' she said, taking the journals from him and putting them in her bag.

'By the way, Valerie, thanks for not telling John and Nancy, certainly not Aunt Jesse, about my family and their misdoings. If we continue the association with Glasgow, I may bring it up in the future, but I did not want to shock them at this stage of our friendship.'

'Yes, Clem, that occurred to me also. It seems the natural thing to do.'

'You could be right, but they made no excuses to turn away from me, and it did not stop John handing me what he considers my due. He offered me what remained of Granny Meg's shares in the factories they run. When he did so, I asked what they were worth nowadays, and he said £2 million or thereabouts, if I wanted to sell them. Meanwhile, he will pay into my account the dividends as they come due. The dividends from the time of Granny Meg's portfolio have been paid back into the company for more shares.

'I could be a wealthy man. I will repay the expenses of this trip to you, Valerie, when I have a chance to go to my bank and see what John has transferred to me. I must say I was shocked by these revelations. I always thought Granny Meg had run out of money after she paid Jonty to take me over. She never mentioned her family and a portfolio of shares to me. That is not something I would have forgotten even in the days when she was so sick and dying. She did not mention it at all. I have to do a lot of thinking about those times to see why she did not tell me.'

Valerie said, 'I am glad for you, Clem. I will be joining my friends in Winchester for a few days after we get home, but I will take the journals and read them there, and when I have finished, I will ring you to meet me at the same tea shop in the mall where we met previously and discuss them. I do not have a home where I can ask you to visit. We have delayed until my granddaughter and her husband return, and we will make a decision where we are to live then. They will be home in a week or two. I haven't received a date when they are to arrive yet.'

'You lead a busy life, Valerie, at a time when most people are retired and playing bingo and scrabble to amuse themselves.'

She laughed. 'Running a bookshop for my living stopped me from taking a government pension, which suited me, and I have never had time for those leisure things and no need of them. I had ample satisfaction and company with the clients that kept coming to the bookshop, and I counted the customers as friends. It has kept my mind clear, and working and physically climbing steps in my house has kept me agile. I cooked because I enjoyed it until recently when I broke my arm, and Alicia has taken over the cooking for me. I have a lovely granddaughter, and her husband is very good to me. Until the fire, we were very happy. Now we have to rebuild our life.'

Soon they were stopping in the driveway of the residential care home to deliver Clem, who leant over and kissed Valerie's cheek and shook hands with Aaron and Tony, saying, 'Well done, boys, I enjoyed our jaunt. Thank you for taking care of Valerie and myself. I will see you soon, cousin.'

Next, they dropped Tony off, and when Valerie handed him the money she had promised, in an envelope, he handed it back to her and said, 'I have enjoyed this trip, Mrs Newton. I do not need to be paid. Thank you for the opportunity of going with you.'

Aaron drove to the partnership office to deliver Valerie and said the same. This time, Valerie said to him, 'Aaron, if it was not for you, we would not have gone on this trip. I have found a lot of new things to mull over, and Clement has been handed his inheritance of which he had no idea until John brought it up. It has been a very successful mini holiday for us. I am glad that you enjoyed it too, but keep the money. I will be calling on you soon. Give my love to Sandra and Jody.'

Going into the office, she sighed. Alone again after a busy week of chatting. It was a relief to sit quietly for a few minutes to go over things in her mind, to sift through the things she had learnt.

The first thing she did was ring Paul Morris, her detective friend, and tell him she was back and what she had learnt on the trip, that she was still unsure of Clement. But though she might be wrong about him with longer knowledge, she would still be careful.

Paul laughed. 'You are turning out to be a detective, Mrs Newton. James and Alicia will be proud of you. I must admit I have been a little worried you would be overdoing things, and I am very grateful you have rung and soothed me. What next have you got up your sleeve?'

'I will go back to Winchester to visit my friend. I will be very safe there. I will read the journals and think more of what we learnt about Clement's grandmother. I think the journals, which no one else has ever read, may bring some insight into Clem's early life and even his own children's.'

'That sounds like a good idea, but do not drop your guard when visiting with Clem. Keep thinking of him as that spider you conjured up until we are sure of him. I look forward to the next episode.'

Finishing the call, Valerie decided she was hungry and went to the coffee shop in the mall for a snack.

She came back and picked up the first journal but decided she was too tired to take it all in. The script was so small for her old eyes, so she put it back in her bag and decided the next day she would go to visit Robert Gooding in his nursing home for a few days. He would be a good person to discuss these journals with to get the most out of them.

She rang the nursing home and made an appointment to visit for three or four days, knowing Rob would be pleased to see her, leaving early the next day.

* * *

The bus trip was uneventful the next morning, and the staff at the nursing home were very welcoming. Sharon, Alicia's friend, was on duty and said Rob was well at the moment. There had been several warmer days recently, and he always flourished with them and went down when the cold weather came back.

She found him sitting in his wheelchair, about to come out to see if she had arrived. The big smile on his face showed his pleasure at seeing her.

Kissing his cheek, Valerie said, 'I have a conundrum to discuss with you to get your opinion, Rob. You were always good at working things out.'

'What have you got for me, Valerie?' he said eagerly.

'A case of a woman—now long dead—who was dosed up with laudanum over her early years, which she may have continued in her later life, although we have no proof of that. We think she would have been addicted enough over the years to have kept up the dosage. These are her journals.' She pulled them out of her bag.

'No one else has ever read them, and we are going to try to find out what sort of woman she was. This is mainly for her grandson, but I am very intrigued as well. Her great-grandson was the one who burnt the bookshop and my house. I suppose we are wondering if her addiction could have run into her family's life or if they were just thoroughly nasty people.'

'Well, Valerie, I have never done this sort of thing before. It's a case of inheritance, isn't it? Perhaps you should take it to the people who do that sort of thing?'

'They are not mine to disperse, Rob. I have borrowed them because I was curious about this woman named Meg. They belong to my cousin Clement, who has not read them yet either, but he allowed me to bring them away to study. I immediately thought this is right up your alley, so what do you think? Are you willing? Or do I have to go away to a corner because I am itching to read them?'

'Put like that, Valerie, I will give them a go. I can see the print is very small. Wait until I get my reading glasses, and we will start. Sit at the table, Valerie, or you will get a sore hand holding them. They look very heavy.'

'They are heavy. Several years take up each book, I think. There are only three of them over a span of thirty years, so that is ten years for each journal. No wonder she wrote small.' She laid each journal on the table. 'How are we going to handle this, Rob?'

'Do the journals come apart, Valerie? I have known some to unclip. She may have done that to write on the pages. It gets awkward to write towards the end of the journal.'

'Yes, it does, Rob. Look, I have just pulled out this spine, and it loosens the pages. How clever. This will make things much easier. We must be careful to put them back in the order we find them.'

'You will have to monitor that, my girl. My fingers are much too clawed to fiddle with such intricate things.'

'I am sorry. I forget you are handicapped sometimes. You are so bright in other ways. I am so pleased to have a friend like you, Rob.'

'Well, I still have my marbles. Sometimes I am not sure that is an asset or not when the pain comes on me. I would much rather not be able to feel it.'

Valerie gingerly peeled off the first page of the journal dated 1914, hoping it would not tear; it was so fragile. The paper was linen by the look of it, very fine, and the fine writing on it seemed right for the delicacy of it. She presumed that by being linen, it would be stronger than the average paper, but she was still careful.

CHAPTER TEN

The first page was written the day before the wedding with Hugh Haskell. Meg wrote that he was too good for her and raged at her parents for arranging the marriage without letting them become better acquainted. Hugh was a shy young man who lived on a farm, and the only other women he was acquainted with were his two sisters. He had been to a boys' boarding college and appeared very naïve about girls and women altogether. He was very polite to her, but they had scant knowledge of each other. She thought they were both too young to be married and once more blamed her parents for arranging it.

She must have stayed up late after the wedding to write her comments after Hugh was asleep. 'So that is what it's all about,' she wrote. 'What a fuss about nothing.' The doctor who had treated her at home had said she might be cured of her schizophrenia by the marriage. 'What nonsense' was her comment.

Some days she missed writing, not many at first. It seemed a novelty to her to have time alone when she could write her thoughts instead of being watched over all day by servants and family. Now she only had a warm older woman, Mrs Bartle, to help her with the chores, and the rest of her day she could please herself as Hugh was out with Mr Bartle, tending the land and sheep. She liked the freedom it gave her.

After three months, she became pregnant and once again became angry at being curtailed from her daily walks and gardening, because she grew too large with the twins she was carrying. She seemed an angry young woman. Not fully understanding her role as wife and mother.

Valerie stated to Rob, 'I suppose because of her asthma, she had been cosseted close, so she was not able to reconcile that this was a woman's lot. She had lived in isolation at her parents' home. With a young woman to teach her lessons, she did not go to school. It must have been a shock for her to come down to earth in a marriage.'

Rob laughed. 'A lot like me, I suppose. That is why I never married. I was afraid of making a fool of myself.'

Valerie looked at him, amazed. 'I never thought of why you did not marry. I accepted that you did not find the right woman. Marriage has its ups and downs, but it has more ups than downs. I was very happy in my marriage but did not want to repeat it after my husband died.'

'Reading these notes, I can see Meg was very naïve, and so was Hugh, but they battled on. It was expected in those days. It was a scandal to be divorced, so they did try to keep it going. She seems extraordinarily angry at her parents,' said Rob.

'Yes, she never wrote to them, and they were unhappy about that. She drifted into doing things her own way, which seems to have made a lot of people unhappy with her. On this page, she said she was tired of Hugh's sisters turning up asking if they could help and sitting around eating and then going home again. She told them she did not need them and not to bother to come again. She certainly cut off her nose to spite her face for when she had the twins. I am sure she could have done with some help, but she stayed adamant that she needed no one.

'Mrs Bartle helped deliver the twins and to look after them when Meg allowed it, but even with Mrs Bartle, she did not grow close to her. She was still doing everything her own way—Meg against the world. It does not mention here yet that she is taking laudanum for the birth pains and nursing pains, but I bet she was. She would have been so addicted by then it would have been second nature for her. If this was true, then the twins would have ingested the opium as well.'

'There has been a lot in the newspapers talking about young people doing crimes because their mother was a drug addict, and they had been diagnosed with foetal drug taking. Could this be one of those cases?' asked Rob.

'It sounds like it to me, Rob, but I will have to ask someone who knows more about it. I have only read it in newspapers as well. I am not sure if opium affects people like methamphetamine does nowadays. I have never been around the drug scene at all.'

'She has not written everyday about the two little boys. How about we stop now and have lunch? I can see the light flashing on my intercom. That heralds a meal. Shall we go?'

After lunch, they gave the journal a rest to have a nap. Valerie lay on her bed, tossing and turning, and could not sleep, so she got up and went quietly back into Rob's room to read a little more whilst Rob slept.

The very next page in the journal was a small cross, and underneath, it said, 'Silvia.' Nothing else on the page. She turned to the next page, and there was script saying, 'Hugh is very angry with me, but I could not bring a girl into the world to turn out like me. I just could not do it. We buried her in the shade of the trees at the back block. Luckily, the Bartle's were having their weekend off the farm. It saved us having to explain.'

Valerie was shocked. No wonder Hugh was angry. It sounded as if Meg smothered the little girl child. This was indeed a case where the opium had kicked in for Meg. If she had taken the opium-based laudanum for the birth pains, she would have not been in her right mind when the child was born, and with no one to help, she had smothered her baby.

She flicked through the journal quickly but carefully and later found another page saying the same thing—a cross marked Cecily. Then a few days after the note about Cecily, Hugh joined the army and was sent to France. Her comment for this was, 'Hugh wants to get away from me. I have never seen anyone so angry. My father never argued or got angry with us, so I do not understand why he cannot see that I am a sad description of a woman and not willing to bring other girls into the world to grow up like me.'

So Hugh had enlisted in the army to stop having more children with Meg. It sounded wise, but he was leaving one type of hell for another. Clement had said he came back after being gassed in France and was never the same man again. What a terrible fate for the poor man who was her grandmother's brother.

Rob woke up and saw her crying and bounded up to come to her. 'What is it, Valerie? Have you had bad news? Why are you crying?'

'I am sorry, Rob, bounding around like that may hurt you. I am only sad because I feel so sorry for the woman Meg, who hated herself, and the consequences for my grandmother's beloved brother. Meg was so horrible to Hugh's sisters, and consequently, the family broke up. I did not even know that I was part of the family. I never knew the name of Haskell.

'Meg smothered her baby girls because she could not bear that they may grow up to be like her, and Hugh was so angry about it that he joined the army to get away from her. Poor Hugh. He came back from the war after being gassed and was unable to manage the farm, so it ran downhill to decay. Within seven years, Meg had caused havoc for Hugh and his extended family. Their twin sons grew to manhood, though they were both killed early during the next war, and only Duncan's son, Clement, was left. Hugh died early after World War II started. So perhaps he died when he heard about the twin's demise.

'This is a terrible history. No wonder her father, on receiving these journals, would not allow anyone else to see them. I am amazed that he kept them even though they were in the attic. I suppose they were the only things he had to remember his eldest daughter by, so he could not bear to destroy them.

'I wonder if Meg knew that it was the opium in the syrup she took that caused her behaviour. Addicts seem to ignore the possibility of them getting worse and keep taking the drugs. There is actually no mention of laudanum in these notes. Perhaps she was unaware of its results. The alternative is too hard to bear, that she was not taking the drug and was a victim of psychosis. It seems too far to suggest she was psychopathic. Her only victims were the two baby girls, to stop them from growing up to be like her.

'Hugh should have reported her to the law, but the scandal would have had far-reaching consequences both for him and Meg's parents. So he humoured her but went to France to avoid her, only to return injured himself. He no longer had to worry about any issue from Meg. He was too sick to perform.

'I am so frightened to read any more. This is only volume 1. What if she continues in this manner? It is gut-wrenching to read. She appears not to realise what she has done.'

Rob patted her shoulder. 'If you do not read on, Valerie, you will always wonder what else has happened in her history. You said that Clement was waiting to hear from you about what you have read. You must go on to the end. She is dead and gone, so she cannot harm you. It may clear up what happened to cause Clement's family to act like they did.'

She thought about it for a few minutes and then agreed, 'You are right, Rob. That was the reason I started to read in the first place. It seems something came down in the genes for Clem's children to inherit. We have not ruled Clem out of that block yet either. He may be biding his time. Paul Morris, my friend in the detective department, said I must be careful around Clem, because he is the father of the group of modern killers, although he hides his possible true personality from me, it seems, if that is the case.'

Sitting up straighter, she said, 'You have convinced me. I must keep going, no matter how hard it is to read, until I come to the end.'

Pulling the journal towards her, she went on turning the pages and reading. Mostly it was about the twins, lively children it seems, and taken up with each other in play. Mr Bartle was trying to maintain the farm, but for one elderly man, it was a losing battle. They were relying on Meg's money—the money her father had given to her at their marriage—to live. They had advertised for help on the farm, but all the young men had gone to war, and nobody answered.

Soon after the twins turned seven, they were sent off to boarding school in the city close by, returning in the school breaks, which Meg seemed to relish for company.

Hugh came home from France, emaciated and coughing constantly, a shadow of his former self. He was unable to manage anything on the farm except the paperwork, which made him even more melancholy. He would sit in the sunshine for hours, not talking, or he would start coughing again. Sitting up seemed better for him. When lying down, his coughing was too much for him, so he would get up again and sit in an armchair.

Meg said Hugh treated her kindly. His delight with the boys when they arrived home made Meg wonder whether to remove them from school and teach them herself, but Hugh said they were very tiring, so he said to leave them at school.

Rob and Valerie discussed this, and both wondered if Hugh was afraid for the boys.

Valerie said, 'Clem said that Hugh had bad nightmares. They are not mentioned here yet. I wonder if something makes them start later on, or Meg has not mentioned them yet because they are not violent.'

They were on volume 2 of the journals by now and stopped for dinner and decided it was enough for one day, and they would continue tomorrow.

* * *

Valerie was very tired after reading the small script all day, she so was happy to have an early night. The next morning, she woke when Rob knocked on her door and said, 'Breakfast time, my dear.'

She scrambled out of bed and into the shower and joined Rob at the breakfast table in the dining room within ten minutes, saying, 'Good morning, Rob. I am fresh and awake, ready to struggle on with my mission at the journals table today, unless you have something more exciting to do.'

'No, Valerie, day follows day here, and they are much the same. I am lucky there is such nice staff here to chat with. Otherwise, I would have given up a long time ago. It is so nice to have you here to be with me. I really appreciate you.'

'Rob, you helped me out so many times when I came to live next door to you. Alicia and I believe you to be part of our family. Even James says so nowadays. We all appreciate you. Nothing will change that.'

'So Alicia and James are now content in their marriage.'

'Yes, Rob, James has fitted into the family so well. I now think of him as if he has always been with us. He is so much like my son. I have to stop myself from calling him the wrong name.'

'He struck me as being a very intelligent young man.'

'Yes, Rob, he is very smart. Did you know that he studied law? I want to suggest to him to sue the estate of Jason Bowering Haskell because of what that man did to the bookshop and house and how he left us destitute. When they arrive back from their holiday, he should be ready to go to court to carry this out. He was completely stunned and upset about the bookshop and house and the apartment that you used to live in. He blamed himself that the bad guys threw themselves at the bookshop door and set themselves alight, and of course, it was not his fault at all, but he was very stressed. I am hoping the holiday with his own family will bring him back fresh and angry enough to sue the Haskell fellows' bank account.'

'That would be a bonus if there is anything in the account. We don't know that. Do not count your chickens before they are hatched, Valerie.'

She laughed. 'You were always the one to bring me down to earth whenever I got het up, Rob. Thank you for the reminder.'

They went back to start the next journal. Valerie was careful with this one. It looked as if it had been damp, at some time. However, the dampness had not penetrated past the cover thankfully, she thought.

All seemed well with Meg's household for a while. She was just reporting the occasional holidays from school for the twins and the weather. It seemed the boys were very exuberant and were always together; it was hard to tell them apart. Hugh was very interested in their life at school and asked many questions, tut-tutting when that told him of their pranks. He said they did not take after him at school because he had been shy. The twins were not shy in any way and spoke proudly about the pranks they carried out on the other students.

As the boys grew older and left school, they declined to do most of the chores on the farm, saying they were not interested and they were going to join the air force as soon as they turned eighteen. Meg was appalled and offered to buy them their own Tiger Moth instead. They were overjoyed with this as they realised that joining the air force did not necessarily mean they would be taught to fly, and flying was what they wanted to do. Apparently, someone from the air force had given a lecture to the senior boys at school, trying to promote them to the services. Both Meg and Hugh wanted them to stay at home for a while and had not counted on them flying off for weeks at a time.

War stories were being broadcast every day on the radio. Hugh had started to cough more as the thought of his sons going to war brought on terrible nightmares for him. His health was deteriorating as he was not getting any sleep, and the lion in his chest would not allow him to eat without coughing it up again.

Meg was worried and begged the boys to stay at home to help look after their father, but they ignored her. A year later, Duncan had arrived home with a tiny baby boy strapped in like a doll on the passenger seat. He presented Clement—the choice of name was the mother's—to his parents proudly. Both Hugh and Meg were astonished at the turn of events. Now Meg had a baby as well as his grandfather to look after.

Meg was pleased that Hugh welcomed the baby into the family. Actually, Hugh perked up with the arrival of the baby. He nursed him each day on his knee while Meg went about her chores. For a while, they were happy until war was announced. The twins enlisted in the air force, and their flying skills meant they were amongst the first to be taken. They went on flying on daily sorties.

It was only a short time later that they were given the news that Duncan was lost in battle over the Channel.

Hugh started to have the nightmares again. Little Clement would wake up and try to comfort his grandfather. The nightmares did not go away, and Hugh would shut his bedroom door. He slept in a single room by then so that he did not wake Meg, but being alone, he found it better to sit up and nap rather than bear the nightmares that woke him up with terrible headaches.

Clem was almost six when they learnt that Adrian, the other twin, was shot trying to escape the prison camp. Hugh, by then, was so thin, and he became very ill, so Meg enrolled Clement into the boarding school that the twins had gone to. Having to pay school fees left the funds very low, but they battled on. Meg then mentioned that Mr and Mrs Bartle had been pensioned off some time previously, mainly because they could not afford to pay them. The vegetable garden that Meg looked after seemed to be their main source of food. She mentioned it often, saying what she had picked or planted.

There were several dates when she did not write in the journal during that time, and then she wrote, 'I have done it! He will not suffer any more. Hugh will be buried in the Greenfields cemetery in hallowed ground because he believed in the church. I can bring Clement home now and teach him his lessons myself and save the school fees.'

Rob and Valerie stared at the page. 'Does that mean that she killed Hugh? I can understand that she did not want him to suffer any more, but that is going a bit too far,' said Valerie.

'You could say that it is another mercy killing as she obviously thought that about her daughters' deaths,' said Rob.

'My goodness, I do not know what to believe. To kill her husband so she would not have to pay school fees sounds a bit drastic.'

'Wait, Valerie, you are jumping to conclusions again. The school fee issue may have been secondary, a way for her to console herself after the event.'

'I feel as if it is me she has killed. How dreadful of her, going around killing people off willy-nilly.'

'Calm down, Valerie. You are being too presumptive. Hugh had been very ill for a long time and probably begged her to do something. I have been there myself, Valerie, once or twice. My body was so full of pain that nothing I took or did would clear the pain for me, and I had wished to die.'

She looked at him. 'I am so sorry, Rob. I know you have dreadful pain from time to time. I have not forgotten how you could not climb the stairs to go to bed and how we made a bed up under the stairwell for you and hid it during the day by a bookcase so people coming into the bookshop could not see it. Even after that, the pain would not leave you alone, so we had to think of this marvellous place for you. That was a sad time for me. I felt bereft at your going from next to me. You had been my faithful friend, always there to help me through some terrible times.'

'We have remained friends, Valerie. That is what counts.'

'Yes, indeed, Rob.'

'Let us go to the dining room and have a cup of tea and come back refreshed. You look a bit shaky, Valerie.'

'Okay, Rob, I would like a cup of tea. I have had a shock from that journal reading and need the tea to get over it.'

Sharon came into the dining room for a cup of tea and joined them to ask how Alicia and James were doing. When Valerie said they were visiting Australia and would be back soon, Sharon exclaimed, 'I have been thinking of going there for a holiday myself! Will you ask Alicia to contact me when she arrives home so she can tell me all about it. The lady I took over from here at the desk went for a holiday there and stayed. So, I am on permanent staff now.'

Rob said, 'We do not want to lose you too, Sharon. You have the happiest face here and stories to make us smile.'

'Oh, Rob, you are the one that makes us all smile. They will put you behind the desk if I do not come back.'

'That would be the day, Sharon. One day and I would come and join you, if I lasted that long.'

CHAPTER ELEVEN

Back at the table, reading the journal, they reached the last page of journal 2 and turned to pick up the third one.

'I am getting tired of this small script,' said Valerie. 'Let's see what she has to say now.'

They opened the journal and took out the spine as before. There was a letter from the army, asking for an interview at the house the next week.

Meg had written, 'What can they do to us now? They crippled my husband and killed our two sons, and Clement is too young to go to war, unless they have asked for children to sign up.'

Clement had arrived home by bus the week before from school. He was a dear child to have around the house. He was neat, unlike the twins, who left mayhem in their wake. He did not raise his voice, was very polite, and was loving towards her. She was pleased to have him home and was preparing lessons for him. She had written to the school and got an agenda of subjects and a pile of books which were to take him through the next three or four years. There was a comment on the bottom of the headmaster's letter to her, saying that the school was closing down because of the ongoing bombing raids and that they had worked out this curriculum for three years, hoping the war would be over by then. As many of their boys came from farms and villages without schools, this was the best idea put forward by the staff.

When army captain Jonty Shepheard and his secretary arrived the following week, she admired the smart uniforms and polite salutation and asked why they were there.

Meg obviously did not beat about the bush, and when they told her they were commandeering her house for a hospital for those men wounded in the war, she asked, 'Why my house?'

She sat back and contemplated them. Clement was there and asked in Meg's place, 'How can you do that? Where will we live? We have nowhere to go.'

The captain said, 'If you have nowhere else to go, you can remain here, but you will be delegated to the attic space. We have acquired a plan of your house from the Lands Department. As the war has gone on so long and the wounded have been returning by the thousands, we have run out of hospital space, and this is our only means of housing the men who have no beds to go to. The department will make the rooms into bedrooms, and we will use the main dining room for meals.

'One room will be allocated to a surgery and operating theatre, and the meals will be brought in or cooked in the kitchen. An outhouse will be built to cater for the overflow needing an extra bathroom. I am sorry to advise you of this, but there is no alternative. Large houses have been delegated as hospitals all over the country, and yours is one of the best of these for the war effort. It is in a safe location, and the quiet countryside will be a benefit to a trooper needing rest.

'You say you have nowhere you can safely go. Have you no family to take you in?'

When Meg said no, he gave her a look as if to say, 'Everyone with a house this size has family.' Meg told of her own husband wounded in the First World War and now deceased and of her two sons killed in the Second World War and saw a look of sympathy come over the captain's face. He said, 'Then we will make you comfortable in the space we have available. A truck will be here tomorrow morning to arrange the rooms and make up the beds. The nursing staff will be sharing your attic space.'

At the end of the interview, he stated, 'The war department will pay you rent for the period they are in residence here. My secretary and I will be amongst the staff. I will be in charge of everything, and if you need anything, you can apply directly to me. If I am busy, my secretary will look after you. Please show me around the house now if you would, so that I can get an idea of where everything will fit.'

Meg and Clement showed them around the house, and Meg asked, 'What will happen to my valuable furnishings?'

'They will be stacked safely in a storeroom you nominate. Only the dining room setting will be required if you allow it. Otherwise, we will bring in other chairs and a table.'

'It is better to be used than stacked away for the rats to eat it,' she countered.

'Choose the furnishings you want to use for yourself, Mrs Haskell, and we will arrange them in the attic room for you tomorrow.'

After the captain had left them, Clement remarked, 'He seems nice, but who knows what he will end up like. Another Hitler? This is a big letdown for someone like you, Granny Meg, who values her privacy.'

She knew then that Clement was all right. He was not flighty like the twins were; he was very down to earth and understood her.

Valerie said to Rob, 'I have just spent a week with Clement, now about eighty years old, and I have been wondering whether he took after Meg. But it sounds like he has taken after his grandfather, possibly Meg's father, skipping the drugs altogether. We shall see. His children seem very much like Meg, although they never met her.'

'What became of Clement after the war?' asked Rob.

'We should read it here because it was Meg who arranged for him to be looked after according to Clement. So far, all Clement has told me has been true. He could not have known about these journals, so he has not copied Meg's story. At least that is good. I have taken all he has told me with a pinch of salt till now, but I have been wrong.'

They went on reading, stopping for lunch and then returning to the journal. Rob and Valerie were getting near to the end of the third journal, and it sounded as if Meg was slowing down. She mentioned twice that her asthma had returned, stating she had been clear of it for some years, and it had returned worse than ever. Perhaps she had no laudanum left to dose herself with. She was enjoying the company in the house for which she did not have to cater, and both she and Clement joined in the evening dinners with the doctors and nurses in the dining room.

In particular, she liked Jonty, the army captain in charge. He was interested in her, and after the first dinner she and Clem attended, he sought her out to ask her about the symptoms of her asthma. When she told him the asthma usually started when she had other symptoms, doctors had told her was schizophrenia, which turned up once or twice a year when she least expected it, and that she had it since childhood, he was sympathetic but could not do too much about it. It was out of his sphere of knowledge. At least he was honest, she wrote. He gave her an inhaler and an antihistamine tablet each day, and it seemed to relieve her coughing. He came back to examine her after a few days and said, 'It is possible that you have had an allergy to something all these years, and you have been dosed incorrectly.'

'It is true. I have felt so much better these last few weeks. I have felt in a daze because I cannot believe that I have been ill all these years from a misdiagnosis back in my early childhood.

'Unluckily, a patient came in to the hospital a few weeks later with influenza symptoms. And although he was isolated from the rest of the patients, the flu went through the hospital like wildfire. Both nurses in the other end of the attic caught it, and so did I. I believe I am getting pneumonia. I have been very sick. I will need to speak to Jonty about Clem. I cannot leave him alone in the world without someone to protect him. He is still a child. I feel as if my last days are numbered, so I must hurry.

'I sent Clement to ask Jonty to come and see me. I will ask him to look out for the boy. I have been saving the rent from the army in the cheques that come each month and will give them to Jonty to look after Clem. He is a lovely boy and does not deserve all that he has had to bear. He has looked after me in my sad days and cheered me, and he is so intelligent. He needs a man to help him into something that will give him a good life.

'Jonty is handicapped with his disease, and Clement could be a help to him in exchange for his attention. Yes, I think I will be doing the right thing by Clement if Jonty will agree.'

Several days later, Meg wrote in a quivering hand, 'Jonty has agreed to take Clement with him when he leaves here. He said that he believes Clem has the ability to be a doctor. He has been helping out in the dispensary and with bandaging since some of the nurses came down with that terrible flu and shows good signs of being a further help. Jonty will help him to study. He is a quick learner. He promised to look after my boy. Now I can go in peace.'

Valerie said, 'We know Meg died two weeks later, and the death certificate was written out by Captain [something indecipherable] of the British Army.'

Valerie sat back and looked at Rob. 'Clem told me all this, and I wondered whether it was made up to suit himself. It is just how he told it to me. I have been wrong in my estimation of him.'

'Have you been to see this big house, Valerie?' asked Rob.

'No, Rob, it was deserted for many years and became really run down. Clem's son Jason has been gradually renovating it with the help of his stepmother, the two who caused the fires in the bookshop. James said it is truly beautiful, although the exterior needs some work to make it look grand again. Jason had purchased it with his partner, who was his boss, as a getaway for if they ever had to leave Africa in a hurry. There is an aircraft in the hangar still from when Jason flew it in on his very last trip.'

'Why don't you ask Clement to take you there? I would bet he has a key.'

'That is an idea. I admit I am inquisitive. It is also my family home too, I suppose. I will think about it. I will have to find someone to take us. Paul Morris has urged me to have someone else with me and never be alone with Clem, just in case.'

'I can understand that, Valerie. After all, he is the father of four of the people who murdered several people. It is a case of "Do not be alone with him for too long". You know more than anyone else about the case. Even the police, now that you alone have read these journals.'

'Do you think I have made a mistake taking these journals from Clem?

'You were not to know that, Valerie, but some of these writings are a confessional of a woman that killed two of her babies and her husband. You were not to know that, and I am sure Clem does not know. But once he has read the journals, he will not want all that to get out to the public. His family are in enough trouble as it is. I cannot understand why Meg's father did not burn these journals.'

'Umm, you are right, Rob. My first thought was that these should not have seen the light of day. I feel quite emotional from reading them. One half of me is so sorry for Meg. The other half is a feeling of abhorrence that such a person was allowed to live. I am sure I will have bad dreams for a while.

'Meanwhile, I have been feeling sorry for Clem. I loved him when he visited us when he was a boy. He was always so polite to my mother and sweet with me. This is a big burden for him, which will ruin his old age if it ever gets out. I will not tell anybody about the journals. It is all up to Clem now. Perhaps he can use them to have at least Fiona's sentence reduced.'

'When will you give them to him, Valerie?'

'I have used up my three days allowed here, seeing as you are not ill. I will ring him this afternoon to meet me at the tearoom in the mall tomorrow at ten. I will feel safer there than going to his residential care home and being alone with him in his room.'

'You are still keeping your distance from him then?'

'I am sorry to say, reading these journals and knowing the history of his children has me still frightened. Enough that I want to take care when I am with him.'

'When do Alicia and James return from their holiday? Have you heard yet?'

'I received a long email this morning. They are leaving Australia to travel to Zimbabwe to see Divit and Derek before coming home. Divit has asked this of them and Percy and is arranging the tickets and visas for them to stay a week before arriving back at Gatwick.'

'I will be waiting to hear the rest of the story after they arrive home and find out what you have been up to. I can just imagine Alicia tut-tutting at you and James sitting with his jaw dropped while you recite all you have found out.' Rob laughed.

'I promise I will keep you up to date, even if it is only on the phone. Once they come home, we will be searching for somewhere to live. I was going to look around for something while they were overseas and have been far too busy to even think about it, but we will not all fit in the office. There is only one small bed.'

* * *

Valerie met Clement in the teahouse in the mall as promised the next morning. He was looking very well and quite excited to see her.

He started to talk to her before she sat down, and she laughed, realising he must have been to the bank and found what John Forrester had transferred to his account.

'I am a rich man now, Valerie, and the first thing I want to do is pay you back for the wonderful trip to Glasgow that you organised so beautifully. I have written out a cheque for you with what I believe is the amount you had to pay out.'

He handed her a cheque, and when she looked at it, she said, 'This is far too much, Clem. Half as much would have done it.'

'Cousin, you deserve so much more just organising the trip, and all you and your friends put into it is worth that and more to me. I feel my whole life is changed with your presence in my life. I am now not the sad old man you first met three weeks ago. Just the thought of my fourteen-year-old self having someone looking for me has uplifted me. I had felt so abandoned at the time. Jonty was a wonderful friend to me, but that is not the same as family.'

'I understand that, Clem, and am glad for you that things have turned out so well. With that in mind, I urge you not to read Meg's journals. It was hard for me to read them, and at one stage, I broke down in tears, so I believe you will be very upset with some of the things she has written about her life. The one thing positive about her is, she loved you, Clem. I believe more than she had ever loved anyone else in her life. Believe me and throw the journals away.'

Clem looked at her, stunned. 'Is it really so bad, Valerie?'

'I believe so, Clem. I found them very hard to read. I felt sorry for her at stages, and at other stages, I felt angry with her. I cannot understand why her father did not destroy them. She was so angry with her family for forcing her to marry Hugh, not because she did not want Hugh, just that they rushed the marriage forward, and she felt neither of them were ready for it. The parents had organised it without waiting until the young ones knew each other. Meg was a very sick young woman, both in mind and body. She never contacted her parents after leaving home. That anger stayed with her for the rest of her life. That is why she did not contact them to take you after she died.'

'I think I became aware of that from what John Forrester told me. He said that her father was sad she had thought of him like that. All he wanted for her was her happiness, but it blew up in his face, and he never got over it.'

'There were some circumstances that proved she was not in her right mind. I believe she kept up the laudanum for several years at least. You will have to do that study about whether the drug passed down the line to her great-grandchildren. It seems a step too far for me, but if her other problems with schizophrenia have been passed down, I can see Ian may have inherited it. Reading the journals made me think psychosis would be a better word for what she had. Is that inherited?'

'They are long words, Valerie, for someone not in the psychiatry world.'

'I know, Clem, and I am not sure of what each one means, but she was a complicated woman left on her own for many years for things to fester in her mind. I did feel sorry for, her but there is a point where sorry is not warranted at times.'

'Instead of stopping me from reading the journals, I am more interested than ever. So much about this business is about Meg. I am the only one left to remember her. I feel as if I do have to learn more about her.'

'In that case, Clem, here are the journals,' she said, handing them over the table. 'I have not looked through the other pages from the box yet. Reading Meg's small print took up the most of three days, and I was so tired after that. I will look at them tonight to see if there is anything worth keeping. I will give them to you next time I see you. I will also arrange copies of the twin's photographs before I put them back to where I borrowed them. My granddaughter and her husband will be back next week, so I have to have everything tidy before they come home.'

'Did you take them from where your grandson put them, Valerie?'

'Yes, he is on the case involving your family, Clement, and went to Bowering House with the police to look for evidence of Jason's entry into the country after the fire at the bookshop. He was involved because the police asked him to look after Divit, Jason's elder stepson, who had amnesia after waking up from Fiona's attack on him.'

'You mean Fiona's supposed attack, don't you, Valerie?'

'No, Clem. She recognised Divit, and so did Faye. Both confessed to it when he faced them at her house.'

'I did not learn that from Fiona. She is saying she did not kill him, so why is she locked up?'

'I am not sure of the laws applicable, Clem, but I would say attempted murder is one of the charges. The boy had many scars from her attempt to kill him. Another charge would have been about the cocaine she was selling, I presume.'

'And Faye, what did that silly girl do?'

'Faye apparently went along to help Fiona out and did kill Edward, Divit's brother, after drugging both young men. Edward was only fourteen, and Divit was seventeen at that time.'

'It is all Jason's fault. He urged the girls to do that deed for him. He had been pushing for it for two years, and Fiona did not want to do it.'

'You knew about it beforehand, Clem?'

He looked shocked that he had revealed his knowledge unwittingly.

'It is your casual, kind manner that makes people say what they do not mean to admit. I must be off now, Valerie. I do not want you telling your grandson-in-law everything I say.' He picked up the journals and pushed his chair back, stood up, and walked away. He was obviously cross with himself.

She watched him go, thinking, *I was right the first time I met him. He does know more than he is making out. It seems Fiona is his soft point. I will have to introduce James to him. That will be an eye-opener. James has a way to get people talking, and he can use Fiona as his leverage.*

She wandered around the shopping mall for another half hour to make sure that Clem had indeed left before going back to the office. It was time to phone the council and insurer. She had left enough time since the Christmas break, and they should be ready to deal with her by now.

CHAPTER TWELVE

Valerie was busy with interviews for the next few days regarding a payout from the insurance company and the council for the land and the proposed cruise-liner office and apartments above. She put her name down for two of the apartments and chose the two at the end above the cruise office.

The offer that the insurance company made, she thought, was generous, but she did not accept, waiting for Alicia and James to come back to advise her.

She rang Paul Morris and advised him of her return to the city office and that Alicia, James, and Percy would be back in one week. She did not mention the journals, wanting to think more about them before telling anybody about them. After all, they belonged to Clement, not her.

She rang Tony Walton and told him that Clement had paid for his time, and therefore the next time she saw Tony, she would give him what was owed to him. That left Aaron to tell the story to, so she invited herself to lunch the next day. She could hear Jody in the background, cheering. What a lovely little girl she was.

The next morning, she walked to their apartment. The weather was still a little drizzly, but it was pleasant to walk with the soft rain on her face, and she was well rugged up. Jody was at the window, waiting for her, and rushed to hug her when Aaron opened the door.

After hanging her coat and hat up, he turned and said, 'I have written a draft of what we did last week, Mrs Newton. You can take it with you to read over later. Have you any more news about Clem?'

She explained about the journals they had brought down from the Forrester attic and that she had read them but thought it best for Clem to read them before what was in them was discussed for Aaron to include in the history.

Aaron looked at her and said, 'That bad, eh?'

She laughed. 'Yes, Aaron, some of it was. I wish now that Mr Forrester Senior had destroyed them. It is no wonder he would not allow Aunt Jessie to read them. I think Clem is going to be shocked when he sits down to read. I did advise him not to read them, but it seems what I said determined him more than ever. I do not expect to hear from him for a while. They are really hard to read, both for the content and the small print she used.'

'It sounds quite a story, Mrs Newton, but I can understand if Clem does not want it bandied around. Having a drug addict as a grandmother is somehow distasteful, even if it was accidental from lack of knowledge of a product.'

'Would you believe that a doctor told Meg towards the end of her life that she was misdiagnosed from a young age and that much of what they thought of as asthma was an allergic reaction of some sort? Perhaps the seeds blown up by the winds at certain times of the year. Taking the drugs were not necessary. An antihistamine would have fixed it for her.'

'My goodness, what a bombshell for her after a lifetime of addiction. The poor woman.'

'That was my reaction as well. I went from one to another reaction all the way through the journals. I felt sorry for her at times, and I was angry with her at times. After I finished reading, I wished I had never started. It was such a terrible history of the woman she became.'

'I am sorry, Mrs Newton, but you have aroused my curiosity even more.'

'That is what Clem said when I handed the journals back to him, advising him not to read them. Do you know she must have only been in her early fifties when she died? Still so young, and she went through so much sorrow.'

Jody came to her and said, 'Do not be sad, Granny. When will Alicia and James come home?'

'Next week, Jody. I am looking forward to seeing them again, and we will have to find a new house to live in. We had such fun together in the bookshop, didn't we?'

Jody looked sad. 'I can't believe it has gone, Granny. I thought it would be there forever, and I could come and stay with you sometimes.'

'I know it will not be the same, Jody. I am too old to start up another bookshop, but you will have to come and visit us in our new house wherever it is to be.'

'Have you any idea where you want to go, Mrs Newton?' asked Sandra.

'Not too far away. I have been asked by the others to choose something, but between the trip to Glasgow and visiting my friend Rob Gooding in Winchester, I have had no time for looking around. The others will be back in a week with nowhere to live.'

'You do not sound as if you are too worried about it, Mrs Newton,' said Aaron.

'You are right, Aaron. Whatever I choose will not be what the others would want. That is the way with families, so I have shelved the decision until their return. I will start the search next week before they arrive so I am arranging a list they can check through. That will be a start for them.'

After lunch, Granny said, 'I am sorry to leave you with the dishes, but I have an appointment with a real estate agent this afternoon. After a lovely lunch like that, I need the walk back to the office to get my mind working again before I see them. I will let you know when Alicia and James will return.' She picked up the papers that Aaron had prepared for her, kissed Jody and Sandra and Aaron, and set off for her appointment, thinking to herself, *I am not too sure what sort of home we need now. A long term one or a short-term one until the apartments above the cruise centre were completed? They could be years off.*

* * *

After getting a list of houses available and their prices, she returned to the office. There was a message left on the desktop for her. Kate and Ken must have called in while she was out. She rang Kate's phone and was answered immediately. Kate said, 'We must have just missed you, Granny. We have just arrived back home. Can we come and get you for dinner? We have recently arrived back from the Isle of Wight, where we had a fabulous time. The weather is better this year. Last year, it was so windy, but although windy, which is what you want for boating, this time the winds were not so chilly. It was great. Ken can be right over to pick you up if you want to come.'

'Yes, Kate, I would like that. Thank you.'

Ken was there for her in ten minutes, and they walked to the house that belonged to Percy but Ken and Kate were renting.

Granny said, 'I have not been here before today. I have often wondered where it was. I knew it was close, and this is a marvellous location for the office.'

Ken agreed, 'We have an option for you if you would like to hear it before the others return so you can think it over.'

Granny was curious. Although friendly, she did not have much to do with Kate and Ken, the office staff, as she rarely went to the office while they were working, until the fire, then she had been in daily for a few weeks until the other group went to Australia for their holiday.

'I am curious, Ken,' she said.

'Just wait until we get inside, and we will tell you our thoughts. Kate as well will want to be there to tell you the news.'

Valerie looked around her. They had entered an iron gate at a narrow entry, just wide enough for a car to drive through, and were walking now on a driveway to the house, set back amongst what was a lovely garden. It was difficult to see the house because it was behind trees and shrubs and seemed very private. She was very impressed with the garden and could see a vegetable garden at the side of the house.

As they parked and went into the house, there was a large hallway with two bench seats from a church lining the hall with a hall table between them.

They moved through the hallway and entered the sitting room, a big room with a large bow window with seating and several armchairs facing a television set. It was an attractive room, and added on was a large dining room with a long table and a lovely cabinet filled with glasses and crystal bowls. They moved through the dining room to a kitchen, much bigger than the one she had in her house, with timber fronted cupboards with a butcher's block at the end, once again timber to match the cupboards. A family-sized refrigerator and a modern stove completed the picture. Then she turned and saw a table and four matching chairs in a nook.

Kate was waiting there for them. 'It is nice, Granny, isn't it?'

'It certainly is Kate. Percy never described it to me, and I have never seen it before. What a surprise.'

'There are three bedrooms. Come, I will show you through,' said Kate.

They went down a passage with a bathroom to the left and two single rooms adjacent. They popped their heads in, and Granny said, 'They are bigger than average.'

At the end of the passage was the master bedroom, a large room with a desk in one corner and an en suite in the other, without a bath, a shower console standing in one corner where a bath had previously stood it seemed. It did not look old, so it must have been renovated, perhaps when Percy's wife became ill.

She turned to look at the bedroom again and said, 'This is huge. It looks as if it has been extended at some time.'

Kate said, 'I think this was first a duplex—two houses side by side connected by a wall—and Percy must have made it into one house instead of two small ones.'

The main window was to the front of the large bedroom, and there was another door to the rear of the room. When Kate pushed it open, it showed a large walk-in robe.

'I never imagined this. It is a lovely house,' said Valerie.

'There is a small addition outside at the rear of the kitchen—a large room with a shower stall and toilet—which can be used for an extra person or guest. Also a laundry and clothesline. It is approached through the kitchen. All you need in a house. All the furniture belongs to Percy. I had been living with my mother until I met Ken, so I did not bring much to the house. Come and have a seat in the kitchen nook, and I will make a cup of tea, and Ken or I will tell you our story.'

They went back to the kitchen and sat down to tea and scones, and Ken said, 'While we have been away, Kate and I have talked things over, and we have decided to get married. The children seem to have accepted me now, so there is no barrier there any more. And we thought'—here he paused and looked at Kate ' if Percy agrees—and knowing his fondness for your family, we think he will—we will buy our own house, and you could all move into this house. We felt so badly for you when your house and bookshop and the apartment were burnt down. We were so sorry for you all, and we know that James was devastated and hope he will be all right now he has had a holiday and time to get over it.'

He went on, 'I have my payout from the police department, and Kate still has hers. Although we will still need a mortgage, but it will not be much more than rent. We think if we moved closer to the school, we will make the whole family happy, as it will be closer to the secondary school as well and not too far from the university. We have chosen a house and have put a deposit down to hold it for three weeks for moving in. Two weeks have already gone while we have been deciding it and having another look through.

'The children like it, which is one milestone over, and Kate and I both think it will do for a few years. It is in a good area and in good condition, so it will not go backward, and we could call it an investment. We will need a car so we can get to work, but that was always on the agenda anyway. We have been lucky this house is so close to the office that we did not need it previously, but it will also mean we do not have to catch a bus on our days off, which will be a bonus. So what do you think?'

Granny was near tears and said, 'What a wonderful couple you are, doing this for us. Of course, all this is up to Percy, and if he agrees, it can be a lifesaver until we decide what else to do. We had never spoken of moving. We were happy with what we had. It was all such a shock to us, to be left with only what we stood up in and all the memories from down the ages gone as if they never existed. I will not pretend I was not devastated too.'

'There is one other advantage too, Granny,' said Kate. 'Tell her about the alarm system, Ken.'

'Oh yes, that is a good thing to have. Percy must have put it in when he was in the police force. As a detective, you can sometimes have callers that are not welcome. Because of the land size, it is quite extensive. He has cameras all over the place so that each window and door can be seen by a screen in the hallway. The front gate can be locked on and off on a keypad and has an intercom so anyone without the code would not get in for a start. After what you have been through, I imagine you will feel safe here.'

'It is so close to the office and shopping and all we have been used to. I would not have to catch buses except to Winchester, and that station is just down the road and around the corner. I will have to wait until Percy gets here. It is only the day after tomorrow. Perhaps I can call him tonight to give him time to think it over before he arrives. I really like the idea, Kate and Ken. We can pay him rent to make it a better proposition for him. Thank you both for thinking of us. When do you start the plans for the wedding?'

'We have not told my mother yet,' said Kate. 'We cannot see the need to wait now we have decided, so as soon as we move house, we will start planning.'

'Congratulation to you both, and I wish you every happiness.'

After a lovely meal, Ken escorted Granny back to the office, and she asked, 'So you have not regretted leaving the Big Smoke to live here, Ken?'

'Not at all, Granny. I like the way Percy and James run the office and the rate at which they so cleverly solve cases. James, in particular, is amazingly clever, and I have learnt a lot from him that I did not learn while a policeman. I can see a good future here, and with Kate and the children thrown into the mix, I am very happy to be here.'

'I am glad to hear it, Ken. I know James likes you a lot. Alicia was a little hesitant at first, but she has got over it now. I think it was because they were working as a family group. Of course, that had to change as time went on, and Alicia has moved on with it, taking on jobs of her own that makes her feel more part of the team.'

'I realised that at the time, Granny. She had a lot on her plate helping you out and working in the office as well. I am pleased your arm has been working better for you. That was a nasty break you had.'

'They will not have to work in the bookshop now on Saturdays, so that will free Alicia's time up for her to do her painting. And if we move into Percy's house, I can see that we will have to do a bit of gardening. That should keep us all occupied. I have been sad at losing the bookshop, but it has had its benefits as well. I was locked up six days a week there with no freedom to do anything else. You can see I am looking on the bright side of things,' Granny said, laughing.

'I think you are brave, Granny, under the circumstances. I sincerely hope James has come to terms with the fire by now. He was utterly angry and devastated, mainly I think because it was your property that was burnt, he felt guilty.'

'You are right, Ken. That was my reading of it as well. He need not think of it that way. I agreed that Divit came to us. We collectively discussed it, and we all thought it was the best for Divit until he could stand on his own two feet while his memory came back. Even the doctors and the police department suggested it as the best answer to keep him safe. It was never meant to be permanent.

'The best thing that came out of it is that the shock of the fire jolted Divit's memory so that he was almost back to normal. I am looking forward to hearing more about him when James and company. return. They are meeting with him as we speak, I believe, so we will find out on Monday when they are all back at work.'

'Well, Granny, here we are at your temporary home. I think this was a good idea of yours to take up residence here. It is so central to everything.'

Granny laughed. 'Comfortable too. I will be sorry to move out. Never mind, better things are happening in the future. Thanks for walking me back, Ken. I appreciate it. Goodnight.'

CHAPTER THIRTEEN

Going into the office, she thought, *I have not even looked at the messages to see if there are any urgent jobs or communication required.* She went to the switchboard and looked up the messages and saw several pages of them. *Wow, they are going to be busy from the word go,* she thought.

Looking down the list, she saw two messages from Clem to her, asking her to ring back. They had been listed while she was in Winchester, so Clem must think she came into the office. She did not believe he knew she had been living here. She shrugged. She had rung him from Winchester, so that would have shown where she was. She was not going to worry now; she only had two days left in the office.

There was suddenly a loud knocking at the front door. She looked through the glass door and saw Clem standing there. She felt her heart clench up but did not show it as she went to the door and opened it.

'What are you doing here at this time of night, Clem?'

'I have come to find you to talk about the journals.'

'Come in, Clem.' She locked the door again behind him and led him into James's office. She sat down behind the desk and indicated for Clem to sit in the chair in front of the desk.

'What is it, Clem? I did tell you not to read the journals. I did not think you would like to find out some of the things in them.'

'They were difficult for me to understand them, Valerie. It was such a shock to read that she had smothered her girl babies and that she may have killed my grandfather.' There were tears in Clem's eyes.

'I never saw that side of her, but thinking all last night about her, I believe it. Besides her love for me, I never thought she loved Grandfather. She was careless with him as if she forgot him sometimes, and I would often get him a meal because she had forgotten him. I was only a little boy, but I remember it because I thought she was cruel to him.

'Strangely, I can remember going off to school and thinking, *Who will look after Grandfather now I have left him?* and feeling very bad about it. I got word at the school not long after I started there that my grandfather had died. There was no mention of me going home for his funeral. It was a very sad time for me. Grandfather was very sick, I recall that, but he always had time for me to tell me stories and watch me play my games. And he would clap his hands and say I was a lovely boy. I was always happy with him and knew he was happy with me. We loved each other very much. Although I was only six or seven, I can remember so well how much I cared for him and how sad I was to hear he had died.

'Now to find out Granny Meg may have killed him makes me feel sick to my bones. How could she! She knew I loved him. Was she jealous?'

'Perhaps that is the reason, Clem. We will never know. Perhaps he was so ill that he begged her to end it for him.'

'No, he would not do that. He was a very brave man and had put up with the illness for years. He would have wanted to stay for my sake. I am sure of that. Although my father and his twin brother were not still alive at that time. I cannot believe he would have ended it then. I am so sure of that.'

'I am sorry, Clem. This is one of the reasons I thought it better that you do not read the journals. Your grandmother did those things and did not seem to realise they were wrong. I admit that I cried when I read it as well. When I finished reading, I did not know whether to condemn her or feel sorry for her. Whatever was wrong with her, I think it may have been the reason your son Ian is like he is. Even Jason, who killed practically a whole family or organised it. I think they should be examined by psychiatrists to find the reason for their deeds, although it is too late for Jason.

'You seem to be clear of the malady, Clem. Why not use your inheritance to have Ian examined? Maybe Faye as well? Although Fiona seems to be okay, but from what I have heard of Faye, she could have been taking cocaine on a regular basis. It is sad to say, but something is wrong with your boys. I only hope Fiona's daughters are safe and have not inherited the gene.'

Clem blanched, his face scrunched up, and she could see the tears ready to spill.

'Hang in there, Clem. I will make you a cup of tea to help you cheer up. I am not a doctor, so everything I say you can take with a pinch of salt. It is only my opinion. You must see that she was a very different woman to anyone else we know. There were several reasons for it that I can see—the opium in the laudanum she had been ingesting for most of her life.There was also the schizophrenia she was supposed to have inherited.

'I presume she bought the laudanum after she left Glasgow from the tinkers who came around to the smaller towns and farms all around the country, selling pharmaceuticals. I remember my mother swearing on Mrs Somebody whose ointment was used on every occasion I fell and had a scratch. Another favourite purchase was an unguent she rubbed on my chest, and I had to lean over a bowl of steaming water to clear my chest and head when I caught a cold. They called on a quarterly basis while I was growing up. Do you remember tinkers calling at the farm? You could buy cottons and fabrics and all sorts of things from them. We always looked forward to them calling. Our city was much smaller in those days, and they would call every three months or so. It was my impression that everyone bought something from them and preorder for next time if your stocks were running low.'

Clem was no longer looking so white and agreed, 'Yes, I can remember them. Granny always welcomed them. She also bought that ointment, and now I think the laudanum as well and odd things. I did not know what she used them for. I was only interested because the tinker gave me a lollipop, the only ones I ever had, so I never questioned what she bought.'

'Come into the kitchen with me, Clem, and I will make that cup of tea and give you a snack Things will look better to you after that. You have to remember that at no time could you have changed things for Meg. In a way, you were a saviour to her. She loved you and cared for you. I think she had never loved anyone before. The twins came in a package of two. Have you ever watched twins? Of course, you have Fiona and Ian, but they are boy and girl. Identical twins seem not to need anyone but themselves. They are so wound up in each other. I think it was like that for Meg with her twin boys, and when you came along, it changed her. For the first time, she had someone to care for and love all to herself. Perhaps she was jealous of Hugh's closeness to you. We will never know.'

'I know she did love me, I have never doubted that. It is the other things in the journal that made me feel bad. Now I am even wondering if she did away with Mr and Mrs Bartle. They were there when I went off to school, and when I came back a year later, they were not there. Could she have afforded for them to go to the village and start talking about her and the baby girls? She does not mention it in the journals, but perhaps she felt someone may read about it after she was gone. It was bad enough about the little babies and a sick husband, but it was another thing to start on your staff.'

'Gosh, Clem, you are one up on me. I had not gone that far in my thinking. There was enough in the journals as it was. What made you think of that?'

'I remember Mrs Bartle looked queerly at her sometimes. By then, Mr Bartle was only strong enough to mend fence posts and odd things that went wrong about the house, and I could see them sitting outside on a bench and looking sneeringly back at the house. I thought Granny Meg must have asked them to do something they did not want to do.'

'Wouldn't someone have come asking about them?'

'They had a son, but he moved away to another district after the First World War, I believe. I do not remember him coming to see them, or anyone else for that matter. The farm was very isolated in those days. Cars were not common, and the bus service was almost non- existent, perhaps one trip past in a week at the most. I know I stayed with you after school because I had to wait until a school bus was going that way because there was no other bus service,' he concluded.

'I will have to look up the death register to see when the Bartles died, if they are not buried under the shade of the trees on the back block. It would have meant that Meg was alone for those months while you were at the school. Anything could have happened,' said Valerie.

'We could go and search, Valerie. I think I know that back patch of trees she has written about. It is quite a long way from the house.' He thought for a minute. 'It was not too far to walk back then, but now we are older, it will seem to be further. There used to be a track, but that is going back sixty to seventy years. I am not sure it would still be there. We did have an old tractor with a digger attachment. She could have used that to help her.'

She blinked. Things were developing too fast for her. 'Clem, I am not too sure if I could manage that. You will have to wait until James comes home. It is more his thing, and he is young and fit. But do you want other people to know about Meg? My reaction to reading her journals was, this is all in the past, and we can do nothing about it now. She is dead and gone. Why bring it up now?'

'That is true, Valerie, but what we may find may explain why my children are so affected. They must have inherited something from her. I would like to know if it went further than what she has written in her journals. I have wondered about Ian since the day he was born. He has always been different. The first time I noticed his impulse to harm people was when he was three years old, and we had Zack come to live with us. It was as if the world had come to an end. The tantrum went on for days. Poor Jenny, she was grieved for her sister who had died, but Zack was not the problem. It was Ian. She had to pretend Zack was not staying, but it went on every time Zack showed his face. It was horrendous, and Ian never seemed to get over his dislike. That was hard on Zack, who was a really nice young boy. Luckily, Fiona would take Ian off for a walk whenever she saw the storm brewing. When we found out what Ian had done to his young wife and Zack, because Zack had stood up to him for her, we were all decimated.'

'Why did he do it, Clem? It seemed a very cruel death for them both.'

'He never explained to us, just shrugged his shoulders. He told us after the deed, when he was jailed for a short term for stealing to hide the deaths, it was as if he did not understand what he had done. Just like Meg.

I did not know until Ian was in court after the cocaine heist about his wife and Zack being tied up. He hadn't told us that part. We had thought it was an accident. Perhaps they were smoking was our thoughts on that.

'It was about then that I moved into the residential care home. Barbara was screeching about going to the police, and Ian was carrying on as if nothing had happened. That is why we thought it was an accident. I felt as if they had me in a cleft stick. I did not know whether I should go to the police or just ignore it and chose locking myself away from it to try and forget it all.

'The only thing wrong with that is, you can never get away from things. There was always a reminder. I kept in touch with Fiona. She was as shocked as I was, but it was too late. Then another shock to us all was when Ian came out of prison. He was given a job where Gerald works, and he began working at a plan to rob the drugs store in the customs department.

'Poor Gerald, he is a nice bloke, and he loved Fiona so much, but Ian would not let him alone. I think Ian thought that Fiona belonged to him and that she was only staying with Gerald for somewhere to live. His idea, Fiona says, was to steal the drugs, and she would go with him overseas somewhere where no one could find them. Poor Fiona, she was a good girl and loves Gerald and her daughters and did not want anything to do with it.

'Then Jason turns up and starts haranguing her to kill those young boys. She had been told she had to move out of her lovely home and possibly lose her children, and she had no money to fight it, so she chose against her will to sell the cocaine. She became scared about that time of both Barbara and Jason. We think Jason had been giving Barbara a hard time about when the house would be finished, and Barbara had, in turn, harassed Fiona about the cocaine Gerald had taken, asking where the money from it was. What a family!'

'How did you feel about the plan to steal the cocaine, Clem?' asked Valerie, looking intently at him.

'At first, I knew nothing about it until Fiona came to me and told me what was happening. She was going into a hotel somewhere, a safe house supplied by the police. She admitted she was frightened of Ian and what he was going to do. More than that, she was worried about Gerald, knowing how scared he was of Ian, and worried about how he would cope with him. Ian could be very scary if you did not do what he wanted, and we were afraid Ian would take it out on Gerald if things went wrong. Gerald had not told Ian that the police were implicated by giving Fiona and the two little girls shelter at a hotel to make sure they were safe.

'We never thought that Ian would shoot those men in the warehouse. Fiona and I had discussed Ian shooting Gerald if it did not work, but we could not see around it. I begged Fiona to come and stay with me, but she countered that she could not bring the girls here, and this way, the police knew where she was, so she would be safe. By then, we did not know what else to do and were not sure when the job would be done. By then, Gerald was totally in a fluster and would not discuss it any further with her, just saying, "The police know about it, and you and the girls will be safe from Ian."'

Valerie was appalled that Clem was telling her all this. And she said, 'Is it now you kill me for knowing too much about your family, Clement?'

He stared at her, absolutely shocked by her statement, and then he laughed. 'You are joking aren't you, Valerie?'

'Not entirely, Clem. After reading the journals and now hearing you talk about Ian, I do not know what or who you are. Has Meg's infamous qualities come down to you? Or did they jump a generation? I wondered about the earlier generation, your father and the other twin, because they seemed to have been intense young men and died too early to judge them. Everyone seems to have thought you were extra intelligent. Perhaps you have been able to hide your blackness because you were so busy over the years with your job?'

'Stop it, Valerie! I can absolutely tell you that I have never killed anyone. Not Jonty, or any of my patients, some whom begged me to assist them to die. I have experienced that many times in my career but never succumbed no matter how sorry I was for them. I would think of my grandfather managing his illness for my sake all those years. No, Valerie, I have never knowingly killed anyone in my life.

'Perhaps someone may have overdosed on tablets I may have prescribed for them, but I am not aware of any. My job was curing, not killing. You are safe with me.'

Valerie realised that she had been holding her breath and was trying not to breathe too hard now to show how uneasy she had felt.

'I am sorry, Clem, but I had to say it and have you confirm that you are not like Meg. Otherwise, I would always have wondered.'

Valerie felt relieved but still would not let her mind believe everything he said; after all, Meg did not seem to realise what she had done was wrong. Could thirty years with Ian not make him believe something was dreadfully wrong with his son and do nothing about it? She realised that she still felt afraid.

'How did you find me tonight, Clem?'

'I have known for some time you were living here on and off. It was just a matter of finding when you were in residence. I must say, it is unorthodox. I have you listed in an app on my phone called Find My Friends.'

She decided to laugh it off. 'It was a matter of convenience. One day here and there between staying with friends and our trip to Glasgow. I came back from Winchester today. My family will be home in a day or so, then we will have to find somewhere permanent to live. The four of us will not fit in here. I could have stayed with Aaron or someone else while my family were away, but I would not have had the freedom as I have being here.

'It is getting late for me, Clem. It is time for you to go home. I cannot function the next day if I have less than eight hours' sleep.'

'Okay, Valerie, it has been wonderful to talk Meg's journals over with you. Otherwise, I would have been sitting home in shock and horror. May I telephone you in a few days? It's a relief to be able to say all these things to someone. I do not have many friends I can talk these matters over with. Also, it is something so strange I think no one would believe me.'

'Yes, Clem, just give me three or four days to work out where we are going to live. You will not find me here in the office after tomorrow or perhaps the next day.'

'Life will return to normal then, Valerie, for you?'

She stared at him. 'Not exactly, Clem. There is no bookshop to return to. There is no comfortable house for me to live in. My family is cast out into the streets, and all our belongings and history have gone. This is not normality. This is frightening! Do you not understand what happened to us for no reason at all, Clem?'

His face fell, and he looked guilty all of a sudden.

'Everything my family have touched has been totally unacceptable in the last few years. I try to shut the bad parts out. If I do not, I would be so cowed I could not hold my head up with the shame of it all, so much shame that is overpowering, that those boys and girls are mine. Even where I live, the staff are aware of the terrible things that Ian, in particular, has done. I feel as if I am battling through life whenever I leave my room.

'That is why I welcomed you back into my life, cousin. I can talk plainly to you as you know all those terrible sequences that my family have done that are not acceptable. I still feel ashamed, but I thought you understood me. Believe me, if I had known what was ahead, I would not have had children. The Bible says it is the sins of the father that are passed down, but my life has been in reverse.

'Now I am aware how the family of a serial killer feels, and it is not good. Believe me! People always look askance at you, and you find that you do not want to go out in public in case someone recognises you. I have been a bit overpowering to be with because I am always waiting for the penny to drop, and they say, "Ian Haskell is your son, isn't he?" It is hell! To think you nursed this child all his life and look how he turned out. Am I a criminal too? I can almost hear them saying it.

'Do not do it to me, cousin. I am not like that at all. I am trying to survive to help Fiona and Gerald overcome it, and perhaps Faye too. She was a pretty little vivacious child, and all I can think of her now is that she too is a killer. Would you like to find out your child is a killer? Not only a killer but sick with it.'

'Oh, Clem, I know it must be difficult for you. You are going to be alone with it for a while. I will not have time for you until we settle down a bit. This had been a break for me to come to terms with everything, and I have stirred up a hornet's nest instead. I am not usually so hard to convince, but what Jason and Barbara did to us is totally unacceptable and leaves one with a sense that everything and everyone could have us next in line, and I am very wary.'

'Perhaps you can call me when you are ready, Valerie. I do not want to lose the only sane member of my family I know,' Clem said with an ironic twist to his mouth. 'It has been so hard dealing with the hard facts about Ian and Jason. Ian has been, from the age of three, very hard to deal with, but do you abandon your children?

'Jason has been the total shock for me. I was so proud of him. All the way through school, he was an honour student and topped his mining engineering course at university. He had the good looks of the Haskells and could be very charming, and suddenly, I hear he has killed a whole family. Can you imagine what it feels like for a loving father?

'I have been totally devastated, and now you wonder whether I am included because I am their father. If I am unable to help at least Fiona out of the mess, I will stay hidden in my residential care place until I die there.'

CHAPTER FOURTEEN

Valerie showed Clem out to the taxicab he had arranged while in the office with her. After waving until he was out of sight, she turned to go back into the office and heard a woman start to scream that went on and on in the car park adjacent to the office.

She went into the office, looking for a weapon, and grabbed her umbrella with a point on the end. Taking her phone with her, she went back out the door, following the sound of the scream.

A car went past her, and she aimed her phone at the window of it and took a photo of the driver and then aimed at the license plate and took a photo of that. Then she went to where a young woman was standing, sobbing as if the world had come to an end.

Valerie asked what was happening, and the young woman sobbed on her shoulder. 'A man has stolen my car, and my baby is in the back in his security chair.' She was crying so hard that it was difficult to understand her.

Valerie led her to the office and called the police and sat the young woman down in the reception area, asking her, 'Do you know who the man is that took your car?'

'No, I have never seen him before.'

Valerie said, 'Let's start at the beginning while we are waiting for the police, shall we? I am Valerie Newton. This is my grandson-in-law's office, and I just happened to hear your scream while I was seeing someone off. What is your name?'

'I am Mandy Lewis, and my eighteen-month-old son Tommy is in the car.'

'It is late for a baby to be out and about, Mandy. What were you doing in the car park so late?'

'I had visitors this evening at home, and when they left, I realised that I had no milk left in the fridge to give my baby a bottle when he woke up in the morning. My husband has been working away for a week, and I had no one to mind the baby at that time of night, so I got into the car, strapping Tommy into his seat in the back, and came down here because all the smaller shops were closed. I went in and bought the milk and had come out to the car and unlocked it to strap Tommy back into his chair.

A man came up to the car, took the keys from the lock, and he did not seem aware of me putting the pram into the boot of the car and drove off. He has taken my car, my baby, and my handbag I had put down on the floor in the back, and my phone is in it. I am sorry I screamed so much, but I was so frightened about him taking Tommy I could not stop.'

'I have called the police, and they should be here any minute. Try to calm down a little so that you can explain what happened to the police. I tried to take a photo of the driver of your car, but it has come out a bit blurry because the car was moving quite fast. But in case you cannot remember the number plate, I have taken a photo of that, and it has come out quite clearly.'

'The only good thing is, Tommy was only half-awake, and while the car keeps moving, he will go back to sleep, so he will not be aware I am not the driver. I am not sure the man was aware there is a baby in the child's car seat. It all happened so quick that I am having trouble taking it in.' Mandy gave another sob.

Valerie heard a siren and said, 'I think this will be the police now, Mandy. Do you want to wash your face before they come in?'

The young woman looked gratefully at her. Her sobs now stopped, and she appeared to be an attractive girl.

Valerie showed her to the bathroom and handed her a clean towel and went back to welcome the two police officers standing at the door. She handed them the notes she had written and told the timing of the event as Mandy came back to the front desk again while Valerie was showing the photos on her phone.

The police decided to drive Mandy home as she did not have any photographs of Tommy because her phone was in the handbag on the floor of her car. And then Mandy said, 'The keys of the house are in my bag as well.'

Valerie said, 'Are you sure you do not have a key hidden under a flowerpot?'

Mandy hit her head with her hand and laughed. 'I have been so distraught that I had forgotten. Thank you, Mrs Newton. Yes, there is a key under a flowerpot in the back garden. I have never had to use it in the time we have lived there and had forgotten about it.'

As the policewoman walked Mandy out to their car, the policeman turned to Valerie and said, 'Good work, Mrs Newton. You acted quickly and appropriately. I notice that this is a private investigations office. Are you one of the investigators?'

Valerie laughed. 'No, this office belongs to other members of my family, and I am only visiting because I had a friend wanting to meet me here. Just wait until I tell them this story. Perhaps they will put me on their staff.'

The policeman smiled. 'I am sure that something has rubbed off on to you, Mrs Newton. I think your prompt reporting may be a saviour to that small child and his mother tonight.'

After she watched the police car drive away, she looked at the clock and said to herself, 'So much for the early night. It is now almost midnight. I will have to sleep in tomorrow to get over it.'

After locking up, tidying around, and turning off all the lights, she lay on the bed for a few minutes, wide awake, thinking of all the things that had happened that day. A week in one day it would have been compared to the bookshop, and she thought she had handled it all well. She punched the air above her and turned over and was immediately asleep.

* * *

Valerie woke up at her usual time and thought to herself, *I did not ring Percy about the house.*

She got out of bed, wondering just where they were at the moment. Had they left Zimbabwe? Were they on the plane? Could they take calls on the plane? Then she decided to send a text message.

'Hello, Percy. Ken and Kate are moving out of your house to buy their own. Can we move into your house for a while until we can see what is around the corner for us all? They cooked me dinner to explain it all and showed me over your house. It looks very nice. Will see you soon. Valerie.'

She looked at the text before she hit send, wondering if she should have sent 'love'. She shook her head and pressed send, saying to herself, 'You are a funny old thing, Valerie Newton.'

Shortly after, she received a text in return, saying, 'On the plane now. Should arrive at Gatwick at 6 p.m. Sounds good to have you in my house for a change. Alicia and James agree. See you tonight.'

She was amazed at the quickness of it and rang Kate and Ken's number. They said they were moving right now in anticipation of Percy saying yes, and the house should be ready for them by six o'clock. James had sent a text yesterday confirming opening the office on Monday.

While Valerie had her breakfast, she thought things over; she would have to be snappy and clean the office up. It was tidy but the floors needed to be wiped over. She had taken the photos for Clem to be copied and would need to pick them up today so that she could put the originals back in the drawer with the album she had been carrying around. All of a sudden, things were going back to normal to become the granny again, an addendum to the others. Laughing to herself, she thought, *I have enjoyed doing my own thing for a while, not having to confirm everything and making decisions on my own. It has been quite fun.*

At nine o'clock, there was a knock on the door, and when she went to see who it was, there stood the policeman from last night's episode. When she opened the door, the policeman said, 'We think you would like to know what happened after we left you last night. We put out an APB to the police cars in the area, and Mandy Lewis's car was picked up a short distance from here. It was driving slowly because the driver was well over the limit and could barely focus. When he was pulled over, he was astounded to be told he had a baby on board. Tommy was still asleep, and the look of astonishment on the man's face made everybody laugh.

'It seems to have been a crime of the moment. He was feeling unwell, as he had imbibed too much beer, and was walking through the car park, taking a shortcut on his way home. He saw the car door open and the key in the lock and did not see Mrs Lewis putting the pram in the boot of the car. He said he thought it was abandoned and he had come into a bit of luck. Obviously, the alcohol had curdled his brain. He has no prior record so will probably only spend a night or two in the lockup until he sobers up properly. It depends on Mandy Lewis and whether she wants to pursue it further. I think she was just glad to have her baby back safe and sound.

'If he had subsequently abandoned the car in a driveway or backstreet, we all agree that in this cold weather, Tommy may not have survived. As it was, he had an adventure he will be able to relate in years to come.

'Taking this into account, my partner and I decided to give you a citation to hang on the office walls to show your grandson how clever you are and how swift you were in calling the incident in.' He handed her a document.

When she opened it, Valerie said, laughing along with the young policeman, 'Thank you for this honour. I will treasure it and make sure it is hung where everybody can see it. And thank you for the update. I would have been wondering forever how it had turned out.'

CHAPTER FIFTEEN

The day went so quickly for her that Percy, Alicia and James were soon crowding into the office on their arrival from the airport.

James went first, after kissing her hello, to see all the messages on the answerphone, saying, 'Wow, there are so many calls. We are going to be busy for a while.'

Percy and Alicia were reading Valerie's citation that she had taped to the entry to the back offices. James too came to read it and, with one eyebrow raised, turned to her and said, 'So you have been keeping the office alive whilst we were gone, Granny?'

They all laughed, and Granny said, 'This has only been one incident, and I am happy it turned out well for all involved.'

Percy turned and said, 'Congratulations, Valerie. We do not all get citations for our work. This must have been extremely well done.'

She smiled. 'I can take it down now that you have seen it.'

James said, 'Oh no. This deserves a frame, and we will hang it in a place where everybody coming in can see it. I look forward to hearing more about it. First, we will make our way to Percy's house and get comfortable. We are all tired from the flight. Oh yes, there is one other thing, Granny. Percy's son, Simon, is arriving in a day or two, and he will be staying in the guest room that Percy has nominated. I am not too sure where that is, so let us go and have a look.'

On arrival at the house, Kate and Ken and the children were just finishing, and Kate said, 'I hope you all want a cup of tea as much as I do. I have only just put the kettle on to get it started, and after we hear of your holiday, we will move off and leave you to carry on and get your bearings.'

Alicia was moving around, looking at everything, and turned to Percy and said, 'Which room have you allocated to us, Percy?'

'The bedroom at the end of the passage, Alicia. I thought you and James would like that. There is a bathroom and a big walk-in robe for you to hang all your new clothes. I thought Valerie and I would have a single room each. We have another room leading out from the kitchen door for Simon when he arrives. His own private quarters—he will like that—when he was growing up, he used it as his den. He could play his music as loud as he wished, and we were not able to hear it. Every young man should have that.'

'The tea is ready, everyone,' called Kate. 'I have put it in the dining room as we will not all fit in the kitchen nook.'

'Good on you, Kate. You know how I like my cup of tea,' said Percy.

Alicia and James were still investigating what was to be their bedroom, and James called out, 'Coming now. Come on, Alicia, you can come back here after your tea.'

Percy laughed. 'I had forgotten how big the house is. Will it do, Valerie?'

'Certainly, Percy, it is a lovely home, and the best thing of all is the security you have around the place. We will all be wary from now on about unacceptable visitors. They will not get into here without due warning.'

Kate said, 'We have enjoyed the conveniences of your house, Percy, and have taken good care of your furniture. Ask the children.

They have not been allowed to jump on their beds or the lounge chairs, so they are all still in good order. You have fresh day-to-day vegetables as we replanted those that chose to wilt in the cold weather, and there are some luscious brussels sprouts ready to pick now.'

Percy smiled at Kate. 'I knew how diligent you are, Kate, and had no thoughts you would not keep the house in order. Thank you both for being such good tenants. It is such a pleasure to come home and settle in right into a cup of tea and scones. You are a treasure, Kate.'

Alicia asked, 'Have you gone back to your mother's house, Kate?'

Kate looked at Ken, who explained, 'Kate and I have decided to get married, and we will be organising the wedding within a few weeks when we get settled. We have bought a house using our payouts from the police force with a small mortgage, no more than we would pay in rent, and we bought a car yesterday. We bought the house which includes furniture, which we will replace to our own taste as we go along. All in all, we are happy with ourselves, and the children both think it is a good idea.'

James, Alicia, and Percy all congratulated them, and Percy said, 'We were wondering where you will be going. We realise that you were making a sacrifice for our sakes. If we weren't in such dire straits ourselves, we would have turned your offer to move out down. This is great news. Now we will not have to feel guilty.'

'This is your house, Percy. There was no need to feel guilty. To us it seemed the ideal time to make our situation clearer, to stop us procrastinating because we were so comfortable. The children will be happy because we are moving closer to schools for now and in the future. The house we have chosen is not as nice as this, but it is a nice size. We will not be getting uncomfortable as the children grow, and who knows, we may have a child of our own at some time in the future. We are happy in our decisions, both to give you your house back and the house we are moving to,' said Ken.

Alicia went and kissed the cheeks of both Kate and Ken and stated, 'Thank you and congratulations to you both.'

James and Percy shook Ken's hand and kissed Kate's cheek.

Valerie watched as all this was happening and said, 'I hope you are refreshed and ready for work on Monday. There is a big list for you growing every day. You are going to be busy, and that does not include any cold cases from the police department.'

'Well, Granny, you will have to come in and be the receptionist for us for at least part of the day,' said James. 'After seeing the citation taped to our door, do not tell us you are not up to it.'

'What citation, Granny? It was not there when I dropped you back to the office on Friday night,' said Ken.

James said, 'Time to tell all about it, Granny. You cannot present us with a citation on our door and not explain what it is about. So fess up now.'

'After you dropped me off on Friday evening, Ken, there was a woman screaming in the car park, and I took my umbrella and went to investigate.'

They all laughed, and Alicia said, 'Your famous favourite weapon, Granny. Has it been in play again?'

Granny joined in the laughing and went on to describe the event in the car park and the comments of the young policeman.

Ken said, 'All the time I was in the police force and never received a citation.'

Percy too was laughing and said, 'Me either, Ken. It must have been extreme bravery because of the weapon of choice.'

James was rolling in his chair with laughter. 'It had to be for that, Percy. Who needs a gun when you have an umbrella handy? I am proud of you, Granny, keeping up with the ethics of our office. We have never used guns, so I will buy you each an umbrella.'

Kate said, 'I see Granny as very brave to face up to an incident when a woman is screaming. Granny went to her aid even though she did not know why the woman was screaming. The police would have turned up with a gun drawn, and all Granny had was an umbrella, but that did not deter her going into a situation she did not know about. I for one am not laughing. I am very proud of her.'

They all paused their laughing, and Alicia said, 'I am proud of you as well, Granny. You always put other people before yourself. I am very proud of you.'

James said, 'You are my favourite person after Alicia, Granny. I am proud to be associated with you.'

Percy and Ken looked chastened, and both said, 'Sorry we laughed, Granny. We know you have your heart in the right place.'

Granny laughed and said, 'Don't worry, boys. I think even the policeman thought it was a joke. His main words to me were about how prompt I was answering the call and notifying the police force. I did not do anything brave. I saw someone driving off, and the woman was still screaming. I could not look the other way under those circumstances. I calmed her down and took some notes for the police so they would not waste too much time questioning her. I think because it was in a private investigation office that intrigued the policeman. He came back in the morning with the citation and to tell me the outcome of the story.'

Kate said, 'How I have missed you all this month. You are such wonderful people, and I am proud to be associated with you. I have worried for you since the fire, but I can see how resilient you all are and moving on. Ken too has been worried, and we are glad you are back looking happy.' Kate had been putting out platters of cold meat and salad and bread rolls on the table as she realised this could be some time while they heard all the stories.

James said, 'I am not usually happy when I am not working, but yes, we are mended to a degree. It is the first time I have been with my sister and parents all together in a number of years. I got on well with my sister's husband, whom I had not previously met, and surprise, surprise, they have a baby son to meet us, born just a few days before we arrived. And my parents were so happy to be grandparents at last.

'We spent a lot of time sightseeing, when we could get my mother and Alicia away from holding the baby, and ate lots of lovely food and drank wine that my brother-in-law made himself. Altogether it was wonderful. It was a little hot for a few days. After the heat it changed to lovely days, so we followed the warnings and always wore a hat and covered up with sunscreen and still got nice suntans that people here will admire in the middle of winter.'

'Do your sister and brother-in-law like living there? It seems such a long way from home,' asked Kate.

'They say the only things they miss are the rest of their families. Everything else is wonderful, and it's only on Christmas and birthdays and anniversaries that they feel they are missing out. They were so happy that we could be there for Christmas and that baby Daniel had arrived in time to meet us.'

'And, Percy, your missing son is turning up here. That is wonderful for you,' said Valerie.

'I do not know how long he will stay. Before he left the UK, he was in police school before he got the adventure bug. One of his friends in police school was killed while on a job, which made Simon unsure of where he was heading, so he left to go on his journeys. After James described our day-to-day work life, he suddenly sprung on us that he thought he might enjoy that and asked if he could come and have a go with us.

'We told him the serious parts of the job, but I think he has got past the fact he could be in danger. Some of the mountaineering and river escapes he had encountered were scary on their own. He volunteered, and it is silly to miss out on living a good life because you are scared. You could be hit crossing a road he said.'

'So he is going to be working with us then,' said Ken.

'For a trial run and moving into what we always considered his den before he went away.'

Ken asked, 'What did you do in Zimbabwe? Is Divit okay?'

James answered, 'He is more than okay. We stayed in what was his grandparents' house—a large house with a lot of servants, including a cook and maids and laundry people. All are African locals who appear to hang on everything Divit says, and Divit carries it all off as if he was born to it, which he was, of course, with a break in between whilst he was here in the UK.

'He has his memory back, thanks to Derek, who goes over everything with him every day, and he has started work in the main emporium started by his grandfather in Zimbabwe and seems happy. I mentioned schooling with him, and he said many people in his country did not have as much schooling as he had and he sees no need to start it up again. He is a very intelligent young man according to Derek and seems to drink information in and retain it as he receives it. The main reason he wanted to see us was to show that he is doing all right. He has worked out the banking system and discovered that his stepfather, Jason Bowering, was stacking funds away here in the UK, in the bank. This was mainly from the sales of the diamonds he was mining. He would not have been able to send money to another country. There were rules against that, so he was using the diamonds to plan his future and had a large sum squirrelled away as a consequence. He could manage to take some diamonds out each flight he made. We have not learnt where the diamonds were sold yet.

'Whilst we were there, he had Derek start up an account here in the London bank, in my name, and transferred all the money that Jason Bowering was saving into that account. I have no idea what the amount is, but he said the rest of the diamond mining was going to the government to help with the economy—in particular, some of his grandfather's favourite charities and schools. His grandfather was always donating to these charities, and he wanted to follow in his grandfather's footsteps and continue that custom.

'The other thing he did was to present to us, James and Alicia and Granny, the deeds to Bowering House. The three of us have joint names now on the title. He said that this was because of the terrible thing his stepfather did, and he was ashamed for his stepfather to be considered part of his family. Divit also said he did not care what we did with the house as he realised it was a long way from our workplace. We could lease it out or sell it. It now belonged to us, so it was our decision. He stated that he had no wish to return to the UK. It had not dealt well with him, and besides us, the investigation team, and Dr Redfern, he never wanted anything to do with anyone else except us and Derek, whom he seems to idolise.

'I must say I was very impressed with the boy—or young man, I should say. He has had such horror and sorrow to overcome. It was hard to hear, and he showed none of it. I sincerely hope he can close it out of his life, but it is a lot to come to terms with.

'Derek seemed to think that our government would take over the Learjet aircraft still in the hangar at the house. He said Divit did not want to think about it because it caused him too much stress. We will wait until the government comes to us on that one in case Divit changes his mind. It has all been a lot for a young person to come to terms with. He said that sometimes he wished his memory had not come back. I can understand that. He lost all his family. It must be hard for him. Derek said because he is throwing himself into learning all his grandfather's day-to-day business, he manages to keep the thoughts of his family at bay.

'At least by turning Jason's bank savings over to us, it saves us from having to sue for substitution of Granny's bookshop, apartment, and house. That in itself would have been a huge outlay for us.'

'When is Derek due to come back? He has a fiancée waiting for him,' asked Kate.

'Divit is not ready yet to be left alone. Perhaps in two or three months. It is hard to say,' added James. 'I am glad we went to see him. He has been on my mind each day since he left, but I think he will make it now. Derek has been an incredible influence on him, and I do not think we need to worry any more.'

The children were yawning and seemed ready for bed, and Kate said, 'I think we had better leave you and go home to our new beds. It has been a very busy day for us all. We will see you on Monday morning, same time, same station.'

After saying goodnight and watching them drive away, Granny said, 'Is that a true story about the Bowering House deeds, James?'

He turned to her and said, 'Yes, Granny. Do you want to see the title?'

'Yes, James, I would. I have a story about that house I will tell you tomorrow when there is no one else but the four of us here. It is too long a story for tonight. We are all tired, so I will save it for after breakfast when we are all settled.'

'Do you want to see the deed now, Granny, or wait for the morning?'

'Tomorrow will be soon enough. It is not going away, but it is a very interesting history of the house if you haven't heard it before.'

'I know nothing about it, Granny, so I will look forward to the story you have to tell tomorrow. Divit had not known of it until he was taken there from Zimbabwe. His stepfather never discussed business in front of the boys. The first time he heard about it they were on the way to it. Jason described the fact that it had been purchased in case they had to leave Africa in a hurry. That was an easy story to believe because white people and part white were being persecuted in that part of Africa at that time.'

Granny was glad to leave her story until the next day. It was not going to be easy to tell, but it must be told. It had been a shock to her when James had said that her name was now on the deed of what she called in her own mind as the infamous Bowering House.

She worried how Clement was going to take that. She was amazed at how the story was chasing her, as if the house wanted her attention. She went to what was now to be her bedroom and unpacked her few belongings, still thinking about all she had learnt this evening. She had thought of the house as belonging to Clem. Of course, it should have been, but things did not go in Clement's way easily. He was cursed by his grandmother it seemed.

She wondered again how much money John Forrester had given Clement. Perhaps he could buy the house. She could not see what James and Alicia would want with it, and she certainly did not want it. She would bring that up with James and Alicia in the morning after they heard her long story. But then if Divit heard that it had returned to his stepfather's family, that for Divit would be like a kick in the teeth. No, they could not sell it to Clem.

Granny went to sleep, dreaming of the house in its heyday, before Meg made it her own. She could see the pictures in her mind of her grandmother as a girl growing up. Perhaps the house was calling her back to it, to its original happy days before Meg arrived to take it over.

CHAPTER SIXTEEN

She awoke the next morning feeling heavy and sorrowful and lay there for a while to orient herself. It was not a normal feeling for her who always woke up happy and rested. She could hear someone moving about in the kitchen, and it took her a few minutes to work out that it must be Percy.

Still not moving, she wondered why she felt so heavy and gradually came to the conclusion that today she was going to have to tell that she was related to the Haskell family and that what she was feeling was dread, knowing that James thought they were a family one would not want, because of the terrible things the grown-up sons and daughters had done.

She felt like pulling the blankets back over her head and staying there, but it was not her way to put things aside. She got out of bed, donning her dressing gown, and went to the bathroom, came back, and dressed and went to the kitchen to greet Percy—a happy-looking Percy, so pleased to be back home and with them, and his missing son no longer missing to him.

He had been setting the table for breakfast, although there was no sign yet of Alicia and James.

He greeted her with a hug and a kiss on the cheek and said, 'Do you think we are ready for visitors yet? I would like to invite my eldest son and his family over to greet Simon when he arrives tomorrow. I have just now had a text that he will be arriving around midday tomorrow. Perhaps we could invite the others to lunch?'

'What a good idea, Percy. I will cook a nice roast lamb and vegetables if you could take me to the shop to buy it. I have only organised breakfast things for a start, because although it is walking distance to the shop, I did not think I could carry everything. Kate catered for us with the meal last night. She is a lovely girl to think of it.'

'No, it is too heavy for you. We will have to reorganise ourselves. With an extra person also, there will be extra goods to cater for.'

'Can you show me the room where Simon is to sleep and the laundry? Kate did not get to them the other night.'

'Out this door, Valerie,' said Percy, leading the way. 'When we were renovating the house a few years ago now, Simon was a teenager and requested a room of his own that he could decorate in his own style. We gave him a small one-bedroom apartment for himself. It has a single bedroom and a small sitting room and bathroom.

'We spoilt him a little. His brother was so clever, and Simon always seemed to be in the background, so we wanted to make things up to him, I suppose. He loved it, and we had stopped him from wandering the streets looking for action. He was happy in his room, making up songs and playing his guitar and having friends over, and we did not have to put up with the music.

'We put in the security about that time as well. Otherwise, we would have had his friends turning up at all hours of the day and night, so we were able to monitor who was arriving. At times he had some weirdly dressed young boys and girls turn up, and I had to put my foot down about how many he could invite at a time. If sometimes they came without invitation, we did not allow them in, although it did not stop them again the next evening. It seems that he was the only one his age to have his own apartment, and he was greatly admired for it.

'He joined the police department when he was eighteen, and there were not so many visitors after that. We were pleased at the time because my wife had become ill and could not cope with all the comings and goings of his friends, but when his mate was killed on duty—a car rolled over, and the two men in the car were injured, then Len, his friend, died—Simon was put off being a policeman after that. When my wife died too, he grew very down, and that is when I encouraged him to take some time off. I did not mean for it to become so long, but he seemed to be enjoying himself, so I never interfered to ask him to come home.

'He is twenty-six now and ready to settle down, I think. It was his own suggestion to James for him to try out the investigation business, and I stood back while they were talking about it so that he did not think I was rushing him into it, but I was pleased when James agreed to give him a trial, re-enforcing that there would be some study involved before he could be licensed. I think he is missing family around him. It always goes back to that, doesn't it? No matter what age they are, you still worry about them, as I have all these years, and I am happy for him to be coming home to be with us.'

Valerie had sat down in Simon's living room whilst Percy was talking and got up and said, 'I had better see where the laundry is. I am sure you all have a bit of washing necessary after your trip.'

'Actually, we don't. The staff in Divit's house picked up the used clothes each day to wash. We have all come home with clean clothes for a change, all nicely ironed as well. The laundry is next door.'

They examined the laundry and washing machine that Kate had left extremely neat and clean and the clothesline outside in the sunshine to dry the clothes, although there was a dryer in the laundry for dull days.

'Time for you to have breakfast, Valerie. I had a cup of tea when I got up, as is my habit. Come, I will show you where the toaster is kept and make a fresh pot of tea.'

When they arrived back in the kitchen, Alicia was pouring a cup of tea and said, 'I wondered where you had got to. I could not find you in the house. Is there more?'

'You have only seen half of the things, Alicia. Did you and James see the security screen in the hallway?'

'What is that you said, Granny?' said James, wandering up the passage to the kitchen to join them.

'You had better show the screen to James, Percy. Ken showed me, but I might need another lesson on how to work it.'

'But you came in via the kitchen door, Granny. Where have you been?' asked Alicia.

'Looking at Simon's private apartment and the laundry next to it, out that door. It is very interesting. Ken did not show me the other night because by the time we got around to it, the sun had gone. It was cold outside and getting dark in a hurry, so Percy has shown it to me.'

'This is a lovely house, Percy,' said Alicia.

'What was it you were going to tell us about, Granny?' said James. 'You were looking very furtive last night and has made me wonder what you have been up to while we left you off the leash while we were away.'

'Gosh, James, it is just as well I am used to your strange way of talking by now, so I will not take offense.'

'Come on, Granny. You looked so guilty last night, and now you are putting off the moment you said you would tell us. You have aroused our interest to breaking point. Sit down. I will pour your tea, and you can start your mysterious story to us,' said James.

'Now I am all flustered,' said Granny.

'Come on, Granny, you have aroused our interest, please begin,' said Alicia.

'You remember the photo album you brought back from Bowering House, James?' she started.

James and the others nodded.

'Whilst you were looking at it, I was sitting at the table with you in the boardroom, and I recognised a couple in the wedding photo of Lady Meg and her new husband, Hugh Haskell.'

Granny saw Alicia frown as she said, 'Who did you recognise, Granny? You were not even born when that wedding took place.'

'No, Alicia, I was not, but standing there, I saw a young couple at the side of the photograph. I recognised my grandparents, and my mother would have been in the nursery upstairs, I believe.'

'You mean that we are related to the Haskell family?' Alicia asked in a pained voice.

'Yes, Alicia. I have spent the last few weeks proving it.' She went on for some time relating the story as it had unwound for her until she had come up to date with the story and sat back and said, 'Please can I have another cup of tea? I feel absolutely washed out after that telling.'

They sat staring at Granny as Percy got up to make a fresh pot of tea and poured her a cup. There was utter silence in the room.

At last, James spoke, 'They say when the cats are away, the mice do play. You have outdone the mice, Granny, and have completely floored all of us by the silence that has greeted your story. You are sure that you are not making this up as a joke?'

'Several times in the last month, I have wished it would go away. I found it very difficult to believe myself, but it is all completely true.

'The only part I have left out is that I believe Meg was completely insane. After reading her journals, I thought that if she was alive today, we would be digging up the farm to find where the rest of the bodies are buried. She killed her own two daughters at birth because she did not want them to grow up to be like her and forced Hugh to bury them under the trees at the back of the farm. She said in the journal that she could not understand why Hugh was so angry with her. Can you imagine the scene? Poor Hugh! Later on, she euthanised Hugh, her ill husband. Perhaps it was a mercy killing. He had been very ill. We will never know. To me it explained Ian and Jason's history, maybe Faye's as well.'

'You are still in touch with this Clement, Granny?'

'I have been up until Friday evening when I gave him back Meg's journals. According to Clem, Fiona and Gerald are guilty only of having Fiona's twin brother pushing them around. Ian, he thinks, is as crazy as Meg. I think I am inclined to agree with him, but he does not know that yet. I have been trying to keep my distance from him, but he is wanting my friendship and is constantly contacting me.

'I have not been doing all this without contacting Paul Morris each time there is a new thing to report, although I have not discussed the journals with him yet, because I only gave them back to Clem last week. You were on your way home, and I thought we could have a meeting with Paul over dinner some evening soon to discuss it all. I have kept Paul in the loop in case I suddenly went missing. I was so disturbed when I met Clement again. I felt uncertain what to do.

'I have to admit I am still not sure of Clement. He seems okay when I am with him, but after he leaves me, I go back to thinking of Ian and Jason, also Faye, and what they did and start questioning all over again. You will have to have a chat with Clem, James.'

'I certainly will, Granny. We will have to work out a strategy to get his guard down. You say that he dotes on his eldest daughter Fiona?

'Yes, he seems to love her and said over the years, she has been the one to manage Ian, and it was only after she married Gerald and moved away from home to her own house that Ian started being creepy. Clem admits there is something very wrong with Ian and Jason and maybe Faye. She has always been the airhead of the family, but I have not heard him say he considers there is anything wrong with Fiona.

'I am frightened to go to Clem and tell him I am on the deed to the Bowering House and farmlands. He is the one who should have inherited it all, but circumstances at the time were against him. I am uncertain what his reaction to it will be, although perhaps by telling him, we will see the real Clem. What about taking him to Bowering House for the discussion?'

'That is a good idea, Granny. What do you say, Percy?'

'I think it will be better than an office situation. I think he would clam up if we tried that, and the house interrogation will bring us all forward to him as the persons his wife and son set up to kill, and that is the reason you hold the deed now.'

Alicia said, 'Me too? Should I go? I think I will be scared to meet with him. But then Granny has been meeting him and even travelling to Glasgow with him and seemed to be safe. I am curious now.'

'I think we all are, Alicia, but he is Granny's cousin, if that counts for anything,' said James. 'The only thing we must hold on to is, Lady Margaret Haskell is not a relation to any of us at all. She is the person that Granny thinks was mad. She married a Haskell who was completely normal, who was related at that time, so that removes her DNA from us all. Of course, it does not rule out Clement as being like his sons though,' said James.

'That is what has kept me on the search for answers, James. None of the Haskells that I am related to before Granny Meg are inclined that way. We were all a meek lot and completely normal too. Quite truthfully, Clem does appear to be completely normal.'

'The story you told us last night puts paid to the suggestion that you are a meek lot, Granny. Nobody I know to my recollection has gone out to save a screaming woman with an umbrella as a weapon.' James laughed.

Valerie laughed too. 'I do not suppose I will ever live that down. I should not have admitted to it. I do not think I would have, except that young policeman came back with the citation. You would get to know about it via the grapevine sooner or later.'

'Do not worry, Granny. We will keep it as our secret,' said James.

* * *

'Do you have any photos of your little nephew and your sister, James?' asked Granny.

'Alicia is the photographer of the family, Granny. They are all stored on her tablet and phone, to be brought out when she thinks is the right time. Percy has just reminded me that we need to go shopping for food. Which do you want to do first? Photos or food?'

'The shopping please, James. Perhaps Percy can take me while you and Alicia do your unpacking. I have unpacked my things, but as I did not sleep too well last night, I would like a nap this afternoon after lunch.'

Percy said, 'I think we can accommodate all that, Valerie. Let's go shopping now and get it over.'

'I warn you, Percy, we will be starting from scratch. I lived from day-to-day while you were away and ate mostly in the coffee shop, so there is not much in the cupboard. We may be a while.'

'I am sure we will manage between us, Valerie, if we both pick up a trolley. We will see you later, James and Alicia.'

James pulled some banknotes out of his pocket and gave them to Granny, saying, 'Don't skint on what you buy. I believe I have a hefty bank account now. I will take time off to go to the bank tomorrow to see how much is in the account.'

* * *

The next day, Simon arrived—a slim medium height young man, who looked like a younger version of Percy. He took his luggage to his apartment and came back grinning and said, 'There is no place like home. It makes me feel seventeen again.'

Percy's other son called on the intercom, 'Let us in, Dad. Has the young scallywag turned up yet?'

By the time the two brothers greeted each other, everyone was grinning at their playful actions, and David's young children were staring at Simon as if they were looking at a twin of their father.

It was a joyful afternoon with a delicious meal cooked by Granny and Alicia.

The next morning, they were all back at work in the office, including Granny, who had been impressed into being the receptionist for part of the day. After the usual Monday morning meeting, James suggested that Percy, Granny, Alicia, and himself make an appointment to go to Bowering House and take Clement with them on the next Saturday morning and include Paul Morris if he was available. He thought it a good idea to go before the office jobs made them too busy. Because there would be six persons travelling, they would take two cars, with Percy taking Granny and Clement and Alicia, James, and Paul going in the office car.

Paul, as the policeman in the group, had the house keys. Paul as yet was unaware of the change of owners, so James would ring him and confirm if he was free for the day and willing to accompany them.

James also made an appointment for the next day with the bank manager, with Alicia and Granny to accompany him at ten in the morning.

The next thing they did was examine the work messages that had come in for the last month. There were several divorce cases for them to chase up, and Percy's comment to them was, 'They are not urgent. If we leave them for a few days, they may decide they have changed their minds, and we will not have to sit out in the cold getting evidence.'

Several insurance surveillances were required, and Ken said, 'Maybe Simon and I can take them to show Simon the best angles to shoot them to get the best results.'

A peeping Tom was reported by a young woman, and Kate said, 'I will take that. It is only a short distance away. I could walk to that one if they cannot come in because of their work commitments. I can work out the surveillance and ask someone to help when I have the full picture.'

'Here is one for you, Alicia,' said Percy. 'Mrs Cooke reports that the Polish girl she had as au pair last year has disappeared. That was only yesterday. Perhaps you can call her today. Do you want me to come with you to see her? That sounds urgent.'

'Yes, please, Percy. In case the husband is behind it like last year. I think a male backup would be handy.'

'Alicia,' said James, 'there has been a call for you from Iris Kumar's son Jamal on Friday. That could be urgent.'

Percy said, 'We should put a call through to the chief of police and tell him we are back. He might be saving something up for us, James.'

'True, Percy. Do you want to do it or shall I?'

'I think he will be wondering if you are ready to come back to work, James. That was a rather nasty end to last year for us, with the fires,' said Percy.

James gave a rueful look at him and said, 'I suppose you are right. It is just that every person I have spoken to since arriving home has treated me like cut glass. It revives for me the terrible time we went through before we went on our holiday, and I would much rather put it from my mind. I still feel angry about it.'

'It is natural for them to feel sorry for you, but there must be other things in the news by now. People have short memories if it does not concern themselves, James,' sympathised Percy.

'You are right, Percy. I will contact the chief as soon as this meeting is over. I want to call Paul Morris as well to put him in the picture about Bowering House.

'Welcome to Gray and Armstrong Private Investigations, Simon. We will just allow you to coast for a few weeks, going out with someone who needs a hand. We do jobs in pairs. As you will be aware, things can get dangerous out there if you have no one to watch your back.

'Okay, we had better make a start. The meeting is over.'

Everyone had nominated a job, so they went off to individually start the year's work.

* * *

James's first job was to telephone the chief policeman in the local force. He knew he could not put it off any longer. When he was put through, before he could say anything, the chief's voice boomed, 'Welcome home, James. It is good to have you back. We are sorting out some jobs for you if you want them, hopefully not as hard as the last ones you had. The department is working on some way to compensate you for having the home and bookshop of your wife's grandmother and your apartment totally wiped out.

'We were the ones to ask you to take care of the young man who had lost his memory. We have not forgotten you, and at the last meeting in London, it was brought up to what we could to compensate you.'

James said, 'We were well insured, Chief, so we will not be out of pocket.'

'We thought you probably were insured, James, but it must have been heavy in the heartache area for you all. Also, we are aware that Mrs Newton's historical house and all her possessions are gone in the fire and realise what a crushing blow it would be for her. Some compensation is due as it was our department and London's who made the suggestion for you to take that young man in.'

'Thank you, Chief. It is nice that you have organised something. I admit it was a terrible few moments when we realised we were going to lose everything. For me it was an especially bad moment as I watched the flames. Alicia's grandmother had not been taking rent from us and had welcomed me into the family home and business, and it was the worst day of my life realising that it was all my fault. I feel it is amazing to me that she still likes me after all that.'

'Well, James, you are a likeable sort of fellow. Give me a few days to come up with those jobs. I have Paul Morris on the job of choosing, so you can blame him if you do not like them. These will be a bit older than the first lot.'

'Fine, we have a bit waiting for us. We left the answering machine on while we were away, and there looks like at least a fortnight's work waiting. We are right on to it. We have Percy's youngest son joining the team. He had studied for the police department here in the early days after leaving school, but had a scare when his mate was killed while on duty. Simon was very young at the time, and his mother had just died. He went off into the wilds until we found him. He is twenty-six now and ready to come back. Both Percy and I think he is ready. He sounds enthusiastic, so we are trying him out to see how he goes. He is aware of the study involved.'

'Tell Percy to bring him in next time you come in. He sounds interesting. I often think we take the young ones in too early. We need to allow them to mature a bit is my personal opinion. They burn out quicker when they come straight out of school. As I said, it is my personal opinion. Not everyone agrees with me.'

* * *

Next, James rang Paul Morris, who answered, 'Is that you, James, or are you the really private investigator we have been dealing with, Valerie Newton?'

James laughed. 'It is me this time, Paul. I believe you have been advising Granny in her pursuit of solving the mystery of the Haskell family.'

'She is a fascinating person, James, and so clever. She had me wondering if I could keep up with her. Also, knowing your reputation within ranks here, I have been told how she probably saved a baby from dying of hypothermia with her prompt action last week outside your office.'

'She will be embarrassed that you know about that, Paul. She had us all laughing to see the citation your policeman gave her, and when she described it all to us, she had us in fits of laugher.

Back to the Haskell family part, we plan to take Clement to Bowering House on Saturday. We have not asked him yet. We wanted to know first if you could accompany us. A few things have happened about it while we were away. We called in to see young Divit and Derek in Zimbabwe on the way back home for a few days at his request.

'The first thing Divit did was hand to Granny, Alicia, and myself the deeds of Bowering House made out into our names. He had been upset for us that Granny's bookshop, apartment, and house were burnt down, and at the time of the fire, he had promised a replacement house. Because Jason Haskell, so-called Bowering, was on the deed, along with Divit's grandfather, the house became Divit's, and he has passed it on to us. With that, he has also transferred Jason's money in the English bank over to us to finish off the house. We do not know as yet whether it is £1 or £100. We have an appointment with the bank in the morning to sort that out.

'We have the situation that Granny is scared about telling Clement about it all, so she wanted some backup when we told him in case he implodes, and she wants us to carry out the interview to see what we think of the man. She says she cannot decide whether he is guilty or not.

'Derek has told us that Divit is going well, and Derek may only have to stay with him possibly two or three months more. He is growing more aware every day and more confident and has said that he does not want to come back to the UK. You can understand that, poor boy losing all his family like that.'

Paul considered, 'Saturday is fine for me, James. I have this weekend off, and I must admit I am curious about Clement Haskell.'

'Good, Paul. You have the keys here in your office. Do not forget to bring them. Granny says she will provide food for us all. You and I and Alicia will go in my car, and Percy will drive Clement,and Granny, in his car. We will not start the conversation until we are all seated at the house, having morning tea after arriving. It will appear a more casual conversation that way. We have not decided on where to start. I think I will leave Granny to do that. Clem seems taken with Granny, so we will let that guide us all for a while. I think this is the most interesting case we have ever had. There are so many facets to look into. I will bring you up to date with the history of the house while we are in the car driving to it on Saturday to save you time now.'

'I will look forward to it, James. The first part of the story was fascinating.'

CHAPTER SEVENTEEN

Meanwhile, Alicia had put a call through to Jamal Kumar, whom she had met whilst investigating a girl who had fallen through a second-storey window of a shop in the mall.

'Hello, Jamal, this is Alicia Armstrong. How is your mother?'

'My mother is dying, Alicia. We have been told there is not much time left, and Father and I think she has been waiting for your return so that she can go. She asked if you would come and see her. Is that possible?'

'We will come straight away, Jamal. We will be with you in ten minutes.'

Alicia went in to see James in his office and asked him to go with her. It was urgent.

He stood up and collected his coat and followed her out the door, telling Granny and Percy as they left the office where they were going.

Alicia was sad; she had struck up a friendship with Iris Kumar while they were visiting her in her house during a case. Back then, Iris had been diagnosed with lung cancer and had already outlived the doctor's prognoses. Alicia had thought of her often while they were away on their holiday, hoping she would be back home in time to say goodbye.

As they arrived at the beautiful home, Jamal was waiting for them outside the front door.

'Oh, Jamal, I am so sorry, but I am glad to be back in time to say goodbye to your mother,' were her first words.

'It is okay, Alicia. She insists on making it a happy occasion for everyone who cares for her, so put away your sad face and smile for her. She is going to meet her Lord. Surely when you are such a believer, it is not a sad occasion. Believing in the Lord, she says, gets you through a lot of sorrow, and being brought up in a convent orphanage, as she was, gives her a huge faith.'

'I hope I can copy her when it is my time to go, Jamal. She is such a wonderful person.'

'I agree with that,' said James.

'Come in. Mother is waiting for you, sitting up in her favourite chair in the sitting room.' Jamal held the door open for them to enter.

They smiled as they walked through towards the chair where she was sitting. To Alicia, she still looked as lovely as when she first met her, except she could no longer get up from her chair.

'Is it all right to kiss your cheek, Iris?' asked Alicia.

'I would like that, Alicia, and you too, James. It is lovely to see you again. Now the reason I asked for you to come is, although things have passed me by a lot for the last couple of months, I did hear of your house and bookshop fire, and I would like to tell you how sorry I am about it. My husband Bharat, Jamal, and I have had a chat, and we would like you to have our house. It is a lovely place to bring up children. There are five bedrooms, three bathrooms, and a study, so it is ample large enough for visitors and for your family to grow. This is a gift for you both because you were so kind to us earlier last year. You made my life happy at a time when I was feeling down, and I appreciated it. So did Bharat and Jamal, so we want to help you out.

'Your little son will have space to run around in the garden and be perfectly safe and will enjoy playing cricket with his father on the lawn and also to dig in the garden, and your daughter too when she arrives will be a happy child and love the outdoors. We are quite well off, and for two people, this house is too large. Both my husband and Jamal will be happy to downsize until Jamal marries and he can choose his own house.'

Alicia and James looked at each other, and Alicia said to Iris, 'You can see us with two children, a boy and a girl?'

'Yes. You do not know yet?'

'I do not understand, Iris. What do I not know?'

'That your son will be born very healthy in seven and a half months' time.'

'No, Iris, I did not know. How can you predict that?'

'I have seen him in my dreams in the garden, chasing the birds. I am sorry. I have shocked you. I thought you would be aware that you are pregnant.'

Alicia looked again at James. 'What a way to learn that you are pregnant. There was a mix-up in timing when we travelled to Australia. I had trouble working out what time it was there to compare with the local time here, and I possibly missed out on taking my pill for a couple of days. It is possible that I am going to have a baby. Whoopee! I am going to have a baby boy. What a surprise.'

James had a big grin on his face, and he said to Iris, 'How often do you do that sort of prediction, Iris?'

She smiled. 'It is always possible if you think positive, but it is not always a happy occasion. Sometimes the news is bad, and people get angry with me because I have brought them bad news. I have always been able to do it from about aged ten. The nuns at the orphanage would not allow me to give bad news, only the good.'

'This is definitely good news, Iris. It also explains why I have been feeling queasy in the mornings. I put it down to all the different time zones we have been travelling through, having meals at what my stomach thinks is not a mealtime. You have caught me by surprise.'

Jamal said, 'Congratulations! Are you interested in this house?'

James said, 'Could you explain that part again? I was listening about the baby stuff and was not concentrating properly as I should have been. You must be used to things like that, Jamal, but for us, it is the first time we have heard about it.'

'I am sorry to hassle you, James, but I learnt of a unit being available today and wanted to get to it before anyone else woke up to it. It is in the same group that Derek Choudhury lives in, and I have always loved his apartment and its position across from the park. If we could put our name down on it and pay the deposit before anyone else does, I think Dad and I will love it. Mother could have a look at it so that she can go in peace knowing we will be happy living there, and she could give it her blessing. There is really no hurry for your answer. We could sell this house easily, if necessary. It is just that when Mother has her dreams come true, she is happy, and she does not think she has much longer. So Dad and I would like to make her happy.'

Alicia smiled. 'I always knew from day 1 that you were special, Iris, and now know how special you really are. I would love to see our son with a garden he can play safely in, a garden of our own. Do you know I have never had a garden to play in? My grandmother's house yard was turned into a community garden before I came to live with her. I love the idea of having a garden, and I love the idea we are to have children. We have not tried for children because we had the business take up all our savings when James and Percy established it, so we decided to wait.'

'You always worried that your grandmother would not have the time to enjoy our children, Alicia, and now a timing mistake has taken place. We are very pleased with ourselves. Thank you, Iris and Jamal, your gift of the house will be very gratefully accepted,' said James with a wide grin.

'Please do not hurry to leave the house, Iris. We would much rather have you around a little longer. We know this house is blessed,' said Alicia. 'Anything we can help you with, do not hesitate to call us. I can see you are tiring now. Can I help you to bed?'

'Jamal is very good with that, Alicia. He knows which pills are taken and when and sometimes has to carry me and get me settled.'

'Gosh,' said Alicia, 'I do not know whether to be happy or sad.'

'Be happy, Alicia, and you too, James. Everyone has their time, and it is not a sad occasion for me. I will be free of pain, which sometimes is horrendous and also for Bharat and Jamal to watch. We will all be free, and I look forward to meeting our Lord. Think of it like that. Goodbye for now.'

On the way back to the office, Alicia said, 'I cannot wait to tell Granny the news about the children.'

James said, 'Are you sure that it is all true, Alicia?'

'Yes, James. Remember when we went to see Mr Patel and he was waiting for us because Iris told him we were coming? He told us she had second sight.'

'Mmm, I would rather wait until a doctor confirms you are pregnant. Isn't there a test you can do yourself, a test kit from a pharmacy? I have heard of them.'

'Stop at the next pharmacy, and I will go in and enquire. I cannot wait until I see a doctor if I can tell from a test kit. I am too excited to wait.'

James let out a hoot of laughter. 'Me too, I guess. We have put it on the back burner for four years already, and I would like a baby to coo over. I think little Daniel has made us clucky. Wait until I tell my sister it is all her fault.'

'You are right as usual, James. When I saw Daniel for the first time, I felt all clucky and could not put him down. I suddenly wanted a baby of our own. I am sure Granny will be happy, but I will not tell her until I have done the test.'

'What do you think of the house idea, Alicia? We have sidelined it over the baby news. Two dramatic news items at once seem too much to believe. I think I will ring Bharat Kumar when we reach the office to confirm Iris's ideas are also what he thinks, although Jamal seemed to believe in it. It is not often a house is given away because of a dream. I have not heard of it previously and can hardly believe it.'

'I feel the same way, James. Perhaps they are only indulging her because of her illness. We must give them time to back out if they feel they want to. It was the last thing I expected when Jamal asked us to visit. I thought it was a visit to say goodbye to Iris. Instead we have been set up for life. If it is true, I think we should pay the rent to the orphanage in India that Iris donated all her life to as an exchange.'

'After we have confirmed it with Bharat, I think we should check with Barry Cross, our accountant, to see what is the right way to go about it. I will bet it will be the first time he has heard about this kind of thing also. I agree to help support the orphanage. That is a good idea. It will be some way to compensate for Iris, in memory of her.'

'Stop the car, James. There is a pharmacy over there. Just pull into the car bay available I can see, and I will pop into the shop.'

Alicia came back with a look of glee on her face. 'I have it, James. I will check it when we get back to the office. Kate may be able to help me with it if she is in. I do not think Granny would know too much about this sort of thing to be able to help.'

'What a day,' said James. 'And to think I was reluctant to return home because of all the problems I could see ahead. Do you realise since leaving Australia, we have been given the deeds to Bowering House, money in the bank from Jason Bowering's account although we will not know how much until we visit the bank, the news of our first child, and to cap it off, a beautiful house. I admired that house, Alicia, the day we met Iris, and Jamal showed me through it to go to the study to print the report Iris gave to me.'

'I admired it also, James, and loved that back garden, the birdbath and the shrubs, and the birds visiting. It was all so lovely and in such good taste. It is so hard to believe it will be ours.'

'Although Jamal seemed to go along with Iris's story, before we tell anybody else, I want to confirm it with Bharat. It is possible that he may have a different view on the whole thing.'

They parked the car in the garage beneath the building and walked upstairs, and James went straight to his office.

Alicia followed him but popped in to see Granny first to ask if Kate was back yet. She nodded to her grandmother when she affirmed Kate was in her office and said, 'I will be a few minutes while James makes a call, then I will be right out.'

James was talking to Bharat when she went in the office. She listened until he had finished and said, 'What was Bharat's take on the whole story, James?'

As he put the phone down, he said, 'Bharat says that the house belongs to Iris, and it is her own wish to give the house to us. There is no monetary connection. It is free of mortgage. She has made a will with a lawyer with his guidance to leave the house to us on her death. He reiterated that the house belongs to Iris and has always been in her name. She worked very hard in the tailoring office from the time of her arrival from India, and they bought the house with the thought of more children to come, but it was not to be. After Jamal was born, she did not get pregnant again to their sorrow. The house was put into Iris's name because if anything happened to Bharat, she would not be left stranded because at that time of purchase, they were still establishing the tailoring business properly.

'They had discussed the will that Iris would be leaving and agreed that Iris should do what she wanted with the house. It was far too big for two people and made sense that Jamal and himself move into a two-bedroom apartment, as Jamal wanted. There would be no garden to worry about. They would get a cleaner in once a week, and they could order in meals. There were several Indian restaurants in the vicinity of the unit Jamal was so keen on and all in all will be easier to maintain.

'When I offered to buy the house from him, he immediately said no. This opportunity for Iris to give it to us was her wish, and they were in no need of the money. I told him that we would make a yearly gift to the orphanage where Iris was brought up, and it was welcomed by him. His statement was, she would be happy about that if we decided to do it. So, Alicia, when Iris goes, we have a house to bring our children up in.'

'Did you ask about Iris's prophecy of two children for us, one of them in seven months?'

'Yes, I did, Alicia. He laughed and said, "Iris is still trying to make people happy right up to when she leaves us. She has always had this ability, and if she told you she saw it, then she saw it."'

'I will go and see Kate, and then I will tell the good news to Granny.'

'Tell me first, Alicia, and then we can tell Granny together, please?'

'Of course, James. It is your news too.'

She rushed out of his office in search of Kate. A short while later, she came back to James with a lovely smile and kissed him. 'Come on Daddy-to-be, let us both go and tell Granny she is to be a great-grandmother.'

'This calls for a celebration. I will order in lunch for us all. I cannot close up the office on the first day back.'

CHAPTER EIGHTEEN

Alicia could not settle down after the huge lunch that James had ordered but suddenly decided to ring Mrs Cooke. She had said it could be urgent when she heard that Cooke's au pair had disappeared. Here it was several hours later, and she had been putting off the call, only now remembering it.

She rang the number listed on the voicemail and reached Susan Cooke immediately. After greetings were over, Alicia asked when and where and why had the au pair, Marta, gone from her house. Susan was a little teary at the sound of Marta's name and said she, herself, had started a new job after Christmas. She came home yesterday after work, and Marta was not there.

She had not left a note and had seemed normal at breakfast and went over the dinner plans for the evening for when Susan got home from work, and everything seemed as always. Marta had been practising her cooking and seemed happy. Her return to Poland was due at the end of the week, and they had discussed it a few days previous whether she would go home as she was enjoying her stay, but said she thought her parents would be disappointed if she was not home to start university. She was to be the first one in her family to go to university, and her mother in particular was very proud of the fact.

As Susan was expecting her to leave by air on the next Friday, she did not expect her to leave without saying goodbye to her. But when she arrived home from work, there was no sign of the nineteen-year-old Marta. Her bed was made up, and all her clothes gone from the wardrobe in the bedroom she had been using. She had tried ringing Sacha, Alicia's friend, an engineer, who was also Polish and had befriended the girl, but there was no answer. By this time, she was getting afraid something similar had happened to her like when she had arrived in the city by ship from Poland last year.

Alicia thought about it and decided that she would have to bring Percy up to date on this and try to find out whether Marta had been abducted again and in the bordello in the wharf area as she had been previously.

She advised Susan that she would look into it and said, 'We may have to advise the police of what has happened. I will keep in touch and go as far as we can on our own. There is more privacy that way for you. Do you realise there will be a fee for our time? Sacha paid us the last time when his brother noticed she was not with you.'

'Of course, Alicia. I am so afraid that she has been abducted for the same reason. That is why I did not delay calling you. If my husband is the party at fault this time, I will sue the pants off him for something. I will think of a reason some way or another. As long as Marta is safe. I have grown quite fond of her, but she is a bit gullible, and someone may trick her into doing something she does not realise. I feel so angry each time I think of it. The girl does not deserve what she almost went through the last time.

'I have not been able to forgive Roland for that. Also, for the other girls, I thought Roland wrong for all those girls. The police just slapped his wrists for it, possibly fined him, and I will bet he has started up again. I have not seen him, nor did I want to since

I left him. My opinion of him hit rock bottom, and I can't believe I turned a blind eye for so long. He had been lying to me for years, and I was gullible just as Marta is.'

'I will see what I can do, Susan, and will keep in touch,' said Alicia.

As she put the phone down, Percy came into her office and said, 'I heard part of that conversation. Is that Susan Cooke of the Dr Roland Cooke business last year?'

'Yes, Percy. James might want to know about this as well. Is he in his office?'

'I think so. Let's knock and see if he is awake. That meal might have sent him off to sleep. I think his jet lag is still making him sleepy. It is hard for a few days to get over the time differences.'

'I heard that, Percy,' said a voice behind the closed door. 'Come in and see for yourself that I am working, not lurking.'

Percy looked at Alicia, and they both laughed and opened the door. Sure enough, James was writing up notes. His system from every job was to write them up as soon as he could or the details might be lost.

Alicia explained to both men what she had learnt from Susan Cooke and how urgent she considered it. Percy said, 'I think we should have the police vice squad make a raid down at the wharf as soon as possible before they whip Marta off somewhere else.'

'I was hoping you would say that, Percy. I will see if there is a Russian or Polish ship departing today or tomorrow in case they are taking her elsewhere. What do you think, James?'

'I agree wholeheartedly. This is an ongoing thing with that group and could possibly have other places they could take her to. Once she is in their grasp, they would not want to lose her, and once she is offshore, we will have no chance of finding her. I will ring the chief straight away to see if we can set up a raid with the vice squad.'

James reached for his phone and rang the chief of police and explained the story. Within ten minutes, they had an answer from the vice squad team leader who asked if James wanted to come along because he had met the girl, so he knew which one to pick up. They knew that most of the girls there did not speak any English.

James answered, 'Affirmative, and we have a photo on my wife's phone. I can get her to send it to you. You must have some details of the earlier case we sent to you?'

'I have someone looking into it right now. Shall we pick you up?'

'Yes, please, there will be two of us. We travel in pairs.'

'No problem, James. We will be there in ten minutes.'

James turned to Percy, 'We are on in ten minutes. Would you rather Ken or Simon come with me, Percy? This may mean climbing a number of staircases and possibly a ship. Do you want to leave it to one of the younger men? I don't think Alicia or Kate should go.'

'It would be a good job for Simon, to break him in. He is tough and fit.'

'True, can you find him? I heard his voice a while ago. Alicia, what have you found on the shipping details?'

'A good guess. The same ship that was involved last time which brought Marta from Poland, the *Balbir*, is in port, departing at midnight.'

'You are a blessing to have around, Alicia. You cannot come with us this time. Percy will stay here also, and I will take Simon or Ken for backup.' He looked at the door and saw Simon standing there and said, 'It's Simon this time. I am not sure how long we will be, but I will phone you at some time if I am able.

'One other thing. Send me a copy of Marta's photo, will you, from your phone, and I will send it to the vice squad fellows.

Thank you. You can ring Mrs Cooke and let her know what we are doing, but wait for a couple of hours before doing so. We do not want to let the cat out of the bag and ruin the surprise.'

He turned to Simon, 'I will fill you in on what the job is on the way, Simon. Put on your jacket. It could be cold where we are going. It sounds as if our transport is waiting for us now. Let's go.' He hugged Alicia and kissed her and ran out the door, followed by Simon.

They climbed into the back seat of a large vehicle as it started down the street towards the wharf without a siren blaring, and they introduced themselves as they went along. It was not far from the area of the wharf that they wanted, and they were soon there. Three large vehicles with twelve men ready for action. Each had a gun, except James and Simon, and they ran beside Charlie, the group leader. Each man had a copy of Marta's photo on their own phones as it had been easier that way when called out on an emergency. They ran up to the door and banged heavily on it, calling, 'Police. Open up.'

Someone from the inside called back, 'Go away! We are a lawful gathering here.'

Charlie said to James, 'Delaying tactics. They always do that. Okay, Jack, use your bollard.'

Jack came forward with what he called his bollard, a heavy wooden ram with a handle on its side. He banged it hard against the door, and it was immediately opened from the inside by a burly man whom James recognised must be Bruce from his earlier case about the loss of Marta.

Bruce said, 'There is no need to break the door down. It is open.'

'Up the stairs, team,' called Charlie. And to James and Simon, he said, 'You two try the ground floor.'

Simon raised his eyebrow at James, and the two went left and found a sitting room and a television set in front of armchairs, about twelve, James guessed. There was no sign of life. They turned and went the other direction down a small passage and into each room. First was a kitchen. They looked for other doorways to get out, but there were none. The next room was a library of books with no other exit until James said, 'Look behind the bookshelves, Simon. When I lived in a bookshop, each shelf was on wheels.' They pushed the shelves, and suddenly, there were three girls crawling out from behind shelves.

'Very clever,' said Simon.

He turned to herd the three girls together and held up his phone with the picture of Marta, saying, 'Marta?'

He looked at each girl in turn, saying 'Marta', and two shook their heads. The third girl nodded. He led the girls out and called out to the man Charlie had left by the front door.

It was Jack, and he said, 'Watch these girls for us, Jack.' Pointing at the third girl, he said, 'This one recognises Marta from the picture. Be careful with her.'

'No trouble,' said Jack, taking some handcuffs from his belt and putting them on to the girl. He took out a rope and tied the girl to his waistband. This time it was James who said 'Very neat' before he turned and went down the passageway past the library.

The next room was a study with three desks. Each desk had a notepad on top of it and a pen and some envelopes in a pack in a holder. He murmured to Simon, 'Plenty to write about here to your loving parents at home who think you are an au pair.'

There was a large room at the end of the passageway, and when James pushed the door open, they saw that this was where the entertainment took place. There was a small stage, a piano, and a number of chairs facing the stage, most around a small table for two. There was a number on each tabletop. They counted twelve tables.

At the side of the room was a bar with room for one person to stand behind, and on shelves behind that were bottles of vodka, whisky, and many other bottles James did not recognise as he was not a drinker.

There was no one in the room, but he noticed another door leading to the rear. James and Simon opened the door, and James said, 'I can smell fear. Look carefully. There is someone in this room here. They opened the rear door using the key in the lock. They looked out, but there was no sign of anyone and closed it again and locked it, leaving the key in place. James went around the room towards a thin cupboard behind a table and single chair. The cupboard was locked, and James said, 'How do we open this cupboard without hurting the person inside?'

Simon said, 'Leave it to me. I have my Swiss pocketknife that I have found very useful on my travels' He unhooked it from his belt and opened it up and chose the instrument he thought would possibly be the right one and moved to the door and spoke, 'If there is someone in this cupboard, I am about to open it up. Try to flatten yourself towards one side if possible.'

He attacked the door near the handle and, within a minute, had the door open. Inside was Marta, her hands tied behind her back and a scarf tied around her mouth so she could not speak. She was standing as it was not possible to sit in the space and looked as if she was about to fall. She looked petrified, and as James held out his hands to her, she fell into his arms.

James said to Simon, 'Go up the passage and tell Jack we have found Marta, but bring me a chair for this poor girl first. She looks like she has been locked up in this cupboard unable to move all day. I will call an ambulance to take her for a checkup after Charlie has spoken to her. After all, this is his operation. We have been lucky to find her so soon. I am sure she would have been put on to the ship before too long. We are lucky to find her before that happened.'

Simon dashed out of the room to get to Jack, and James sat Marta on to the chair and said to her, 'Do you remember me, Marta? I came to visit you the day you were taken to the house of Mrs Cooke after you came from the ship.'

The girl nodded; she was shaking, obviously in shock, so she could not speak. He said no more except, 'We will look after you, Marta. Do not be afraid.'

He walked over and carried another chair to place it facing the girl and sat down.

Charlie came into the room and, summing up the situation, said, 'Well done, James. What do you want to do now?'

James grinned. 'You are obviously taking statements from the rest of the girls and Bruce and Madam, if she is here. I am told she does not leave the premises between shiploads. The shiploads come into this port three months with girls from Russia and Poland. They drop a load of girls here and take some back. Most of the girls thought they were coming as au pair girls. Few of them speak English, and it is a big scam. Dr Roland Cooke seemed to have been the instigator, a local doctor whose wife had been unaware of his employment in the scam, until we discovered that Marta was missing, and the good doctor had promoted his own address for a reference. Susan Cooke was not in on the scam and helped us find Marta. Needless to say, the Cooke's are now headed for divorce.

'We got Marta from him three months ago, after she arrived here, thinking she was going to be Susan Cooke's au pair, and Susan reported to us today that Marta was missing again. Marta is due to fly home to Poland on Friday, and when Mrs Cooke came home from her job as a nurse and found Marta gone, she rang Alicia, my wife, and reported it again.'

'Most of the girls upstairs have given statements that they came here under the guise of being an au pair. What do you want to do about Marta now?' asked Charlie.

'Ring for an ambulance to have her checked out, and we will look after her from there. I will ring my wife to pick Simon and myself up and to tell Mrs Cooke where we found Marta, and she can make sure she takes that flight on Friday. I will take a statement from Marta after her medical checkup and fax it to you tomorrow. She is not fit to give a statement at the moment. She has been locked in that narrow, cold cupboard much and is ready to collapse. I believe the reason she has not collapsed yet is because the walls of the cupboard held her upright.'

'A good job done, James, and you too, Simon. We could have kept taking the statement from the other girls, and the bully bloke could have smuggled Marta out the back door. It looks as if it is not the first time it has happened. This time they were aware of our usual run through the house. We surprised them by having you with us to do the ground floor simultaneously. It outfoxed them.'

Charlie went on upstairs, and James rang for an ambulance. He also rang Percy because Alicia had left to go home to cook dinner. Percy promised he would ring Mrs Cooke and would come and pick up James and Simon and would go to the hospital and meet Mrs Cooke there. It was getting late, so Percy would lock up the office before coming.

James rang the chief policeman and reported they had found the missing girl. He also rang Alicia at home and told her the story; it had always been her case.

Percy arrived at the same time as the ambulance, and they watched as the paramedics wheeled her from the house. They followed in the car with Percy. They waited at the hospital until

Marta was declared fit and took the girl with them to meet Susan Cooke coming up the stairs.

At last, Marta broke down; she sobbed as she told of Bruce coming to the Cooke house about nine o'clock in the morning after Susan had gone to work, and he had forced her to pack her bag for departure—as he had put it. He made her lie down on the back seat of the car and drove her to the wharf and took her through the back door of the house and put her in the cupboard. She did not know what happened to her bag. She had been locked up in the cupboard all day with nothing to eat and drink. Here she looked baffled. 'Did he think I am a dog?' she asked.

'Did he slap you, Marta?'

'He did not need to. He held my arms so tight I could not get away from him.'

She rolled up her sleeve to show the extensive bruising on her arms.

Charlie had delivered Marta's suitcase to the hospital while they waited there for her. He had found it in another cupboard upstairs.

Susan said, 'I have booked the two of us into a hotel for the night, she flies out to Poland on Friday. After that, so I know she is safe, she will ring me from her home with her parents, to make sure she has arrived safely. And then I will sue Roland for everything he has got and take out an order to keep myself safe.'

Percy said, 'Simon and I will be at the hotel at nine o'clock in the morning to take your statements. Both Alicia and James have a ten o'clock appointment in the morning, so they will not be available till the afternoon. It is always better to give a statement while everything is clear in your mind, so we will come to see you. Statements have been given to the vice squad already at the wharf side house by the other girls, but Marta was not in any condition to give one, and as you know, we must have it for the prosecution.

I hope some of the other girls have spilled the beans on how they were at the brothel.'

Susan wrote the hotel name and room number on a page from her diary and said as she handed it over, 'I will notify the hotel that you are the only ones to be allowed to come or call.'

Percy drove them home, and Alicia and Granny came to ask, 'How are they doing, and is Marta safe?'

Percy answered, 'Locked up in a hotel room by now. Simon and I will go and take their statements in the morning because you and James will be going to the bank. So Kate and Ken will be in charge of the office for the morning tomorrow.'

Granny said, 'How did you do, Simon? Could you follow easy enough?'

'Well, Granny, you have to have all your senses available when you are following James. He seems to see things before anyone else and is halfway to the girl before anyone else has even moved. I think the only thing I got to do was use my splendid old Swiss knife that Dad gave me for my tenth birthday to open a locked cupboard. It worked though. Do you know that expression "He could smell fear"? James used it, and it made him walk to a cupboard door. And there Marta was locked in with her mouth covered and her hands and feet tied, and because it was such a slender cupboard, she could not move. You would not have believed a woman could be in it, and anyone else would have walked by it. James though could smell the fear. I was so impressed.'

Percy said, 'You are learning your trade from the best, Simon. You have seen it in action. If anyone else had got the call, they would still be asking, what do I do next?'

'Yes, Dad, I can see what you mean. I was chatting with Ken yesterday while out on a surveillance, and he said the same thing.'

'Come on, boys. It is just a matter of hearing the story, listening carefully, and counting the dots, and it is all there.' James laughed.

'Oh yes, the only trouble is knowing where the dots start and finish,' said Percy.

James looked at Percy and said, 'The only thing I am worried about is what Roland Cooke will do about us. This is the second time we have thwarted him. I think we may have to ask the chief for protection for a while. That man thinks he is God's gift to all women. I am scared he could pick on Kate and Alicia as redress. What do you think, Percy?'

'That has crossed my mind. Kate has Ken to watch out for her. We will have to be vigilant that Alicia is safe from him and Bruce. Do not dismiss the bouncer. He is a bully.'

'I thought that myself when I saw him today. I had not seen him previously, just heard about him from Alicia after her cooking lesson next door.'

'Speaking of which,' said Alicia's voice from the kitchen, 'dinner is ready.'

As they sat at the dining room table, Alicia turned to Granny and said, 'Would you mind terribly if I did not come with you to Bowering House on Saturday? I would like to go and see Sandra Dunston. I have not seen her for so long, and I would like to tell her our news before it becomes too obvious. Also, I would like to be free in case I get a message from the Kumars. It cannot be too long now for Iris. Jamal said she was still alive because she was waiting for us to come home so we could say goodbye.'

'Of course, my darling, you can go again another day. I only hurried it up so that James and Percy could meet Clement to see if they can see the same things I have discerned from him. I need to be more secure in my belief that he is not like his sons and Faye. There is no one better at getting information from someone than James. You all recognise that. Also, DI Paul Morris needs to have James's impressions as well of Clement, so the three men can reinforce me in what I have been doing with Clem or whether I should break off the relationship.

'You do not need to be there this time, Alicia. I know you are not happy about going for the time being, so we will go another weekend, because I think you will be amazed as I am prepared to be at the house, from when James described it previously when he was looking for Jason Bowering.'

'In that case, are you doing anything at the weekend, Simon? Would you be prepared to watch over Alicia on Saturday while we are gone? We have just been saying that we should watch over Alicia in case bully boy Bruce gets wind of her or Dr Roland Cooke for that matter. Both could turn up. I will ring the chief tomorrow to get someone to come around on Saturday as a watch to make sure she is safe.'

'Thanks, James, but will they know where to find me? We have moved house. Surely that makes it safer,' questioned Alicia.

'They could follow us home, Alicia. I am just taking precautions while Percy and I are out of the city.'

'I realise that, but they would have to get me while I am away from the house. I feel quite safe here in this house with the security.'

'Yes, but if we have both Percy's and the office car, you will have to walk, and that makes you easier to follow.'

'Well then, the solution to that is to buy me a car. It would make it so much easier while you are working on a case for me to do the shopping.'

James looked flummoxed; he thought for a minute and said, 'You will need a car to take the baby around. Okay, what colour and type of vehicle do you want?'

'Stop there. I have never needed a car before. We will have to speak to Barry Cross. I have no idea what sort of car I will need, and I have no idea what car is best for carrying all that baby stuff around. Barry should know. His wife has a car and a baby.'

'We will have to speak to Barry in the next day or so. We will ask him then.'

'Dad and I will do the dishes, Granny. You and Alicia put in a full day at the office, and you have cooked dinner. What do you say, Dad?'

'That is a good idea, Simon. I can see you have remembered your early lessons.'

'I like also the way you talk over issues at the office at home. That must put you in front of everybody who knocks off at five o'clock to go home and wait until the next morning to start up again,' said Simon.

'Yes, we worked that out a couple of years ago, and we all believe that is our strong point. Mind you, that could also be our downfall, because we rarely get enough rest from our cases, and when something terrible happens, like the fire in Granny's house and bookshop, it nearly wiped me out,' said James. 'Then again, because we are such a tight-knit community, the help we give each other keeps us going. Once again, in the circumstances like we had prior to Christmas, I would have folded if I did not have our group support.'

Simon went on, 'You say about your experiences, but my brother told me how you supported Dad when he was shot in the neck with a needle, possibly a lethal dose from a mad nurse in a healthcare home. You took him in to your family until he has become part of your family, it seems. And still is. I do admire you all.'

'It has all evolved over time, Simon. We are close-knit, and we like it that way, despite the differences in age. You are part of that family now.'

'I am grateful to you. Thank you, all. After Mother died, I had felt so alone. Instead of standing up and asking for help, I shot through by myself. I can see now I should have stayed. Dad would have helped me, and I could have helped him. We were both in the same boat really, so I have wasted all those years.

'There is one more thing I think I should bring up now. I have a girlfriend in Australia. When I left her, it was said between us that I should come home and try things out, or I would wonder all my life about how things would have been. Stephanie is an Australian girl, and the reason why I stayed in Australia for so long, besides the climate, the friendly people, and the great food, of course. She is the daughter of a station owner of 100,000 acres, where I stopped to work for a few months. As it turned out, we fell in love, and I stayed longer than I initially counted on.

'When we found out that Dad was looking for me, we talked it over, and we decided that I come back here to try things out. If I am happy here, she will come and join me, and we would get married. I am finding out that I am missing her already and hope she is missing me the same amount. I have not spoken to her since I arrived.'

Alicia had stopped to listen and said, 'This could be the best thing yet. We know Percy missed you and worried about you while you were travelling around. If you do stay, you could move into this house, and the rest of us will move to Iris Kumar's house, which she has given to James and I. I am sorry we did not tell you about that before now. It has five bedrooms, three bathrooms, and a study and is absolutely beautiful. Iris is leaving it to us in her will. We were wondering what we would do with it. It has lots of space, and Granny and Percy could have their own rooms. You could have the freedom of your dad's house until you have decided what you want to do permanently and bring your lady to stay with you in complete privacy. What do you think of that, folks?'

Granny said, 'Why did you hold that news back about the Kumar house, Alicia?'

'We all seemed happy here together. We thought, well, Iris has not gone yet, and it gives them time to change their minds if they want to. It seems strange that they give a house away to acquaintances. That is all we are really. I know that Jamal is their only relative, and Iris has not made many friends in the community, but she seems to have appreciated our friendship from the beginning. I also think she thought our help with Divit was a good thing and was sorry her illness prevented taking him in, so she appreciated us for helping him. Then when we lost the bookshop, the apartment, and Granny's house because of it, she was sorry for us. It is not complicated at all really if you are on the inside of the story. Bharat and Jamal agreed to it, so when Iris dies, which could be any day now, the house will go to us after it is probated.'

'Wow,' said Percy, 'I am glad I am on your side.'

They all laughed, and Alicia said, 'We are glad too, Percy.'

CHAPTER NINETEEN

At ten the next morning, James, Alicia, and Granny went to the bank as arranged. They felt overwhelmed when the manager came out to greet them personally and ushered them into his office. They were offered tea or coffee, and when it arrived, there was a nice little cake on a plate at the side of the saucer.

Alicia and Granny looked at each other and then at James, who winked at them. They had never received this service before.

After James explained the circumstances of their meeting, the manager nodded and said, 'Yes, that is the same explanation given to me by our director in London.' He pulled a large journal over to the middle of the large desk and opened up a page with a long list of numbers on it, saying, 'This is the account of Jason Bowering Haskell, now deceased. The balance showing here is the balance that Mr Haskell's stepson in Zimbabwe, whom we have contacted, has approved and we are to change into your names.

'We need some photo identification if you would have it on you, such as a passport or a driving licence. Under the circumstances it will be hard for you to give us your permanent address, I understand, so your office address would do for the time being until you have that permanent residence, if you could notify the bank when that is available. Is this to be in one account or divided between you?'

James said firmly, 'One account each, please, Mr Burford. Three names if you would. The house and bookshop that burnt belonged to Valerie Newton, who is my wife's grandmother. However, I have been told by Jason Bowering Jr that the account is to be in my name. I take issue with that as at that time, I was living above the bookshop and paying no rent as the husband of Mrs Newton's granddaughter.

'I would like to share the account three ways if that is possible. So far, I have no idea how much money is involved. I work in a precarious business where the property burning down is not the first occasion it has been attempted, and this time, it was only by the grace of God we were not in the buildings when it was torched. We had chosen that particular evening to go to a restaurant for our dinner.

'I would like both my wife and her grandmother to have part of the account in the case of future grievances by the population that may take me from them. Do you understand what I am trying to say?'

Mr Burford harrumphed and said, 'I do understand, Mr Armstrong, and sincerely hope it does not happen again. It seems terrible that someone with a grievance could be so destructive. I think I will stick to banking.'

James laughed. 'I am sure you get some laughs from banking. You have to see the funny side of life, or you will go crazy. How much are we looking forward to, Mr Burford? For all I know, it may not be worth breaking up into three.'

The banker pushed the journal over the desk so they could see the figures. 'It's £3 million at the moment. I believe there is some interest to be added to that at the end of the month.'

They did not look stunned because they were guessing it would be a large amount, although not that large, and James said, 'Well, that will not be too hard to divide.'

He turned to his wife and her grandmother and nodded, and they nodded back. He turned back to the bank manager and said, 'If you would, sir, three separate equal accounts, please.'

As they left the bank, they could see people looking at them, and James said out of the corner of his mouth, 'No giggles for the moment, girls. Wait until we are around the corner.'

Granny said, 'We are doing well between us. With £1 million pounds each here, a house there, an insurance payout next, and two apartments from the council when they are built, I think we are each multimillion heirs.'

'It would seem so, Granny. The business is in the black as well. I will have to rearrange my thinking. It seems, Alicia, you can have your car for your little joey.'

Granny looked at him. 'You have chosen a name for your baby already?'

'Not yet, Granny. That is what the Australians call the kangaroos' babies that they carry in their pockets at the front of them—joeys. They are so cute. From conception, the joeys live in those pockets, and for several months after they are born, it is wonderful to see quite large joeys crawl out of the pockets.

'Sorry, that just slipped out. We have not had time to discuss names yet. It is all too new to us at the moment.'

Alicia said, 'I feel I am in a state of shock at the moment. Every day there is a new revelation. I am waiting to see when the other boot falls. It is all so hard to believe. How long can it continue?'

'It does mean, James, that any time you want to leave the undeserving public and go do an easier job, you will have the means to do so,' said Granny.

'True, Granny, but where am I to get my excitement from, that race of adrenaline when we solve a case? We will die of boredom, don't you think?'

Granny made a sound like James did when he laughed sometimes, the hoot as she called it. She said, 'You are right, James. Even down to my level, I get excited when we are on a case. Do not laugh because I said *we*. You do let me help sometimes, and I find it exciting.'

'We could not have solved some cases without you, Granny. I think you are the breach between the generations. You think differently because you belong to the earlier generation, and that is what I will be counting on when we meet Clement Haskell on Saturday. Have you rung him yet to ask if he will come?'

'No, not yet, James, and I am glad I didn't. He would be wondering why Alicia is pulling out of coming, and now he will not know that she was coming at one stage. He is still anxious to please me, and I do not want to throw him out until we dig a little deeper.'

'Good thinking, Granny. I agree with that.'

The team were busy with various cases until Saturday arrived, and each prepared for their day. Granny had a big hamper ready for lunch and did not worry about flasks of tea, remembering James telling her they had made tea and toast the last time they went to the house.

Percy drove with Valerie to pick up Clement. And James went off to pick up Paul Morris from the other direction. They were to meet at Bowering House.

Simon opted for a sleep in, and Alicia said she would see him later as she was having coffee in the mall with her friend Sandra and her daughter Jody.

After her coffee date with Sandra and Jody later in the morning, coming out of the mall, Alicia saw Roland Cooke peering into the window of the private investigation office. She was startled. James had said that Cooke might come looking for them or perhaps her, so as he had not noticed her, she ducked back into the mall and waited half an hour before venturing out again cautiously.

The coast looked clear as she came out again, went into the office, and picked up Granny's umbrella, laughing to herself as she walked away from the mall in the direction of the house, looking around herself constantly as she walked briskly, saying to herself, 'It is a good weapon. Granny is right about it. It is not conspicuous as every person in this climate carries an umbrella at some time, but if used correctly, it could do quite a lot of harm.'

She reached the end of the street and looked carefully in the direction of the house. There were several cars parked outside of the houses, but their own driveway looked to be free. As she went to turn the corner, one of the cars started up, and she jumped back in time so that the driver did not see her. He was faced towards their house, and she heard the bark of a gunshot. The car went racing down the street, luckily to the opposite way where she was standing.

She waited until it had turned around at the corner of the street and drive back up the street again. She watched, peeping around the corner, and saw the vehicle driving slowly, looking at the house in the rear-view mirror, so the driver missed seeing her slip into a gateway to hide behind a bush. She took a photo of the vehicle on her phone and tried to get the driver in also. She called the police emergency number as she ran towards the house and filled in the code number for entry.

As she closed the gate, she saw the car coming back and sprinted towards the shrubs near the front door to hide amongst them. She looked around for Simon but could not see him at first. Then she saw a foot move behind another shrub, and she called out, 'Simon, can you hear me? Are you all right?'

Simon answered very weakly, 'I have been hit in the chest. There is a lot of blood, but I am okay.'

'I have rung the police, and I will now ring an ambulance. Hang in there. We will have help quickly at this time of day.'

As she finished speaking, they heard a siren.

'Keep still, Simon, until I see that it is the police or ambulance. The shooter is still in the street, I think. I saw him turn back to have another look. I managed to stay out of sight. I think it is Roland Cooke. I took a photo, but the face is not clear and is only clear of his body and he is wearing a hat. But I got a clear photo of the car. That could be enough evidence.'

The siren moaned to a halt at the end of the driveway, and Alicia peeped out and called out the code for the gate to be opened.

Two policemen came cautiously into the property, and Alicia stood up to show herself and called, 'There is a family member here that has been shot. I am Alicia Armstrong, and behind that shrub there is Simon Gray, son of Percy Gray, whose house this is. I have called an ambulance. I have no idea how badly Simon is, as the shooter was making a return trip towards us, we had to hide before I could look at him, but there seems to be a lot of blood.'

By this time, she was standing up and walking to Simon. He was still alert, but she could see a pool of blood where he lay, and he made no attempt to stand up. Then they heard an ambulance siren, and she said, 'Thank you, Lord.'

The gate was still open, and the paramedics came quickly in, carrying a gurney to convey Simon to the ambulance. Simon looked up at her and said, 'Thank you, Alicia. That was quick.' He gave a short laugh, holding his chest, and said, 'I see you have Granny's umbrella.'

'If I was two minutes earlier, Simon, it would have been me lying there. I am sorry. I was out of umbrella range.'

'Don't make me laugh, Alicia. It hurts.'

'I will ring your brother and tell him where you are and ring your dad too. Get better soon.'

The ambulance went off with its siren blaring, and one of the policemen said, 'Can we go into the house? You look very shaky. You need to sit down.'

The door was open, so she led the way into the lounge room and sat down, indicating chairs for the policemen. One of them asked, 'Could I make you a cup of tea to steady you?'

'No, thanks. I have only recently had a cup of coffee. I will be right in a few moments. It is only the shock of it, even if we were expecting something to happen.'

The policemen introduced themselves, and one of them, Ben, said, 'Are you related to the Armstrong and Gray group of private investigators?'

'Yes, James is my husband. He is carrying out an interview in the country today, and I do not expect him back for some time yet. Percy and DI Morris are with him too.'

'I met your grandmother last week,' said the younger policeman. 'She too was in private investigation mode and wrote up a splendid set of notes for me and my partner at the time regarding the loss of a car with a baby in it.'

Alicia laughed and said, 'Yes, we have seen the citation you gave her. She was chuffed about it.'

She looked at the policemen and said, 'Do you mind if I make a phone call to Simon's brother? He is a surgeon at the general hospital and will want to know how Simon is.'

'Sure, go ahead.'

She made the call and described why Simon was on his way to the hospital and listened for a while and then said, 'I would like to hear that he is okay. I have not rung your dad yet. He would only worry, and he is having a sort of day off and will be back by teatime this afternoon.'

'Now,' said the policeman, 'you have a little colour in your cheeks and look a bit better. Tell us your story and show us your telephone. We presume, like your grandmother before you, that you have a picture of the car and driver?'

She laughed. 'A hard act to follow, my grandmother. Yes, James and Percy have trained us well, and I do have pictures, but let me go back to the beginning to put you in the picture.'

Telling the story of the original time they had to find Marta and the story of the latest time that she had disappeared, she brought them up to date with seeing Roland Cooke peering into the office about eleven o'clock this morning, her hiding in the mall until she thought it safe to go home, then almost walking into a gun blast when arriving. Hiding in a neighbour's front garden until she heard the car leaving, and realising the shot must have been at Simon as he was the only person home at the Gray house.

Ben, the younger and more talkative policeman, said, 'You folks are really out there, aren't you? After your grandmother's episode last week, I was reporting in the office, and they told me that her house and bookshop were burnt down by a couple of crims before Christmas.

'Now one of your staff and almost yourself have been hunted and shot at. I had always thought that being a private investigator would be fun, but fun like that, I can do without. I think we are less obvious because we are in uniform. It seems to be some type of protection that covers us for the fault of investigating these people who cannot look straight.'

The older policeman, who had not said very much, joined Alicia in laughing at Ben and said, 'I think I will stop him there before he puts his foot in any further. We will report all this to our office, and perhaps DI Morris can follow things up. He sounds as if he could be part of this investigation.'

'Yes, the chief has made Paul Morris part of our reporting team. We do need backup from time to time and since we are not able to do more than make a citizen's arrest, it is handy to have Paul assisting where necessary. Although, I think I have it from my point of view, and it is us that are assisting Paul. We seem to keep running into people who want to take things out on us. I think we should call ourselves the "impersonal private investigators". That might give us a bit of slack.'

'I like the way you fill us in with photographs and the background in what is happening. It certainly makes things easier for us,' said Ben.

'Thanks for being so prompt this morning. I think because you turned up so prompt that you saved us from a further volley of bullets. I saw the car coming back at us, and the siren behind him made him put his foot down and take off. I will call you if I see him come back, and I will not move out of the door in case he does return.'

The older policeman answered his phone and had a short conversation. He turned to Alicia and said, 'There is a policewoman coming to stay with you for the afternoon until your family comes home. The chief apologises that someone was not allocated earlier. It was a busy night last night, and staff were not available. Apparently, your husband alerted them yesterday that there could be a problem.'

'Thank you for your company till now. I am feeling better and do not really need anyone. I think Roland Cooke or his henchman will think twice about coming back today. You were so quick in arriving they must have heard or seen you and the ambulance, so I think they are probably thinking about leaving town for a while till things cool off.'

Ben was quick to say, 'Are you sure you do not need anyone?'

'No, it is safe here with the security. I do not know why Simon was outside. Perhaps someone rang the buzzer, and he thought it was me and went out to investigate why I had not come in. That is why he was the one shot. When will you interview Simon?'

'I called the hospital a few moments ago, and he is still in surgery. His brother is with him,' said the older policeman. 'The hospital will let us know when he is awake and able to talk.'

'I know he is in good hands if his brother is there, so I may have a nap for the rest of the afternoon until the rest of the family come home. They will be worn out with their day's outing, so I might have to start the evening meal early. My grandmother gets tired nowadays. Percy will probably want to go into the hospital to see Simon as well, so it may be a long evening. I think a nap is in order.'

'Well, if you are sure, we will cancel the policewoman. But do not go outside just in case they come back or unless you are sure of who is talking on the intercom.'

'Thanks for the advice. I will go to bed now, at least for an hour. I will wait until you lock the gate first,' Alicia said.

She was yawning as they got into their car and drove away and said to herself, 'I am so tired I do not think I will even hear if someone is at the gate. I feel as if I could sleep for a week.'

* * *

She was awoken some time later and looked at the clock and saw she had been asleep for three hours and felt shocked. Lying there for a few minutes, she realised that what had woken her was James returning home.

Jumping out of bed, she went to the bathroom to rinse her face to wake herself up. This was not her normal thing, sleeping in the afternoon, and felt quite guilty and hurried out to put the kettle on for a cup of tea and ran out to greet James. He kissed her and held her at arm's length and said, 'You are flushed. Are you all right?'

Alicia blushed. 'I have been sleeping and suddenly realised I was asleep for three hours. It must have been the result of Simon being shot. The shock of it made me tired.'

'What!' exclaimed James. 'Did I hear you right? Did you say Simon was shot?'

'Yes, I saw it happen as I was turning the corner. It looked like Roland Cooke in the car. I took a photo as he passed me, but I was hiding in the neighbour's yard at the corner so that he would not see me, because I think it was me, he was looking for.'

'Come on in quickly, Alicia. Do not show yourself. Whoever it was may come back.'

'Simon was shot over three hours ago. If they came back, I was asleep and did not hear a thing.'

'How is Simon? Will he be okay?'

'The last I heard he was still in surgery, and his brother was with him. I have not heard since, but I was so sound asleep I would not have heard the phone if someone called anyway. I did not ring you or Percy because there was nothing you could do at the time, and I thought it better to let you carry out your investigation into Clement without interruption. Is Percy far behind you?'

'I can ring him now, and he can go straight to the hospital. If he is driving, Granny will answer the phone. In fact, I will ring her phone, and she can tell him about Simon. You say you think it was Roland Cooke?'

'Pretty much so. I had seen him peering into your office twenty minutes before I arrived at the top of our street. Luckily for me, but bad luck for Simon, Cooke arrived here before me because I was walking and taking my time, never thinking he was going to ambush someone with a gun. I was carrying Granny's umbrella, thinking if someone grabbed me, I could stick the spike into them, but I never got close enough. Neither the police nor I had time to ask Simon how it all went down, because we could see he was bleeding quite badly, and the ambulance was so quick he was gone to hospital before we had time to ask questions.'

She went on to relate the story as she had seen it, ending with, 'I think Simon thought I needed entry at the gate and came out to see why, and got the bullet. I had rung the police while I was still up the street right after I heard the shot and saw Cooke turn the car at the corner to come back to have another go. Then the police came so quickly, and hearing all the sirens, he put his foot down and roared off.

'My god, Alicia, you had Granny's umbrella for a weapon? What did you really think you could do with that?' James sounded so horrified.

Alicia, in turn, sounded offended when she said, 'I did not have anything else, James. If we are going to mix with people like Roland Cooke, we need something to defend ourselves with. I had seen him looking into the office and did not really think he would go any further, but I remembered Granny's umbrella and picked it up for my walk home, just in case I saw him again.

'How was I to know he had a gun and was prepared to shoot someone? Give me a little slack for good sense, James. My reasoning was that if he physically attacked me, I might get a swipe or two in before he did me any damage. If you remember, I am quite practised in self-defence. You of all people would know I am quite able to defend myself, but not anyone with a gun who is prepared to shoot it.'

James reached over and pulled her close. 'I am sorry, Alicia. I was not thinking clearly. I was too worried for you. I know how you can defend yourself. You have been practising for three years now at Harry's barn, and you are very good, Harry tells me. But you are my Alicia, and I want to be the one to defend you. And of course, we have to think of our little joey too now.'

'Ring Percy, James. He needs to know. Do you want to go to the hospital yourself to make sure everything is all right for Simon? Shall we eat out tonight? I am sure Granny and Percy are tired. It has been a big day for them. I am lucky I have had my sleep. You could tell me about your day while we have dinner somewhere.'

'Good idea, Alicia. I do not want to let you go after you gave me that fright, so yes, we will go Italian tonight. Okay, I will ring Percy now.'

As he said that, the gate opened, and Percy and Granny drove through. James said, 'That has saved me a phone call. Wait here until they come in. I will make a cup of tea to calm Percy down when he hears about Simon.'

'I will put the cups out, James. I will leave you to tell Percy and Granny about Simon.'

James went out to greet Percy and Granny. Alicia could hear the consternation in their voices as James went on, and Granny hurried inside to see if Alicia was all right.

Alicia laughed. 'Yes, Granny, I am fine. It is Simon you should be worried about. I was asleep all afternoon and did not hear if my phone rang, but I presume they were waiting for Percy to get back to hear all about it, allowing Simon to sleep off the anaesthetic. If Percy rings now or, better still, goes into the hospital to see for himself, you will have a better idea of how he is. James proposed we all go to the hospital and then go on to our Italian restaurant for dinner. What do you think?'

'I think you are all correct on each point, Alicia. I can see you are fine. It just makes the old heart jump a little when I hear you were in a fight of sorts, just like when you were a child, not that you were in many fights.'

'Not me, Granny. I like to think of myself as a pacifist. I do not like to upset people, although thinking that comment through, you had better keep Roland Cooke away from me for a while.'

They decided to go into the hospital, and Percy rang his eldest son and asked him if he would arrange for them to see Simon for themselves.

The answer to that was that Simon was in a private room, being watched over by a policeman until they could say he was safe. Anyone could visit if they could prove themselves safe by showing their ID.

They set off to the hospital after a quick wash-up, and David came out to greet them when they arrived outside the room to tell them that Simon was fine. They had got the bullet out easily where it had lodged in the flesh beneath his collarbone, and he would heal well because the flow of blood had kept the wound clean. He would be out of hospital within a day or so.

Seeing Simon made Alicia teary, and she said, 'I can see you are not too badly off and your wound is clean. I just felt faint when I saw you drive off in the ambulance, knowing it was my fault. That the real person he was trying to kill was me. If something worse had been wrong with you, I would not be able to forgive myself.'

Everybody looked at her in amazement, and David said, 'I hear you are pregnant, Alicia. You have just proved it to me. Pregnant women always get teary in the first few months, sometimes for no reason at all.'

'Does wanting to fall asleep at a moment's notice also happen for the same reason?' asked Alicia.

'Yes,' said Granny and Percy together.

'Well, I guess I do not need to go to a doctor to prove I am pregnant then,' said Alicia with a grin. 'I have all of you to tell me I am in the family way.'

She went on, 'What I was trying to say, Simon, is that the policeman outside your door is a good sign. The one thing you will have to watch out for though is, Roland Cooke is also a doctor and could easily get past the policeman by wearing his white coat and identity gear and saying he was a doctor who came to check you out. Had anyone else thought of that possibility?'

They all looked at each other, and David said, 'That is a very good deduction, and I believe Simon will be better off at my place for a few days, where I can watch over his wound and know Cooke cannot get to him to finish him off.'

Percy said, 'That could put you in danger, David, and you have your family to think of. I think we will take him home with us. We will not be going out tomorrow, but you could come in the morning, David, and have a look at him to make sure he is okay. He can have my room in the house, and I will sleep in his den for a couple of days. He would be safer all around.'

'I second that,' said James. 'That is one angry doctor, and we will have to prove it was him and close him down.'

'I think that I have proved it, James. I gave the police who came all the details and photographs, and they are probably right now trying to find him to lock him up,' said Alicia.

'Then, Percy, who do you suggest I ring to find out the latest on the case?'

'Ring Paul Morris and get him to chase it up. He would like to be kept in the loop anyway. He knows about Roland Cooke from our earlier case last year.'

David said, 'You had better go out of the hospital to make your calls. Phones can upset the works in here.'

James said, 'Gosh, yes, I had forgotten all that in my anger at Simon being shot. I will pop out and make the calls. Will someone organise Simon for going home while I am gone.'

'While you are making calls, James, can you organise takeaway dinner tonight to save us going to the restaurant or eating bacon and egg sandwiches?'

'Anyone have any other suggestions? No? Okay, I will organise something. I will be back in a few minutes,' James said, walking out the door.

Percy said, 'Suddenly it has dawned on me. We should not be walking around by ourselves. I will be back shortly. I will catch up to James. It is better to be sure than sorry.' He disappeared out the door, calling to James, 'Slow down, mate. I will follow you in case you find someone you do not want to meet.'

James called back, 'It occurred to me also as I came out the door and saw the policeman. Thanks, Percy, I will slow down for you. Just stay a couple of feet behind me.'

Outside the hospital, the telephoning went without issue, and they were able to go back and James said 'It appears we are safe for the time being.'

'For the moment only, James. Until Cooke is put away, we will have to be careful, and I think taking Simon home is a good idea,' said Alicia. 'Roland Cooke heard the ambulance come to the house, so he will be looking around to see if he can find Simon. He thinks Simon is the only witness to the shooting, because he did not see me. He will not want Simon to give evidence against him. He will be saying by now, "In for a penny, in for a pound", and go all out to get to him, and he knows how to access the hospital system.'

'Being pregnant has not affected your brain, Alicia. You are coming up with all the right things to do,' said Percy.

Alicia grinned. 'I think it is more likely that long sleep I had this afternoon. I feel like it is mid-morning rather than evening, when I often think my brain wants to sleep after a long day.'

Simon had gone quiet, and Granny said, 'I think we have tired him out. We must try to remember in the next few days that he needs to sleep to get his wound better and speak quietly. We are so used to talking loudly and interjecting with each other when we are on a case.'

David had gone to organise an ambulance to take Simon home, with the constable on duty to accompany him, and came back now and said, 'I will go with you in my car and make sure he is settled correctly. Luckily, he has had a light meal. That should sustain him till morning. Could you sleep in the same room tonight, Dad, in case he needs to attend to nature? He will be a bit woozy for the next day or two and should not be left alone.'

'I can organise that, son. There is a spare bed in the den, and I will bring it in and set it up when we get home.'

The paramedics came in with a gurney and shifted Simon on to it and took him to the waiting ambulance. The constable was to share the ambulance. The rest of them picked up their things and followed out the door to the car park.

When they arrived home, James called the pizza place where he had placed an order and added an extra pizza as the policeman would be staying for a while. 'Can you deliver now, please?'

The policeman sat at the table with them, and Parl Morris also turned up, so trying to keep the voices down was a little difficult. After David left to go home, Granny tiptoed in to see if Simon was disturbed but saw he had gone back to sleep. She shut the door so as not to wake him again.

CHAPTER TWENTY

Alicia arranged a cup of tea for everyone sitting at the table and then sat down herself and asked, 'Can someone tell me how everything went today at Bowering House?'

Granny said, 'That seems so long ago now. James, you tell the story. It is new for you, and you can include me in it, then we will see it from your perspective'

'Okay, Granny. As you know, Alicia, we drove out separately, and I believe that was a good idea for Clement to meet us one by one instead of being overwhelmed with strangers all at once. Paul and I arrived first, and we had the door opened and ventilated the house which has been closed up for two months and needed a touch of fresh air. We had the kettle boiling by the time Percy arrived with Granny and Clem, who had made friends with Percy on the way, so everything was working well for us.

'Granny brought out the snack things as it was too early for lunch. We sat around that beautiful sitting room with the art deco furniture and arrangements, and I admired it all over again. If Barbara had decorated that room, she had good taste, I thought as I looked around. What did you think of it, Granny?'

'Lovely, James, truly lovely. I could see Clem thought so too. He seemed very pleased to be there, and it relaxed him.'

'My opinion too, Granny. He seemed very relaxed as if he had come home again, which he had really, I suppose. We spoke generally about the farming of the property at first, but he did not remember too much about that side of things. He was very young when they sent him off to school as a boarder. We started speaking about the war years when the house was used for a hospital, and he seemed to remember more about that and showed us around, pointing out where the soldiers had slept and where the surgery and operating theatre was situated, and then up to the attic as he called it, although it is more like the third storey of the house and was divided into sections separated into three.

'He pointed out where the nurses slept and where he and Granny Meg slept, which had been made into a mini apartment for them to live in for privacy. It was not a large area compared to the rest of the house but quite sizeable for the two of them, and they had their own bed-space and sitting rooms. They had a little methylated spirit stove for cooking, but Clem said they did not cook much. His Granny Meg was afraid of starting a fire, so they went down to the ground floor dining room after a while for their meals with the rest of the staff. He said his granny had been reluctant at first to join the staff downstairs but came around to it after a few days, giving it a trial. At this stage, he said his friend Jonty Shepheard had chatted with Meg and asking her to give it a trial. I think Jonty must have been a very personable young man. She seems to have trouble agreeing with most people in her life, but according to Clem, Meg liked to chat with Jonty.

'We had a look around the outer areas but had to take the cars to drive to where Clem thought the bodies were buried. But too much time has passed, and we could not make out any graves or signs of any digging. We are talking about at least 100 years. I would have thought the earth had settled very quickly with the rain and winds over the years, so we were disappointed there.

'When we got back to the house, we asked Clem whether he wanted to take Jason's belongings back home with him, and he gave me a queer look. It dawned on me about then that he was thinking he would inherit the house from Jason in time. I had not thought of that previously. It was the look he gave me that brought me up to what he expected. Everything went quiet for a little while. I looked at Granny, and she nodded to me. So I went to the car and brought my bag out with the deed in and brought it into the house and told Clem, what Divit had done for us and showed him the deed, and he went so white I thought he was about to faint.

'He had not expected that. I told him about Divit giving us those deeds in compensation for what his stepfather had done to Granny's properties. He sat silent for quite a long few minutes, thinking things over. He looked at Granny and said, "Did you know about this Valerie when we went to Glasgow?"

'Granny said, "No, Clem. We did not know until Divit asked James to drop in to Zimbabwe for a few days on his way back from Australia, and I did not know until they arrived back home. It was a complete surprise to us. Did you know that Divit's grandfather had left all his houses and properties, both business and private, to Divit? Jason would not have inherited them anyway, which is why he wanted Divit dead, so he could take over as next in line."

'Clem stayed silent for the next half hour, and then it was time we came home. I do not think he said anything else to myself or Paul. Did he say anything of interest, Granny, while you were in the car with him?'

'Most of the trip back he was quiet, and he said to me just before we arrived, "What are your plans for Bowering House, Valerie?"

'My answer was, "We have had no time to contemplate it yet, Clem. As I said, we were unaware of Divit's ideas towards it until last week, and we have been busy starting work again, all of us. We will have to seek out our lawyer and ask his opinion on things."

'Clem started to talk as if he was justifying things to himself. "I would be interested to know who sold the property after Jonty and I left it. I always presumed it would go down to me as the heir and the only one left, but being so young, I did not follow things up. I have meant to research the loss of the house to our family, but trouble in my immediate family always took over my time until it was too late. When I did find out it was neglected and for sale, Jason and I discussed it one of the times he holidayed back home.

'After a while, he told me that he had talked 'the old man', as he called Douglas Oliveri, into buying the property in the event they had to leave Zimbabwe in a hurry. He talked Oliveri into including his name on the deed as it had been in his family at one time. I never knew Jason's mind after that. I would ask him what he was planning, and he would clam up and say, 'One day we will be back living at Bowering House, Dad, just like we should be. Someone sold your inheritance, and it was illegal. You never knew. Nobody told you what happened, and you were given no choice. You should be back there, Dad.'

'The next thing I knew about it was, he wanted Barbara to help him renovate the house, just the inside for the moment, and they would do the outside when we moved in. Quite frankly, I thought it was all pie in the sky, but one day he came to visit me and said he would take me for a drive. He had not mentioned Bowering House to me for some time, so I was surprised when suddenly we were driving into the driveway. I was captivated at what he had Barbara do.

'"It was just like it was when I was a lad before the war, before Grandfather died. He always loved the house, poor old man. But do you know, when I sit thinking things over, I realise that he was not old, just very ill, my grandfather, I mean. He would have only been in his mid fifties by the time he died, and here I am in my mid eighties.

'"He had such an unfortunate life with Meg. I realise it now, but as I was so young and Meg treated me okay, it never dawned on me until I read those journals."

'He was quiet for a while, and I thought he had dozed off. Then he said, "At least your name and Alicia's is on the deed, so it has come home. Will you allow me to visit sometimes, Valerie?"

'I felt so completely sorry for him. I started to cry, and Percy turned around and said to me, "Are you okay, Valerie?"

'"Yes, Percy," I answered, but I wasn't. All I could think of was the shy young boy who came to stay with my mother and me in the early stages of the war. I had loved him like a brother and missed him so much for the rest of my life really. I had never had any family to speak of, and I would have loved a brother. Why could not someone in the family have come forward for him when Meg died? Meg must have really got their backs up. I suppose they thought Clem could be as mad as Meg, because I am sure that is what they thought of her.

'I then told Clem I would keep in touch with him and let him know whenever we were able to what we planned for the property, because it was all new to us at the moment and had no time yet to organise anything, and this was the first time I had been there to see the property. I think he was happy at that. He had no family now to keep him company, so he was back to the beginning again. Poor Clem.'

Paul Morris turned to Granny. 'You no longer think of him as the spider in the web, Mrs Newton?'

'At last, I do not, Paul. I think I was still wound up in the loss of my home and bookshop. Clem had come out of the woodwork at that time, and I was still angry enough to want to blame someone. And he was Jason's father. It seems to me that the only ones that cared for Clem was Jonty and Jenny, Clem's first wife. He has had a bad trot all his life, poor man. It was no fault of his own. It all goes back to Meg. Now I feel as if I want to make it up to him, as even I thought of him as a bad guy because of his children.'

'It is unfair the he has had to take all the blame for what Meg created. She has ruined so many lives and continues to do so,' said James.

'Do you have anything in mind, James?' asked Alicia.

'We will have to think about it and, meanwhile, not let Clem out of our minds and lives. I do not know how we will manage that yet. You will all have to rack your minds for something suitable. After Granny telling her tale, I admit I feel sorry for him too.'

Percy said, 'While I was driving, I also felt sorry for him. All those things his children have done have not been his complete fault. He recognised from the start that Ian had a problem. Fiona is normal by the sound of it and, like Clem, has been involved because of her brother, but unwillingly. And Jason seems to have gone bad only in his latter years. Perhaps he was tied up in his work, and that stopped him until the possibilities jumped out at him. All that money was too hard for him to resist. Living in a world by himself in a strange country may have affected Jason as well. Like Meg, he was cut off from what we think of as the normal world, and that could have brought it all on. We will never know.

'I am sorry, folks, but I am completely worn out by the day. In case I do not wake up if Simon wakes up and I do not hear him, can you give me a call? I have to go to bed now myself.'

'Thanks, Percy, for all you have done today. Sleep in if Simon is still asleep in the morning. After my sleep today, I will probably be up early,' said Alicia.

Paul said, 'I must be off too. It was an interesting day. I will call by tomorrow to take a statement from Simon, and I will chase

Roland Cooke up if no one has done so already. I will update you on it from the police point of view.' He turned to the policeman Bill Waters, and said, 'I understand that you are sleeping in the den tonight. Do not sleep too heavily in case you are needed to fight Roland Cooke off or even bully boy Bruce. He may be the next one to expect.'

Granny was the next to go to bed, and James said, yawning, 'Come and rock me to sleep, Alicia, if you are not sleepy. You will not have to wait too long. I too am tired. It has been a long day for us all.'

* * *

The next morning, although it was still dark, Alicia woke up after having a dream of Roland Cooke waving his gun around, and then she wondered about Susan Cooke. Was she all right? If Roland is on the rampage, would he be thinking straight? It was not normal for a reputable doctor to go crazy enough to shoot another citizen. Had Susan contacted Roland about Marta leaving and her abduction by Bruce? She jumped out of bed and grabbed her phone and dressed quietly and went into the sitting room at the front of the house to make a call. There was no need to wake the rest of the household up so early.

Phoning Susan's number, there was no answer. It was Sunday, so she would be at home. She had told Alicia that she worked only Monday to Friday as a nurse in a day clinic. She tried the number again and still no answer, and she started to worry. They had become friends after Alicia's first case of finding Marta early last year, so Alicia knew Susan still lived in what had been the family home.

Pondering this, she decided she would have to go to see for herself that Susan was unharmed. So early in the morning, Susan should be at home, and the phone should have woken her up.

Decision made, she went back to the bedroom and woke up James and explained her theory.

James showered quickly and dressed while Alicia put on some warm clothes, and the two of them slipped out of the house, leaving a note for Granny and Percy on the kitchen table to say where they had gone.

They took the office car, as it had been parked in the car bay at the side of the house overnight, and drove through the quiet streets, marvelling how it was to have so little traffic early on a Sunday morning. It did not take long to reach Susan's home. They saw her car parked at the side of the house in a carport, so they presumed she was at home. Alicia tried her phone number once again and let it ring until it went to voicemail.

'I am going to knock on the door,' Alicia said. 'I do not like this. Susan should answer her phone. She is obviously here if her car is.' Saying that, she got out of the car and walked to the front door and knocked, but there was still no reply. Peering through the lounge room window, she could see a light on in the kitchen area, so she went back to the door and tried knocking again, this time a little louder.

James too got out of the car, and as he did so, the next-door neighbour popped his head over the fence and said, 'If the car is here, Susan must be here too. There was a lot of shouting coming from the house yesterday afternoon. I know there has been trouble in their marriage, so I thought they were only having a barney as people do and did not intervene.'

'Do you have a key by any chance, sir?' asked James.

'As a matter of fact, I do. Susan gave it to me some time ago in case of emergencies. We have been neighbours since the children were small. Susan worried in case the children locked themselves out, and they knew they could come and get the key from me.

Do you think we should try the door? It is strange Susan is not answering.'

'Yes, please, mate. We think it is strange too. My name is James Armstrong, and that is my wife, Alicia, peering through Susan's window. Roland was around at our place yesterday, and he shot one of our staff. My wife has been trying ever since to raise Susan without getting through, so when we woke up this morning, we thought we had better check up to see Roland had not included her in his rampage.'

'Roland shot someone? That is not like him. We think of him as the suave, clever doctor. Mind you, he has not spent much time at home lately. Susan is not one to complain to the neighbours though. She keeps to herself since the children have gone on to university and rarely come home. My wife and I worry about her being alone. That is why I popped out when I heard you knocking. Something is not right.'

'What is your name, mate? Bring your key, and we will go in and see where she is.'

'Right,' the talkative neighbour said, 'I am Ray Willard, and my wife is Angela. I will pop in and pick up the key and warn Angela while I am about it.'

James walked over to where Alicia had given up knocking on the door and was waiting for his next move to help her.

'Ray and Angela, next door, have a key and have gone to find it. They were given it some years ago when Susan's children were small. They will be right out with it, and I am afraid we will have witnesses to what we find. They seem very friendly with Susan and said they heard loud arguing going on in here yesterday but did not interfere, although they thought it strange because they did not usually argue. Roland thought himself above that sort of thing.'

The neighbours came out of their front door and down the drive to Susan's door and put the key in the lock and turned it. As the door opened, they were immediately struck with the smell—a mixture of blood and faeces. James said to Alicia and Angela, 'You may not want to look, ladies. I think we need to call the police before we go any further. It seems someone has gone crazy here.

'Can you call Paul Morris, Alicia? I will have a look in the next room, which is the kitchen, isn't it? To see what has happened for you to tell him what we have.'

As he walked carefully into the kitchen area, he saw on the table four glasses, half full. There were two bodies. Both were lying sprawled—Susan with a bullet hole in her heart area and blood spilled on the floor beneath her and Roland sitting with his back to the wall. It looked as if he had shot himself also in the heart. James thought it a strange way to commit suicide. He had read that most people shot themselves in the temple; it was a quicker death.

He looked around the room. It did not look as if they had been fighting. There was nothing thrown around as angry people are likely to do. James walked around the table and saw bloody footprints smeared towards the back door. His immediate thought was that there had been a third person in the room. The rear door was unlocked, and James looked out and saw another smeared bloodstain on the step leading down towards a gate.

He went back inside to where Ray, the neighbour, stood in the sitting room and asked, 'Does the gate in the back lead out on to a road?'

'There is a small park behind this street and a walkway down from the top to the park for neighbours to use to walk their dogs. Each of us on this side of the road have a gate straight out to the park. The people on the other side of the road have to use the walkway which comes down at the side of this house. Are you asking if someone could come out unseen through the park? The answer is yes, because the houses on the other side of the park are identical to this and have the same accessway.'

Alicia had been crying silently, from the redness of her eyes. James went to her and held her, and he said, 'I am sorry, my darling. Both Susan and Roland are dead. I think there must have been a third person involved in their deaths. To me it does not look like suicide. Is Paul on the way?'

'Yes, he was at home, but he said he would ring his office and organise a forensics team to come too. They should be here any minute.'

'That is good, just as well you had your dream last night and woke up thinking of Susan. Otherwise, it may have been days until they were found,' said James.

He turned to Ray and Angela and said, 'Ray, you said you heard loud arguing yesterday. What time was that?'

'It was about six o'clock last night. It was not quite dark. I came into our sitting room after dinner to listen to the news on the television and heard the loud voices. Now come to think of it, they sounded like Roland with Susan's voice as well. We cannot hear voices from here generally, and it is too cold to have the windows open, so they must have been yelling at each other.'

He thought for a moment. 'I knew Roland and Susan were having a few problems, and Susan had served a divorce notice on him. To be honest, I had never heard them argue before yesterday. Roland was a supercilious sort of fellow. Arguing a point would have been too low for him. His idea was to turn his back on Susan rather than argue a point verbally. It was the silent treatment that Susan hated always, she told Angela.'

Angela was nodding and added, 'Have you ever tried to have an argument with someone who will not argue back? Susan used to get so frustrated with Roland. She said it was worse than being slapped.'

'Therefore, you are saying that you did not see a third person or even a fourth person yesterday?' said James.

Ray looked guilty and said, 'No, I am sorry. I turned the TV up louder to drown them out and never thought any more about it. In fact, only because I saw you arrive this morning that I have thought about the loud talking I heard yesterday. I did not hear shots either. Did you, Angela?'

'No, I was washing the dishes, and Ray always turns up the TV, because he says I am making too much noise for him to hear the news.'

James could hear a siren coming towards them and said to Ray, 'Can you hear the sirens?'

'Sirens? No, oh yes, I can now.'

'So you are a little bit deaf, Ray?'

Angela put in, 'I am always saying he is going deaf, but he will not believe me. He says I mumble, and that is why he cannot understand what I am saying. But I do not mumble.'

'I think that is the reason you did not hear gunshots, Ray. I suggest you have a hearing test.'

The sirens had come to a stop, and James and Alicia stepped out the front door to show the way for the team to see the murder scene. Paul Morris looked at James and said with a twinkle in his eyes, 'Have you worked out the sequence yet, James?'

James grinned but ignored the remark. Instead, he introduced Ray and Angela and explained the circumstance of where they met, leading to the discovery of the bodies.

Ray had obviously got over James's remark that he was deaf and told his part of the story again to Paul.

Paul listened politely and said to the neighbours, 'Thank you for your help on what happened, and we are very grateful to you. You have been able to put a time on what happened here, which will be very important to us in our investigation. Now if you don't mind going back home to leave our forensics team to do their job, we will appreciate that. There will be a lot of coming and going for a while, so we need the space.'

After the two had left, James said, 'Well done, Paul. I thought they would never leave. Now what about us, do you want us to go too?'

'Not until I hear all about your theory, as I am sure you have one.'

James grinned and said, 'I would laugh, but it is not the right place right now. I think that there were three or four people in the kitchen sitting at the table, having a drink, and an argument started. Roland and Susan were living apart. They have been separated at least three months, so it would have not been a convivial meeting from the beginning of the conversation. She was very angry that "Bruce from the brothel" had taken Marta from her house and returned her to the brothel. That would have been part of the argument at least.

'Ray, next door, said he heard Susan and Roland arguing, but I am almost sure there was at least one other person present, and I predict we will find Bruce was here. Can your forensic team check for fingerprints? Ray also said there is another way to enter the property from the rear. There is a walkway to the dog park outside the gate, which anyone can approach from either end of the park.

'I wonder if there was a fourth person here also and suspect Madam from the brothel made up a foursome so that a walk through the park would not look so obvious. Perhaps they have a big dog too. I did not see a dog when I went there last week, but then we did not go out of the house. But I imagined I could smell a dog, perhaps a large one to frighten the girls with. I am sorry now I did not chat with Marta last week, but I do know she was petrified. When I took her out of that cupboard, she was looking around over my shoulder and turning her head. Maybe she would know about a dog.

'I think we have her address on Alicia's phone. Luckily, we did not wipe it off yet, as I saw it when I was looking for Marta's photograph to send to the vice squad fellows. I will give her a ring later today and have a chat to get the idea of the place, if there is a dog, and most of all, the relationship between Bruce and Madam.'

'Good, that will be a start. It is lucky Alicia thought of ringing Susan. It could have been days before anyone found them. It makes it easier having practically fresh hand and fingerprints. I wonder if there is any doggy doo in the back garden. I presumed they tied the dog up before they came inside, in case of an argument, which would arouse the dog.

'Let's look while we are thinking of it. Even that could identify who was here, showing the size of the dog and how much it eats. It is a long shot but worth trying. Anything unusual helps in moments like this.'

'Okay, shall I send Alicia home in my car if you want me here? She is upset. She had become friendly with Susan while she was helping her last year.'

'That is a good idea. I will drop you off later at home.'

Alicia agreed she would be better off at home and drove off, saying, 'At least we do not have to keep looking out for Roland now. We know exactly where he is.'

Paul and James went around the back of the house so as not to disturb the forensic team. Looking around at the neat garden, Paul said, 'If we find anything, we will know it is important because this garden is so neat. The lawn looks like it has been combed rather than cut and not a weed in sight. I did notice how clean and tidy the inside of the house is too, so anything unusual will stand out to us.'

'How about these marks near the gate, Paul? It looks like a dog has scratched and turned around here to lay down as dogs do while they are waiting for their owners.'

'Look for hair, James. Most dogs lose a little in the process.'

'There is very little here. I think the forensic chaps though would like a look at these marks. They could sift the ground where it is dug up, maybe to find hairs, or even slobber. To be quite truthful, I know very little about dogs. Wait, look over there. Could that be from this dog we are looking for? If so, it is not a small dog to produce all that faeces, but it is away from the gate into the park. It could be any dog.'

'I am sure they could work something out from it, so we will tell them about it when they have finished inside the house,' said Paul. 'If it was from a local dog, the owners are supposed to pick it up and put into a bin, aren't they?'

James shrugged his shoulders. 'I think I have heard that somewhere. I am looking for footprints now. If they came in this gate, they may have left some prints. Surely they would need to touch the gate while they were opening it and tying up the dog. Inside the house, they may have wiped down anything they touched, but out here for entry from this gate, they may have not thought of it. We would not be looking for a dog except that it is that sort of park.

'I saw a slight blood smear from someone's shoes on the lower step to the house. Come and see whether we can see any tread mark in it. It is a good sample surely of a shoe belonging to the shooter. There was another one close to Roland's body. It looks altogether like there was an argument, but whomever it was there came prepared, and it was a premeditated decision to bring a gun. Otherwise, there would be no forensics needed for the park gate. They would have come via the front door in a car.

'We should try to see something or ask around if anyone else saw anything at six o'clock last night on both ends of the dog park. It was not quite dark, and it was not raining, so there may have been other dog walkers out and about. Perhaps someone just came home from work and took their dog for a walk, although it was Saturday. When I am out running at that time of night, I see a lot of folks out walking their dogs,' said James.

'We have quite a bit for the forensics to go through,' said Paul, who had been taking notes and measurements. 'Have you been through the rest of the house yet?'

'No, I had Alicia call you straight away after I realised there were dead bodies lying around. I did not want Ray wandering around messing up with the evidence, so I had to keep him with me, talking in the sitting room. Anyway, I do know better for me not to wander around myself in these circumstances. I have big feet, so I took a quick look into the kitchen and could see the drinking glasses on the table and the bodies, so I retreated.'

'With that quick look, you saw the blood smears and saw there were four glasses on the table and deducted that there were two other people besides Susan and Roland in the kitchen at the time of the killing all in a few minutes. You are good. It would take some detectives longer than that.'

James looked at Paul, who looked quite serious, and said, 'You are kidding me, aren't you?'

'No, James, I mean it. My expectation now, because you have been here with me, is that we will wrap this up quite quickly. You and I have done all the footwork needed here already, and I will send some police officers to question other dog walkers about who walks their dog at about six each night. Most of those people will know or recognise the usual walkers, and strangers will stand out to them, I believe, because strange dogs will act defensive in another dog's territory.'

'That makes sense, Paul. Of course, the usual people and their dogs would recognise strangers in their territory. The dogs would have made their owners aware of another strange dog.

'The one thing I am cross with myself about is, I did not question Marta properly when I had a chance. As soon as I get home, I will try her number in Poland and ask those questions which keep popping up for me to find answers to. She was in this house for three months. Did she have any visitors here during that time? We did not think it necessary to question her. One reason was, she was overwhelmed at being locked in a cupboard all day at the time, but we thought Susan had it in hand.

'Now we do not have Susan to question. And why did Roland shoot Simon? Was it Roland? I will have to chase up those photos Alicia took of the car on Saturday morning and have someone look at them and see if they can make them clearer. All I could see was a blurry figure as it drove past where Alicia was hiding. She believed it was Roland because he had been peering through our office window, and twenty minutes later, she saw someone shoot Simon. I will not ask her again whether she is sure. But I will take a copy of the photos in to your office to see if you can identify him.'

'I think that is a good way to go about it, James. Anyone gets cross when you question them about what they saw or, I should say, what they think they saw, even us, and we can be wrong too.'

They went together back into the house after wiping their feet thoroughly. They checked the forensics team was still busy. Paul gave them the list he had made out in the garden, to do when they finished in the house. He told them that he and James were going to look through the remainder of the house to see if the argument had spread at any time and asked them to give him a call if there was anything else they wanted him to do.

The bedrooms were all very tidy, nothing strewn on the immaculate beds. They reached the room that looked as if it had been recently used and guessed this was where Marta had spent her three months in the house.

As James looked around, he said, 'Both sides of this double bed have been used. It looks as if she had a visitor from time to time, of the male variety. Quite often too by the impressions on the pillow. It seems she was not the innocent we thought she was. The sheets and pillowslip have been washed, but the imprints are still here. Have the forensics look at this room. They may find more than Marta's hair on the carpet around the bed. Well, well, this is a turnaround. We thought she was a good little girl just out of school, but we were wrong again by the look of these clues. We seem to have taken everybody's word for things in the old case, but it was wrong to take things at face value. I can see that quite well now.'

They searched the room thoroughly, looking for anything that would point to what had happened there over the previous three months, but found nothing. They checked the nearest bathroom which Marta would have used and did find some hair in the bin, obviously missed in the last cleaning before she flew to Poland. The hair was clinging to the plastic liner in the bin. Paul picked up the plastic liner and found a small piece of paper also clinging to the liner with small wording written on it.

They took the paper to the desk in the room and examined the writing under the desk lamp and agreed it looked like a doctor's script in what they both thought was a doctor's hand. It was unsigned, the writing saying only, 'Saturday, between 5 and 6 p.m.'

They looked at each other, and Paul said, 'A time for someone to call at the house?'

James said, 'Yes, but not to visit Marta. She left Friday for Poland. Could this be Roland's note left behind? Someone was coming to visit this house, and if not for Marta, it must have been Roland's message taken from his phone while he was here in this room. Someone rang him while he was here, and he wrote this reminder for himself. Because he was busy when they called, he wrote it down to remind himself. Busy at what, I wonder. Having sex with Marta? Surely not. I find that hard to believe. Although why else would he have been here?'

'All of our thoughts keep coming back to Roland. He moved out three months ago, and yet he was here yesterday, drinking at the kitchen table with Susan and two others,' said Paul.

'It looks as if he was sleeping with Marta in this bedroom, unknown to Susan. She worked, as you said earlier, in a day clinic from nine to five, leaving Marta alone for the day by herself. We now think she was not by herself but occupied with Roland during that time, perhaps not every day. He had clinics of his own and patients to see, but some of the time was spent in this room with Marta. This is all so queer.'

'Yes, it is queer,' said James. 'Marta was brought over from Poland by Roland, and he supposedly rescued her from the brothel. He moves out of the house—this was Susan's idea—and Marta moves in. Then when things quieted down, he moves back, but unknown to Susan. He was undoubtedly here and not so long ago according to this note. We now have to question who sent the note. Did you see Roland's phone anywhere? Or Susan's?'

'No, James, unless the forensics team found it. Possibly in Roland's pocket or Susan's handbag. I will go and see them. Back in a minute,' Paul said as he went through the door.

James went back down the passageway to the master bedroom and looked around and went in to the en suite bathroom. There was nothing new to see. This time the bins were properly cleaned. There was hair in the hairbrush, but it looked like Susan's, so there was no mystery there. He could not see a handbag in any obvious place and no phone anywhere, although he looked in drawers where he thought he might find them and on a shelf in the wardrobe. No, she must have had her phone with her, which was the obvious thing to do. He even looked amongst the towels in the bathroom but still found no phone or handbag.

He looked in the other rooms. One obviously a son's, just as he had left it, waiting for him to come home again.

The next was a girl's room, with posters on the walls, pink design on the bedspread. She must be the younger sibling. The room was designed for a teenager, and it looked left behind.

So Marta had been allocated the last bedroom, or perhaps it was the guest room, with its own bathroom, at the end of the passage, away from the other bedrooms, and also had a door leading out to a small pergola in the garden, with a seat incorporated. *Very nice,* thought James, closing the door again and thinking. *Has its own access too, no doubt with a key to let visitors in privately.*

Roland would have known about this access. Very quiet, away from anyone else in the house, he could come any time of the day or night, and it would have been unknown to Susan, who trusted Marta, no doubt.

Paul came back and advised there was no sign of a phone or handbag. The team had tried pockets, cupboards, and shelves and even the refrigerator. They also looked in the television room and the sitting room without any sign of bag or phones.

James told of what he had found and also no phone or handbag.

He said, 'Wait, I will ring Alicia and see if she has any idea where either would be hidden. This could be a female secret thing.' He laughed.

Other than the places they had already searched, Alicia could not come up with any ideas. She ended her statement, 'There is the car, of course, parked out in the carport space. If she had been out shopping as working women often are on a Saturday and she arrived home the same time she saw someone in her house, i.e. Roland or others, she may have rushed in and left the bag with the phone in the car to bring in later. And there will be groceries in the boot of the car. Look under the front seat. It is where I would shove them if I was in a hurry.'

'Thanks, Alicia. I still do not know when I will be home, but it will not be long.' As he closed up his phone, he said to Paul, 'I have just been reminded why Alicia is so valuable to have around. She suggests we look in the car parked in the driveway carport, particularly under the front seat. It is possible that Susan arrived home from shopping and saw someone in her house, either Roland alone or with the other suspects, and left her bag with the phone in for safety.'

Paul reacted, 'She is right, of course. Susan would have been shocked to see someone in her house, and never having seen Bruce before or Madam, she would think there may have been a break-in and Roland had caught them. Alicia is clever. So is her grandmother. Why didn't we ring her earlier and ask?'

They went out of the house and looked in the car. It was unlocked, which to James indicated that she left the car in a hurry, the key still in it. Under the front seat, squashed down, was Susan's handbag, and searching through it, they found the phone they wanted.

They both gave a sigh of relief. Paul said, 'I would have been so embarrassed if I gave up the car to forensics, and they found the handbag and phone. I would never be able to live it down. This sort of chiacking goes on for years in our office. I must buy Alicia a box of chocolates for this.

'We will give this phone to the forensic guys casually. As they are now aware, we have been looking for both the bag and phone, and let's tell them to give us any information they find on it.'

James laughed at Paul and said, 'It sounds like a good way to handle it. Give them the key to the car as well so they know where we found it. After all, they have been here the same length of time as us, and they did not wake up to it either.'

Paul said, 'When I went in, it looked like they were about to finish up. They will organise the bodies to be taken to the morgue. Now I have to go back to the office and notify the son and daughter. This is always the hard part of a case. I will ring Roland's office on Monday to arrange a search of it. Do you want to come along?'

'We work well together, Paul. Yes, I would like to see what is there. There may also be another phone that he contacted Marta on, as it looks like whomever killed Roland also took his phone, and also to contact the brothel. It could give us some clues because he would not have rung either of those places on his work phone. The office would also know where he has been living since leaving here. That could yield up a few clues.'

'I will pick you up tomorrow then at nine o'clock. I doubt anyone would be available till then to talk to us. We can do the office first, and that should lead us to where Roland lived. You said previously that he worked away up the coast a bit. I suppose we will have to go and see for ourselves what is left in that office. Is that all okay with you?'

'I will ask Percy for permission to be absent from our office for the day. He can run the Monday meetings that we always have, and I can bring him up to date with things at home tonight and tomorrow night. It is a real asset to live in the same house, although Simon pointed out to us last week that it means we never get a rest from work.'

'How was Simon this morning?' asked Paul.

'There was no one else up when Alicia and I left the house early this morning. It was barely light, but Alicia could not sleep because she was worried about Susan, thinking she may have been caught up in Roland's rampage, little knowing that Roland had been caught up with her in somebody else's rampage.'

The forensics were leaving the house now, and the cars were arriving for the bodies. There was also a contingent of police officers to follow Paul's plan of knocking on doors.

'We will have a couple of policemen guarding the house overnight and this afternoon. I will organise now some to question the neighbours, to see if they heard anything or, better still, if they saw anything. They can question those on the other side of the park as well. It would have been dusk when the visitors arrived. Someone must have seen them,' said Paul.

'Wait, Paul, I have just had a thought. I have a picture on my phone of Bruce, taken as he opened the door to us at the brothel last week. I will send it to your phone, and you can organise some pictures for the police officers to show around. It may trigger some memories to dog walkers.' James took out his phone and scrolled through it and said, 'Here we are, a nice, clear close-up. You should get some reaction from this picture.' He sent it to Paul's phone.

'Well done, James. You may have a winner for us here. I will drop you off at home as soon as I have spoken to these police persons, and I will post these photos of Bruce to their phones. Being Sunday afternoon now, it is a good time to ask around. They will find most homeowners home generally at this time on a Sunday or out walking their dogs. If we wait until tomorrow, they could be at work.'

'Good, while you are doing that, I will look through Susan's car more thoroughly. I do not expect to find anything, but you never know,' said James.

There was nothing else to find inside the car, but in the boot, James found the shopping Susan had left the house to get. It looked mainly like food, but underneath, he saw a notebook that looked as if it was for shopping lists. He turned the pages over and saw a note Susan had written for herself. 'Ring Alicia Armstrong about Marta and Roland and their romance. Tell her I saw them together on Thursday night in the pergola when they thought I was asleep.'

James punched the air. 'Yes, I read it right. They were in cahoots. Roland boy, you never missed a chance, did you? What were you doing playing around with Marta right under Susan's nose? That was a cheeky thing to do. You must have known that if Susan found out, there would be hell to play.'

CHAPTER TWENTY-ONE

James told all this to Paul as they drove back to Percy's house and reminded Paul that he was going to try and contact Marta. On second thoughts, he said, he would ask Alicia to ring Marta because of her language skills. She might learn more through the nuances in the conversation, and respond better to her. He would tell Paul in the morning if he felt the need to get going to his office about what they could find out from the girl.

Paul and James both went in to the house to let the other's know what had happened, and James asked for a snack and a cup of tea because neither he nor Paul had breakfast or lunch and were about to faint.

Granny looked at them and grinned at James and said, 'Sit down both of you in the dining room, and I will tell everyone that you are here. We have all been on tenterhooks, wondering how things were going. Alicia was so upset when she came home and told us that both Susan and Roland were dead, and we all want to know all about it.'

They sat down as they were told, and food and tea were brought to them quickly, with Alicia saying quietly into James's ear as she passed, 'We cannot have you fainting before you tell us everything you have been up to. We will give you a few minutes to eat, and then we want to hear all about it. Did you find the handbag and the phone?' When James nodded, she said, 'In the car?' Another nod. 'Stuffed under the front seat?'

Both Paul and James laughed, and James said, 'You know we did. I told Paul it would be a woman's secret hiding place and that you would know.'

'What else did you find out?' she asked.

'Would you believe that Roland and Marta were having an affair?'

Alicia raised her eyebrows, and James continued, 'In Marta's bedroom in the house?'

'And how did you find that out?'

James had come prepared for the questions and picked up the notebook from his pocket and turned to the page where Susan had written about it and passed it around the table. By then, everyone had raised eyebrows.

James said, 'I found the notebook in the car boot. I would think that Roland was not aware that he had been found out. This must have been written the day before Marta flew out to Poland, I would say. Perhaps Susan invited Roland back to the house to have a go at him about it, that was the note in the bathroom bin and they were interrupted by their killers.

'Perhaps Bruce and Madam had come calling, coincidently bringing a gun with them. Or maybe even, Bruce always carried a gun. Overhearing what Susan and Roland were fighting about, they joined in, accusing Roland of stealing the girl from the brothel for his own purposes, and things went from bad to worse. In the heat of the moment, Bruce brought out his gun and shot the pair of them. He looked a violent sort of person. Perhaps it was Bruce who had also shot Simon. It seemed out of place that Roland shot him. He did not know Simon, but Bruce did.

'Maybe even, Marta told Bruce about herself and Roland the day he picked her up and took her to the brothel. After putting two and two together, Bruce and Madam had talked it over and decided to have it out with Roland and just by chance found him at home with Susan not knowing Roland did not live there any more.

'There, we have several instances we could conjure up. Which do you think it would be, Percy?'

'Any of the above, James. I was wondering with any of these instances, why did Roland shoot Simon? It does not make sense.'

'Only if Susan had phoned Roland and said she was going to see Alicia Armstrong [as in her note to herself]. Roland had been afraid that if enquiries were made by Alicia, it would get back to big bad Bruce, and there would be hell to payif he knew that he was keeping Marta for himself That is why he brought the gun to scare Alicia off, and Simon accidently got in the way.

'The agreement in the brothel business was possibly a three-way business affair—Roland finding the girls, Madam accompanying them to and at the brothel, and Bruce making sure the girls do not leave before their time is up. If it was a partnership, then Bruce and Madam had every reason to want to have a go at Roland breaking the rules.

'Susan would have been a byproduct of the conversation, and she wanted them out of her house, not knowing who they were and what they were doing there. This put her in line for brutal Bruce to take his angst out on her. There was also the fact that Bruce and Madam would not want Susan to identify them, as they were going to kill Roland anyway. We have to wait for the coroner to tell us who died first. I think it would have been Roland. But then again, it could have been Susan, to show Roland what was in store for him. Either way, they are both dead.'

Paul was looking at James, astonished at what he had read in the scene at the house that morning, but could find no other reasoning in his mind that it would have been different to what James had said.

James turned to Alicia and asked her, 'Would you ring Marta for us and ask her whether she told Bruce of her affair with Roland? I think she started this chain of events, unaware of what she was dealing with.'

'Now, James?'

'Yes, please, Alicia. I want you to act sympathetic to her, not telling her of the murders, until she confesses if she had the affair with Roland. If she denies it, tell her we found proof in the room. The police had found a message for Roland in the bathroom bin from a phone call the last night he was in the room with her. Ask her if she had told Bruce about her affair when he abducted her or if he had asked about it. That part is very important. We have to link Bruce and Madam too if we can get her included. Ask her too whether Bruce has a dog and what sort of dog it is. Can you remember all that?'

'Yes, James, I have written it all down.'

'Good girl. Think carefully and speak clearly. We will have a recording of the conversation. I have been linking your phone up to our recorder while we have been talking.'

'Okay, James, here goes.' Alicia dialled the number of Marta's parents' home, and when Marta's phone was answered, Alicia described in Russian to the man who answered about herself, as a friend Marta had made while visiting England, and she was ringing to see if Marta had arrived safely so that she, Alicia, could tell everyone how she was enjoying being at home with her parents. She also asked if she could she speak to Marta.

All this took part in Russian, and Mr Novak answered, 'I will bring her to the phone. She is just finishing her lunch. Wait one minute.'

Alicia said before he put the phone down, 'I will speak to Marta in English, Mr Novak. I know how she likes to practise the language. She is very good at speaking English now.'

'Okay, that is good,' said the man, and Alicia heard him put the phone down on a table and call out to Marta.

When Marta came to the phone, she said in Russian, 'Is that you, Roland?'

'No, Marta. It is Alicia Armstrong. I am checking up that you arrived home safely without any more trouble from Bruce.'

'Oh, hello, Alicia. Yes, I am fine, and my parents are happy to have me home. Have you spoken to Susan?'

'Not lately, Marta. I have been asked to find out a few items from you. When you were taken to the brothel by Bruce, did you tell Bruce about your relationship with Roland Cooke?'

Alicia heard an intake of breath. 'Roland told you about us, Alicia?'

'Not exactly, Marta, although I know about it. Did you tell Bruce that Roland will be cross because he took you to the brothel that day?'

'I did not tell him. He already knew, because he had been spying on Roland, following him around. He told me, and he only wanted me to confirm it, but I would not tell that horrid man or Madam anything about us. Roland and I are going to be married when Susan and Roland's divorce becomes final. Bruce laughed at me and said I was kidding myself. Roland would not marry anybody like me. He could have anyone he wanted. When I said Roland wanted me, he laughed and said, "He would see about that." He locked me in that tiny cupboard with the dog to sit outside to get me if I broke out.'

'Did he really say that, Marta? How cruel! What sort of dog was it?'

'A huge German Shepherd, a big brown beast. I was so frightened of it and was so happy when your husband came and rescued me.'

'Where did the dog live, Marta? James did not tell me about that.'

'He lived out the back door in a kennel and was chained up all the time. The girls said it was taught to be vicious. Bruce would threaten that if we went out of the door, he would let the dog off the chain and tell it to find us. That is why we did not stray, and I was so happy Roland came to get me from that place.'

'Did you and Roland start your affair straight after he rescued you, Marta?'

'Yes, we fell in love as soon as we met. It was love at first sight, and Roland told me he would teach me to appreciate lovemaking, that it is a beautiful thing between two people in love. He can make me feel so special.'

'Marta, I am sorry to tell you, but I have to tell you now that Susan and Roland have been murdered. They were both shot dead. It only happened yesterday, so we are still looking for whomever shot them. We think it may be Bruce, but we are not positive yet. We will let you know when we are sure.'

Marta screamed, then whispered, 'I told my parents I am to be married, and now you tell me Roland is dead?'

'I am sorry, Marta. It is true. I am very sorry.'

Marta slammed the phone down, and Alicia turned to James, 'Was that enough?'

'I am sorry, Alicia, to put you through that, but none of us could have got so much from her. She confirmed all we wanted to know. Paul would not be allowed by his office to speak to Marta about those things, but now we know that Bruce was aware of the romance and that he has a big brown dog. So any dog hairs we find at Susan's property can be compared. Very well done, Alicia. Your phone call may have dropped the last piece of the jigsaw puzzle in place for us.'

Alicia said, 'I find it hard to believe that Marta entertained Susan's husband in Susan's house while she was in the other room. We should have left her in the brothel. That is obviously what she is worth, looking out for any man she could get on her conditions, never mind who she hurts on her way. It seems unethical somehow to me.'

'That is what I feel about her too, Alicia. Poor Susan, she did not realise what her cruel husband was capable of. It was his dabbling into brothels that caused all this, and some of this type of people will not be crossed. It is a dog-eat-dog business,' said James.

Granny said with a grin, 'It sounds like dog-shoot-dog sort of business to me.'

Everybody laughed, even Simon, who said, 'I hope you are not including me as a dog into that category, Granny', which brought more laughter.

Paul stood up, 'I have to report to the office. Thank you for the entertaining lunch, everybody. Thank you too for your instincts into the case, Alicia, and that phone call is a little gold mine for picking up Bruce to charge him. I will wait until the policemen finish their interviews around the block and in the park and then arrest him this afternoon. Otherwise, he may disappear. He will know his business will be dead in the water after all this. May I borrow your recorder, James? I may have to keep it until the end of the case. I will also have one of our chaps look at Alicia's photo she claims is Roland. With what has been happening, I believe it may be Bruce in the car shooting at Simon. After all, Roland has not met Simon, so why shoot at a stranger? But Bruce had come face to face with him at the visit he made with James to the brothel, and

I think it likely he recognised Simon as he was following Roland down the street.'

'That is all right, Paul. Keep the recorder for as long as you need it. We have another recorder in our office. I agree with that statement about Bruce. I think that was the beginning of his mayhem. He was so angry the brothel was invaded and Marta was taken, for the second time, from him and the business. It was enough for his anger with Roland to take him over and set him off on his rampage.

'See if the dog was in the car as well. Although, he may have gone back to pick it up, and he picked up Madam at the same time.'

'Okay, I will see you in the morning, James. I am pleased to see you up and about, Simon. Do you think you will be okay from now on?' asked Paul.

'It is a clean wound, Paul. The grogginess I had last night was mainly from all the gunk shot into me at the hospital. I could not keep my eyes open, but I could hear every word you said. Magic really.'

'It seems to have fixed you up. You seem very clear today, thank goodness,' said Paul, as he reached his car.

As Paul drove away, James said to the others, 'I am requesting a day off at the office tomorrow, Percy, so I can go with Paul to the various offices belonging to Roland to tell the staff he will not be returning and to search for any evidence he may have left there. We are looking for a phone that Roland did not have on him when he was killed. We really think Bruce may have taken it but want to be sure and to see if he had another phone somewhere.

'We think, for instance, that he would have had a different phone for his local sex girls other than at the brothel. He would not have wanted them to get mixed up or their numbers to get out to anyone, such as a reporter.'

Alicia said, 'Do you really think Roland would have married Marta?'

James said, 'Personally, no, but Marta seemed to believe it. It seems to me he was only leading her on, and then he would send her back to the brothel or install her with the other women he has in his sex trade.'

Granny said, 'When you first met Marta, you thought she was very naïve, Alicia. Have you changed your mind?'

'I do not know what to believe any more, Granny. This has all been way out of our comfort zone. We have had nothing like this before and cannot say we are experienced in the sex trade, but we are certainly learning fast.'

James said, 'I am going to have a sleep. It was barely daylight when we left the house this morning, and it has been a big day. A real mind stretcher. Poor Paul, he was at the scene not long after us, but he still has a lot of work to do. I hope he brings a driver with him tomorrow so he can nap on the way. It may be a long day tomorrow as well.'

Alicia said, 'I will come with you to nap, James. I have not been resting because I did not want to miss you if you called, but I am tired now.'

As they walked towards the bedroom, Alicia said, 'You think it was Bruce who shot Simon? I was sure it was Roland, but then again, from where I was hiding, it was hard to be sure. I was trying not to be seen myself and pushed the phone through the bushes. I had seen Roland only minutes before at the office and presumed it was him.'

'Roland possibly came down the street first, but Bruce was following him, we believe, and then he saw Simon, whom he recognised from the brothel visit we made. That made him angrier than he already was, so he fired his gun. I think by then he was so angry at Roland and anything to do with him. He had already gone a little crazy.'

'That makes sense, so then he went back and picked up Madam to make a plan for Roland's demise?'

James laughed. 'I am not an oracle, Alicia, but something like that.'

Back in the dining room, Granny had seen that Simon had suddenly looked pale and sweaty.

She then said, 'Simon, you should go and rest too. It is the best thing for healing. Take a tablet to help you sleep. Percy, shall you and I go for a walk? We seem to be the only ones not in need of sleep. It is still fine outside, and we can pick up some fish and chips for dinner for us all on our way back.'

Percy put on his coat and hat and held out his arm, and they went off towards the gate.

CHAPTER TWENTY-TWO

Granny was still worried about Clement Haskell's reaction to her family ownership, not his, to Bowering House. At the end of Saturday, he had seemed okay with them showing him the deed, and by the time they dropped him at his residential care home, he was back to normal. But after a day alone to think about it, what was his mood now after brooding on it overnight? she wondered.

She rang his number as soon as she woke up, thinking to catch him before he started his day. She was greeted by him cheerily, and she gave a huge sigh of relief.

'I was worried about you, Clem, after the news that my side of the family now owns Bowering House. How are you today?'

Clem laughed. 'Do not worry about me, cousin. I am used to bad news and learnt many years ago to accept things I cannot change. I am happy that the house has not gone to a stranger. At least with your ownership, I can visit occasionally, and what else was I going to do with it alone anyway? My original thought was to set Fiona and Gerald up in it to run it as a farm, wishful dreaming only for me. Gerald is a city boy and has no idea how to run a farm.

'I have gone off at a different tangent now. After our visit to the Lake District, I had thoughts of setting Fiona up in a B & B place to run. When Gerald arrives, he can get a job around in one of the villages. During the summer, the tourists flock to the towns, and there is a definite problem of staffing the different venues. I thought Gerald may get work somewhere there. He is quite handy with tools and made a lot of the furniture in their house in his spare time.

'The two young girls could go to the local schools, and even Fiona may find work. And they could share the B & B between them. If Faye ever gets free, she could help in that venture. I am only thinking this since I saw the size of the cheque our cousin John gave to me as compensation. I will now be able to comfortably afford the B & B with that in my bank account. It has come at a good time for me to help the girls. I cannot see that Ian will ever be free. If he survives the prison, he will be put into psychiatric care. There is certainly part of Meg in him. I am convinced of that. I am sorry to say.

'With Faye, I believe, as you yourself said, she was on cocaine. She was erratic in her childhood, but that was Barbara's fault, not Meg's. And until the cocaine was available to her, she was a dizzy girl, but normal. In fact, she did very well at school and was always high up in the records at exam times. Perhaps there is hope for a normal life for her yet if she is taken away from temptation. I can only hope she will recognise that I am giving her a chance and she does not blow it. Do you know she was a cute little girl in her early days and she used to follow Fiona around everywhere?'

'It sounds like Fiona had a heavy load, first with Ian and then Faye. I wish her well. Have you found a lawyer to take on her case yet, Clem?'

'Not yet, cousin. It is all still conjecture until I can find access to Fiona. There is no use going ahead with it until she knows what is in my mind. She may decide something else for herself. I have had to put it to one side until I can visit her again.'

'I may be able to help with that, Clem. I will not ask James or Alicia, but I can go straight to the chief of police. I believe he will talk to me from past meetings I have had with him. Not business meetings but casual ones, and he is always happy to have a chat with me. What if I ask for an appointment with him and you come too? He is a very reasonable man, or has been, whenever I have spoken to him before, and if we explain everything to him, we may get some sympathy.'

'Would you do that for me, cousin? It would make me so happy. I knew you were the same cousin from my childhood that sympathised with me because both our fathers were killed in the war.'

'A word of warning, Clem, this will only be a friendship deal with the chief. I have no capacity even though James and Alicia are aligned with the police. That compliance does not run down to me. I will be only a lowly citizen asking on your behalf.'

'I will take anything at the moment. Like you, I have been left with no family to help me out until you introduced me to John and Nancy Forrester. That is so hard to believe when I once had four children or five, if I count Zack amongst them, which I always did.'

'Well, I will call his office and see if he will make an appointment with us. It may take a day or two to organise, and I will ring you when I get an answer.'

'Thank you, Valerie. I look forward to your call at any time.'

After she put the phone down, she went to the kitchen to talk to Percy about it. He seemed to think the chief would make an appointment with Clem and herself. He was a very caring chap if you were on the right side of him, Percy concluded.

Valerie felt a little bit nervous about ringing the police chief. After all, she had only met him two or three times. He had always been nice to her, she thought, so perhaps he would agree. She decided to wait until James had time to offer his opinion about it. Granny waited her opportunity, waiting for a moment when James was relaxed after he had returned with Paul Morris, and went into his office and closed the door.

He looked up and smiled at her. 'This must be a serious moment, is it, Granny, if you are closing the door. You do not want me to escape? What do you want me to do?'

'You know me so well, James. I want to have a discussion with you regarding Clement Haskell and Fiona and Gerald. I have told you their story of life with Ian, whom we all consider a person who will never walk in the local streets again. I also want you to consider what it must have been like for Fiona and Gerald, who were his almost constant companions because of the twin situation. He had Gerald so afraid of him, and Fiona was only afraid of Ian, because of Ian's influence on their lives. Ian obviously thought of Fiona as his, not Gerald's at all, and that made life a misery they could not get away from.'

James did not say anything yet and waited for Granny to get to the point.

Granny took a big breath and went on, 'I believe that Gerald was doing his best to display to you the position they were in without being explicit about it when in his workplace because of the walls having ears and Ian getting to know about it and exploding with anger, which both Fiona and Gerald were afraid would happen.

'I listened to you and Percy when you came home from the customs warehouse, and even I got the impression that Gerald was afraid. He knew what Ian had done with his wife and Zack, his cousin. He had to be careful that Ian did not wake up to the fact that Gerald had brought you in, knowing on the city grapevine that you were good at what you do, or Ian would take out his anger on Gerald and take Fiona away with him somewhere. For Gerald, it was a huge balancing act.'

'Go on, Granny. I can see all that.'

'I have always believed Gerald was being taken advantage of because of his fear of Ian, and speaking to Clement, he has agreed with me. The other point is with Jason. He was the big brother, someone they had all looked up to, because he was so clever. He had been in Africa for a long time and had grown into a different person. We will never know why, but I believe that hiding your thoughts always from the people around you and living a life the way you do in those circumstances alone, not loving your circumstances any more or the people around you as life changed around you the way it did for him, it made him feel separated from his day-to-day companions. And with his Granny Meg's history, I believe he became like her and did not realise that what he did to Douglas, Divit's grandfather, and Douglas's wife and then his own wife was wrong. It did not completely register with him. By then, he too, like Meg, was mad and taken over with dreams of past glory in the family.

'All this madness was carried out away from his family. They had no idea what was happening till after the event, and he had died. When he arrived back here, he had become heavy on Fiona to kill his stepsons. She resisted for two years until her life was at a low ebb. She had lost her husband to jail. She had sent her daughters away to keep the news of their father locked away from hurting them. She had lost her loved house, and she had no money, so she had to produce the cocaine that was hidden by Ian and Gerald to sell for a living.

'Up to this point, Fiona had been the steady one in the family. She had kept Ian on the straight and narrow until he went crazy after she married Gerald, and for the first time, he had no one to guide him.

'Enter stage left, we have you, James. Not knowing anything about the family history, you had Ian and Gerald arrested and later on Fiona and Faye. Not that they did not deserve to go to prison. What the two women did to Divit and Edward was inadmissible, but once again, you were not given their family history.

'You are a lawyer, James. Is there a way you can get Gerald and Fiona and their daughters back together again? Now you are aware of Granny Meg and her possible inheritance down to the Haskell family. Can you leave them in prison? Ian, yes, he needs to be in a psychiatric ward of a hospital being checked out. There is no doubt about that.

'Although, it is my belief that Fiona and her husband can be rehabilitated with their daughters in another town, far away from Ian and his influence and with Clement's help.'

Granny had ended her long story and now waited, looking at James to see if there would be a reaction. If James could not be persuaded, what hope had she talking to the police chief?'

James stretched his long legs out and sat thinking for a while, tapping the desktop with his pen.

'So it is a challenge to me in my lawyer role, Granny? Lock them up in my investigative role and let them out in my lawyer role. That is a good way to make an income. Does it mean I get paid twice?'

'You are making fun of me again, James. Isn't my role as grandmother to you reason enough to give an opinion? Which is not biased, by the way, I will still love you if you do not agree with me.'

James gave his hoot of laughter and said, 'Oh, Granny, you know I cannot resist you. I will have to try and find holes in your story. That is what lawyers do so that they can put their story forward. Let's take it to the after-dinner forum tonight to see what the holes are. We have to have it watertight before we can put it through to the public, or we will be cried down by the said public very quickly. They were abhorrent acts that they both committed, and there will be an outcry if they are let free.'

'Thank you, James, for listening to me. I have become really wound up about these cases against my will, and I keep finding excuses for them. Can we ask Clement to dinner tonight to give his views on the case?'

'Sure, Granny, you do not have to ask. You are the cook. If you can squeeze one more potato into the pot, yes, go ahead and ask Clement. I found him an interesting character. I have not seen Alicia today. Did she come to the office?' he asked.

'She was feeling very sickly this morning, so we suggested we could manage until she is feeling better. Some morning sickness last all day, and some only an hour or two. Actually, I thought I heard the door a few minutes ago. I will go and see how she is now.'

Alicia was looking pale but had stopped feeling ill and was talking on the phone when Granny went to the reception area.

She finished her call and said to Granny, 'I must tell James that Iris Kumar died yesterday, and the funeral is Friday at ten o'clock.'

James had come in behind Granny and said, 'Yes, it is something we must go to, Alicia. We must not miss that.'

Granny said to Alicia, 'We are having an additional guest to dinner and discussion tonight. I am going to ring Clement and invite him. Do we need anything from the shop?'

'No, Granny, I think we are fine at the moment. It feels as if we are moving the office to the house. We have had a different case study every day since we arrived back home.'

'I only suggested this one, Alicia, to help Clement feel like family. I am not sure that what we have in mind after I discussed it with James is doable, but I want him to know we are trying to help him. Just that knowledge would help him. He feels so alone in his misery.

'We would not do it for anyone else. It is going beyond our job description. If after discussing it tonight we cannot come to a solution, he will have to make his own mind up whether to contact a lawyer. We have spent enough time on it already between us.'

That evening after dinner, the group sat around and had a cup of tea, and James brought up the theory that Fiona and Gerald were imprisoned because they were so afraid of what Ian would do to them if they did not back him.

Granny saw a look pass between Clement and James—a look so grateful to James that she thought Clem was going to cry.

She realised when she came back to the conversation, James was saying, 'Both Fiona and Gerald were picked up and jailed because they did deeds not acceptable to society. The job of the police was over when the pair were convicted individually. So a visit to the police chief, in my opinion, would be out of place.

'The case for a retrial is now in the hands of a judge and the parole board. We can submit a brief requesting for the case to be looked at again. We would have to check first what stage they have got with Ian before we start. If in the opinion of the medical personnel and if they knew the facts, which I do not believe they do at the moment, we would stand a better chance of working for Gerald, who did not actually combine with Ian in murdering those chaps in the warehouse at customs. He was charged with being an accessory. I believe we may be able to have Gerald released if we are careful in our summary. Ian would, however, have to spend the rest of his life in a psychiatric ward or prison ward. It would not be safe for the public to have him released.

'The case of Fiona is different. She did try to murder Divit, although all she caused were multiple stab wounds, none of which were deep enough to kill him, but combined with the drugs given to him, it caused amnesia. I am not sure, without talking to Fiona, if she was aware that her brother Jason had arranged the killing of Divit's whole family. Divit was already traumatised, and that stabbing Fiona rendered to him, in my opinion, worked on his subconscious so that he did not want to wake up to face the horror of it all.

'I am no doctor or psychiatrist, but even I could see that Divit, who was only seventeen at the time of the stabbing, was unable to face any more horror. His younger brother was stabbed by Faye. He did not survive, and Divit had probably viewed that and could not intervene because of the drug he had been given to immobilise them, so that was one more sorrow on top of all the others. I have to ask at this stage, how would any of us cope with that, even us, at an older time in our lives?

'I know I would not have wanted to remember it all. So if we want Fiona released, we will have to make up a good case from the journals you have in your possession, Clem. We have to have a watertight reason on why the law should allow Fiona to walk free. Without a good reason for her compliance to kill Divit, I cannot see anyone agreeing to free her back into society for a long time. It is not in the public's interest. If we can tie it up with Ian's insanity—and it will be hard to prove because it was Jason who manipulated her into doing wrong—therefore we will have to prove Jason insane as well. I do not see it happening, and it could take years.

'As for Faye, she is younger, and it can probably be proved she was not in her right mind because she had been taking cocaine on a regular basis. She will have to serve her time, which is eight years. If she survives in the jail, she may grow out of her silly ways by then. We would hope.'

The entire table of people sat stunned by James's summation of the events. James looked at them and said, 'Can you, all knowing the history of the case and events recently, tell me whether you agree or not agree with what I have said? You go first, Granny. What is your opinion?'

Granny had been gripped with James's summation, and turning to Clem, she said to him, 'I am sorry, Clem. I agree with James. It is a case also of proving Jason insane along with Ian. Otherwise, it does not make sense to free Fiona. She would have to live with people forever judging her, because news travels fast in this world, and everybody will know what she did was not acceptable.'

Percy said much the same but added, 'It is a matter for you to decide, Clem. Do you want the world to know about your grandmother? To me she was insane as well, and that is where the family had it passed along to them. This can also be recalled if let out to the public wherever your granddaughters go in the world. It will be uncomfortable for them for the rest of their lives.'

James turned to Simon and said, 'I know you came in late in the story, Simon, but do you have an opinion?'

'I think you brought it together very well, James. I am afraid I will have to agree with you on all points. One thing to remember, if Fiona behaves herself in the jail and does not get into trouble, she could be released by the pardon board for good behaviour early in her sentence. After all, she did not kill Divit.'

James looked at Simon with interest. 'That is a good deduction, Simon. However, it is entirely up to the pardon board. If we try to interfere, it could go back to the beginning, with nothing gained. I think Percy has it right. We should let it stand and hope for the best. If we muddy the waters with the story of Granny Meg, everyone will become fascinated with the story, and it will follow Fiona with "Are you like your great-grandmother?" It could become very hard for her to live through the barbs, especially for her children. Now, Clement, you have heard all of our opinions. What do you want to do?'

They could see that Clem, although interested in what everybody at the table had to say, was not yet convinced. 'But Fiona did not kill that boy. Why should she be in jail for so long? They put her in for five years. The children will be grown up before she is released.'

'It is your choice, Clem. We are only telling you our opinions.'

Clem turned to Granny and said, 'So we have not changed anything?'

'It is your choice as James said. You can arrange a lawyer, but you will find you may not get any further than you have here tonight, and your pockets will be a lot lighter. Lawyers are expensive. What you have had the benefit of tonight is a qualified lawyer in James for one and an upfront jury on the case, in the persons of Percy, Simon, Alicia, and myself. We have all got the same opinions. Take it or leave it.'

Clem turned to Alicia and asked, 'Why did you not speak tonight, Alicia? Is it your opinion as well?'

Alicia said, 'I did not want to hurt you, mainly for my Granny's sake. I have met Fiona. We were the ones who had her arrested. I am sorry, but my opinion of her is not the same opinion that you have. I found her a thoroughly nasty person throughout her dealings with us. At first the way she terrified Derek Choudhury to keep her cocaine stash safe by saying she would send messages to his faculty at the university that he had raped her and so end his promising career and ruin his life. The next for her stabbing of an innocent boy who had done her no harm.

'I do not want her set free to wander the streets and hassle the likes of Derek and Divit ever again. I do not believe you know your daughter, Mr Haskell. You still think of her as your favourite child. Wake up! Fiona is long past childhood and made those decisions for herself.

'Your other daughter, Faye, was obnoxious as well. First of all, charging that Derek Choudhury had raped her, which was entirely untrue and caused a lot of trouble between Derek and his father. When she admitted to us that she had stabbed Edward to death, she was so cheerful about it we thought she was making it up until Divit faced her. She admitted it was true but was still laughing about it as if it had only been a bit of fun on her part.

'I have brought from the office the file showing Divit and Edward, apparently dead on their bed. You think Fiona did not want to kill Divit? I know she tried her level best to kill him. The reason it was not successful was that she was not tall enough. The girls drugged the boys and then went on to kill them when they were lying drugged upon their bed.

'Because the room was so small, the one bed was pushed against the wall, with Divit lying against the wall and Edward on the outside. Faye, although smaller than Fiona, was easily able to stab Edward several times and deeply, so he died quite quickly from her efforts. Fiona's efforts failed because she had to stand at the end of the bed, or kneel on the bed, to reach Divit, who is quite tall, and stab. If you look at this picture of the boys lying on the bed, most of Fiona's efforts were wasted. There was a lot of blood, but she was not able to dig deeply enough to kill him, and she missed his heart altogether. Most of the blood is from slashes, not deep enough to kill. Most of Divit's injuries were mental. He was drugged as I said, and he was unable to move. He had to lay there and watch his younger brother die and put up with the twenty or so slashes that Fiona made on him.

'I must ask you this, Mr Haskell, who supplied the drugs? Was it you?'

Alicia waited a moment or two before she went on, and looking Clem in the face, she said, 'I do not admire your family in any way, Mr Haskell. The very thought of Fiona back on the streets is abhorrent to me, and as far as I am concerned, they were given sentences that were not nearly long enough.'

James wanted to laugh but hid his smile. He could see that everyone else at the table was amazed that Alicia had lashed out. Everything she had said to Haskell was what was in their own hearts.

He almost said, 'Hurrah, Alicia', but he bit his tongue. This was a man who had lost his family as much as how Divit lost his and was grasping at straws. He would go home tonight and rethink his family and leave them to their fate if he was as smart as everyone said he was. He wondered what he would do if faced with the same thing. 'Keep struggling,' he supposed.

The discussion ended there. They had made the effort for Granny's sake but could not find a reason to forgive what Clem's family had done to Divit.

Clem called a cab to take him back to his residential care place. They waved him goodbye, and James said to all who listened, 'Well, we told it like it is. That is all we can do.'

'Yes, we tried, James. Perhaps that will be the last of the unpaid jobs, except you still have not told us what happened today out with Paul, looking for Roland Cooke's secrets,' said Granny.

'The best I can say about it was that it was a nice day out in the country. We did not find a telephone connected to Roland. We still do not know where he moved to when he left home when he was told to go by Susan. He was a very private man, even to his nursing staff. They said they had a number to ring if a problem came up, but it was only an agency to take messages. Where do we go next?'

On Sunday evening, Paul went to see Bruce at the brothel, but he was not there. Madam answered the door and said Bruce had not been in all day, and she had no idea where he was. The day before had been his day off, but he had not come in for his duty last night and had not come in this morning. She would not loosen up any more about the man and kept denying any knowledge of what he did in his spare time. She said she did not go to the house of Dr Cooke on Saturday night; she had no idea where the doctor lived. He came to the brothel on a quarterly basis to examine the girls, and that was all she knew about him.

'I have not spoken to Paul about the police search for Bruce and his partner in crime on Sunday night. The results were not in from the chaps on duty by the time we left early this morning, and I have heard nothing since, as I have been tied up all afternoon and evening, thanks to Granny's cry for help.'

'Thank you, James, for answering the cry for help from me. I seemed to be going around in circles with Clem. One minute thinking he was a part of the crazy family and the next feeling sorry for him because he was my long-lost cousin and needed company to pull him out of the pit he had dug for himself. I will try to keep away from him for a while. He must be aware after today's talk that we are not big fans of his family. I suppose it was because I had never met them myself that I could believe he could free Fiona, because she did not kill Divit after all. But Alicia is right. She is a grown woman now. She did not have to follow her brothers any more. She made the decision.'

'Good, Granny, I am glad you can see that point. At the time of the arrest, Alicia was particularly angry about the way both women, Faye and Fiona, were so careless and laughed about the boys' stabbings,' James said.

'I am glad all the same that we may have been able to convince Clem of their culpability. I liked the way she said "Wake up" to him. No pussyfooting around. I think he needed someone to say that to him just like that. He might be cross about it now, but left alone to think about it, I hope he comes to the belief that Alicia is right.'

Alicia came back into the room and said, 'Someone had to say it. He has been hiding from the fact that his children turned out to be so terrible, probably because before the journals came along, he had no one else but himself to blame for them, and they did turn out nasty, didn't they?'

Granny turned to Simon, 'How are you keeping up, Simon? Is your brother coming in the morning to check you over?'

'Not tomorrow, Granny. He has a heavy operating schedule, but he is sending a nurse to redo my bandage and make sure the wound is okay.'

'Good, you have looked much better tonight, almost back to normal, I would say, with your insightful comment to Clem,' commented Percy.

'Well, I feel chuffed about it then. The old head was not affected after all.' Simon grinned. 'I wondered about it for a while because I could not stay awake. It must have been the painkiller treatment they gave me to swallow.'

'It is good to see you awake and looking better, and that was a good comment you made. Why didn't I think of it?' James said.

'I think you did well on the spur of the moment,' said Granny. 'It sounded as if you had spent days on it, and I know you had no time to prepare it.'

'Something still there from my law school training then, Granny?

'Definitely, James. You have a good retentive memory. That is always a bonus.'

'Hooray for something. You have been very quiet tonight, Alicia, or should I say counsellor? What is on your mind?'

'I keep thinking of the funeral for Iris on Friday and feel so sad. She was too young to die so soon, and I will always remember her. She never complained of her fate. She accepted it. I think that is true fortitude for her and an example for everybody else.'

'Where is her funeral being held, Alicia?' asked Granny.

'In St Francis, the Catholic cathedral in the main centre.'

'Do you think we should all go?'

'No, Granny, James and I will go. It could take up a big part of the day, so the rest of you will have to keep the office going. We do not want to go broke because we are all away and do not want the clients to get cantankerous with us as we have only just come back after five weeks of being closed up.'

CHAPTER TWENTY-THREE

The week went quickly, with everybody catching up with jobs. Alicia was coming into the office mid-morning after she got over the morning sickness, so Granny had been coming in her place to fill in until she arrived.

James went in to the office early on Friday to check jobs for the day and then home again to be ready to go with Alicia to the cathedral for the funeral beginning at ten o'clock. They walked to the cathedral as it was just around the corner from the office and home and took their places in the unfamiliar church.

After the long service, the guests were invited to the hall next to the church for a cup of tea. James and Alicia elected to go. They had not intruded on Bharat and Jamel during the service, so they wanted to pay their respects.

The hall was crowded with people to their astonishment, and as they stood wondering what to do next, they were greeted by a tall nun, asking how they knew Iris Kumar. They explained that they had met her only a short time ago but immediately struck up a friendship.

The nun said, 'You have possibly heard then of Sister Angeline from the Indian orphanage?' When they nodded, she said, 'I am Sister Josephine. Sister Angeline was my older sister by fifteen minutes.' She saw that they were surprised at this and, laughing, said, 'Our parents were deeply devout and went out to India for a spell doing charity work amongst the poor. However, the climate was not good for my mother's health, and they had to come home again. After my sister and I left school, our parents decided to take us for a visit to India as a graduation present. I'm so pleased to meet some of Iris's friends. I think of her as family, through Angeline's involvement over the years with her. We were visiting the Sunday service at the church of St John and had a tour through the orphanage attached to it because my parents had been contributing to it from the time of their earlier time there. My sister never came home. She became a nun especially to serve in that particular orphanage. She said when we asked why, "I feel as if I have come home, and my previous life in England was only a lead up to it."

'She was adamant that she wanted to be there, and the priest organised it for her to become a nun. She never wavered in her intention and took holy orders and never left the orphanage again.

'It was Angeline who discovered Iris in the cardboard box on the steps on the church. She heard dogs snuffling at the box when she went out to pick flowers for the altar and shooed them away and went to pick up the box to dispose of it and found the newborn baby. She called for help, and the other nuns came running. Iris became their little baby. A child for each of them that the nuns would never have. My sister, in particular, grew very fond of her. Part of the orphanage rules not written down was, "Do not grow too fond of the children. One day they will leave."

'You will know the timing of Iris leaving to get married, and she and Bharat sailed here where my father helped establish them.

My parents would have done anything for Iris as Angeline's letters were always full of her. To them she was the grandchild they would never have for themselves.

'Iris and Bharat have paid back over time all that they borrowed and have kept up donations to the orphanage so that there would be no hungry days as Iris experienced. They have been very generous. They were hardworking and became successful in their tailoring business almost at once and helped so many other immigrants to settle in when they arrived in this country.'

'When and why did you decide to join the church as your sister did?' Alicia asked.

'I told you we were twins—identical twins—and how Angeline thought also was the way I thought, like we were one person. I also felt the pull of the orphanage, but our mother was not well, and I could not leave her to die on her own. So I came back here and waited until after her death to join the order. It is not an orphanage this time. I am a teacher in early education, and I love what I do.'

'You are not wearing the black and white that we recognise as a nun's outfit,' observed James.

'Things have changed over the years. We no longer wear that stifling outfit. Rather, we have modernised, or those in many orders have. Those in closed order still wear it, but on a hot day, I am glad I do not have to. My parents were very devout, so it is no wonder the church called both of us, and I have been happy in my choice. Nuns have more freedom nowadays than in the past.'

Just then, Bharat came over to them. He kissed Sister Josephine and Alicia on the cheek and shook the hand that James held out to him.

Before they could say anything, Bharat said, 'Jamal and I will be moving into the unit at the end of the week. The paperwork for the house has gone through successfully. I look forward to helping with anything that comes up about it. I think you will be very happy there. The only furniture we will remove is Iris's chair and her bed. We would like to keep them for a while in memory of her.

'Will you let us know when your baby arrives? I would like to come and see him. Iris told me he is the spitting image of you, James. I would like to come and see if Iris was right. To date she has never been wrong.'

'Bharat, I hope that will not be the only visit from you. Please come whenever you need to talk to someone. Do not bottle yourself up in the apartment trying to get over your sorrow. Remember, you have friends who would welcome your company. We would like to be amongst them,' said Alicia sincerely.

Bharat smiled at Alicia. 'That is a nice way to put it, Alicia. I have promised Iris I will not lock myself away. It may be some time until I come to terms with her loss, but when I do, I will remember your invitation.'

He kissed Alicia again and shook James's hand and turned to the nun and said, 'I will see you on Sunday, Sister Josephine.'

He moved to the next people waiting to greet him. Alicia looked around for Jamal and saw him talking to a group of young adults. She pointed him out to James, and they excused themselves from Sister Josephine and moved over to hug Jamal, who hugged back fiercely and said, 'Thanks for coming.'

They left then to return to the office. On the way back, James said, 'We are going to miss this closeness to everything. It has been such a pleasure walking back and forth between the office and home. I feel each day we are getting exercise even at a low level, but it has kept us fit.' He gave a laugh and continued, 'I hope little Joey is going to approve of the move and appreciate what we are doing for him.'

'Bharat seems to believe absolutely that Iris was right, and we will have a son. It is wonderful to know that he is going to look like you, James. It is what I want in a son,' she said, hugging his arm.

'As long as our daughter looks like you, Alicia, I will be happy.'

'I feel so lucky, James. I know it was dreadful when we had the fire, but we seem to have got over it much quicker than I expected. Being given a house has a lot to do with it. We are all getting along together in Percy's house with the addition of Simon. Percy seems so happy to have him with us, and I am pleased for Percy.'

'I am too, Alicia. He is such a good chap and partner. I do not know what we would do without him. Also, he seems to have become part of Granny's family.'

Alicia laughed. 'Including Simon too now. She is a rare person, our granny.'

When they reached the office, Ken said Paul Morris had been waiting for some time to talk to James.

They went directly to the boardroom because they knew Granny would be giving Paul a cup of tea and a snack, and sure enough, they were sitting and chatting. Paul looked up at James and Alicia and said, 'No, I have not joined the partnership. You just cannot get away without one of Granny's cups of tea.'

Alicia and James joined him at the table. 'To what do we owe this visit, Paul? Did you want to get out of your office for a breather?' joked James.

'I was bringing you some old files to work on and report that we have found Bruce from the brothel, who was away for the weekend in Bournemouth, catching up with old friends. His story was collaborated by said friends, saying Bruce had stayed over the whole weekend.'

'Oh dear, so that idea is dead in the water. Who else can we blame for Susan and Roland Cooke's demise? Perhaps they shot each other,' said James.

'I do not think that was possible,' said Alicia, 'Because the *Balbir* was in port, do you think it is possible that Pieter came back from Poland on it and he shot the Cookes? Susan did mention she tried to ring Sacha, and there was no answer. Perhaps he was out with Pieter and did not take the call. I know this is way out, but we are short on possibilities. Shall I try and ring Sacha now?'

'It would not hurt, Alicia,' said Paul. 'We are short on possibilities at the moment, and it could eliminate them before we go on looking for someone else. The test with Bruce's photo around the street and with dog walkers came up blank. We are still waiting on ballistics for the type of bullet they took from Simon and the Cookes. Apparently, it is not the usual bullet taken in similar cases and has the staff flummoxed at the moment. I should hear soon what sort of gun it is. What they do know is, the gun used was the same in both cases. The bullets were the same. At the moment, they are trying older guns. Nothing modern fits.'

'Well, I will try the call to Sacha to eliminate him and his brother.' She searched the index for a number. It was over three months since she last called him. Eventually coming up with a number, she called it and waited for an answer. Besides a 'Leave a message' spoken in Sacha's accent, there was no answer. She said, 'I will not leave a message. I will keep trying every hour or so. If he is at work, perhaps he cannot answer his phone, but he should be finishing up and going to his rooms within an hour or two.'

James had a thought. 'Let's try a what-if story. First of all, I will call in Percy and Simon. Did Simon come in to the office, Granny?'

'Yes, he is on light duties for a day or two or until over the weekend at least. I will get them to come in.'

James waited until Percy and Simon were seated and said, 'I want you all to hear my what-if story. Alicia checked up when Marta was missing and confirmed the *Balbir* was in port, sailing on the tide at midnight the day Marta was picked up by Bruce.

'Alicia confirmed the next day that the ship had sailed on time. Now what if Pieter had arrived on the ship with the purpose of seeing Marta again? He had been very concerned previously as he had thought Marta a lovely, innocent girl. It was time she would be going home to Poland, so he wanted to make sure that Susan had kept her promise that she would go home when her au pair duties came to an end at the end of three months.

'When he tried to contact Marta, he learnt the story of the abduction and, for whatever reason, started to follow Roland Cooke. He had picked up a gun on the ship or brought an old Russian gun from home. I am certain they would be readily available in Poland. When he was in your street, Percy, he saw Roland get out of his car and took a shot at him. Roland ducked back into his car and drove off, because the shot hit Simon, not Roland, as it had been intended.

'Pieter then gave up the chase and went to the Cookes' house and waited. He had sent a text message earlier, saying he wanted to meet Roland at the house. Roland had no idea who the text message was from but turned up out of curiosity. I think Roland was aware he was being followed but did not know who it was.

'When the argument started in Saturday evening, Pieter blamed Roland for corrupting Marta. As yet, we do not know who told him, but I suspect Sacha, his brother, at this stage of the what-if. It may have been another sailor or, even possibly, Bruce, you never know. It would have been Pieter's third journey, and he would have been friendly with the other men on board by this stage. Don't tell me that the men on board were not in on the fact that girls come in and girls go out. I can imagine there is a lot of gossip between the girls and the men.

'He would have been angry that Marta had joined the girls, albeit one on one with Roland, and not aware that Susan was not in the act—she too was a bystander—he included her on the people he had to get rid of, in his mind, to rescue Marta. I could see that one of the reasons why Susan was included was because the corrupting was going on in her house, virtually under her nose, even when she was at home but in another room. Even we were amazed when we realised that. So that is the end of my what-if. Anyone up for commenting?'

Simon was the first voice heard. 'No one really asked me why I was out the front of the house when I was shot. I admit I did not remember for a few days. I was so full of drugs for one thing and another, but it has gradually come back to me. It was when you said Dr Roland Cooke that my ear pricked up. That was the name a man said on the intercom before I was shot, something about being followed and that he wanted to speak to James Armstrong or Percy Gray about it. He apologised at calling at the house because the office was closed. So I went out to see what he looked like, and I heard the bang loudly a second before the bullet hit me. I knew it was not him that shot but someone behind him in a car.

'I also heard him get into his car and drive swiftly away, and another car followed, then came back down the street slowly before speeding away again. So the bullet was not meant for me.'

James leant forward and asked, 'Did you see either person properly?'

'Not really. I know I am supposed to take note, but I was too busy getting off the ground and skittering away to hide in the shrubbery when I saw one of the cars coming back down the street. By then, I was having trouble staying awake, and soon after, first Alicia found me and then the police and then the ambulance. But I am not sure which order they came. I was going in and out by that time with the loss of blood.'

'Did you get the make of the car, Simon?' asked his father.

'Not even that, Dad. Sorry.'

'Don't be sorry, lad. We were so glad to see that you were still breathing by the time we got to the hospital. We were all so shocked. We have Alicia to thank for calling the ambulance and the police so quickly. I believe she was trying to keep up with Granny's record at the time. She was carrying an umbrella as a weapon.'

Their laughter was so loud Granny, with a big smile, turned to Alicia and said, 'I am glad you have still got the brains you were born with. I sometimes wonder about the rest of them.'

James, whose laugh was the loudest, leant over and kissed both women and said, 'I am glad they are on our side', which started the laughter up once more.

'So we have proved that Roland Cooke was being followed, but the shooter was not an experienced shot.'

'Alicia, could you try Sacha's number again, please?' asked James.

She dialled the number and waited, but nothing happened. The number went to voicemail again.

'I think it is time to check if Sacha is okay. Susan told us a week ago that he was not answering. Perhaps he is having a holiday at home in Poland and does not know what his brother is up to. I had thought that he might be helping Pieter, but if he has been gone that long, he left before Pieter arrived. The other thing is that Pieter did not go back home on the same ship that sailed a week earlier when Marta was still here.'

'Alicia, will you check if a Polish or Russian ship is in dock, please?'

'Kate, can you ring the management of the new big grey building next to the railway station? You must know it. You lived close by for the last few years.'

'Yes, James, it has been named the Orbit Inn. It is not a big plain grey place any more. It has become the place to stay when you are in town, with rooms upstairs and shopping on the ground floor.'

'The old town is looking up, and I heard today that it is official. Where the bookshop and house were is to become a cruise centre with restaurants and shops and apartments upstairs and offices above the apartments. With all that advertising, I presume you can get a phone number from it, Kate.'

'I have it now, James. Do you want to speak or shall I?'

James held his hand out for the phone and said, 'Good afternoon, my name is James Armstrong. Is there anyone who could tell me if the building has reached completion stage? I want to speak to someone on the building team.'

He listened for a while and closed up Kate's phone and handed it back and announced, 'The building was opened before Christmas, and all staff working on it was dispersed before the shopping centre part of it was opened up.

'It looks as if Sasha has gone home and went before Christmas. We were away so that is why he did not come to say goodbye. He did say he wanted to go home for Christmas, and it sounds like he got his wish.'

'Why is his phone still answering?' asked Kate. 'Someone else must be recharging it. I wonder if Pieter is using it now.'

'Good thinking, Kate. Alicia, would you ring the number again and leave a message for Pieter to ring you back. He may fall for it. He does not have many friends around here, if that is where he is. First, can you tell us if there is another possible sailing soon from this port?'

'Yes, there is another sailing due this evening, at midnight again because of the high tide at that time. They would not give out any information on passengers, for privacy's sake, they told me. You might have to follow that one up, Paul. I have written all the details down for you.'

'Thanks, Alicia. It sounds a possibility. I have been wondering about the car Pieter possibly hired, or does anyone believe it is

Bruce's car and he is letting Pieter do all his dark work for him?' He gave a grimace. 'I have not let Bruce out of my story yet. He seems to fit the picture too well,' said Paul.

Percy said, 'It must be the policeman in you, Paul. I think Bruce is still in the picture as well. What about the car that Alicia got the plates on her camera?'

Paul sighed and said, 'I had forgotten to get them followed up. I have been so busy in the past few days. I do not know whether I am coming or going. I will ring the forensic department and see if they have anything for me and also see if the result for the street cameras picked anything up.'

He went off to a corner to make his calls, and they could see they had come up with something by the look on Paul's face.

He smiled at Percy. 'That policeman's hat does work, Percy. The car that someone fired at Simon in your street belongs to …' He paused.

Then Percy said, 'Bruce.'

'Right Percy. It was Bruce's car but an unknown driver. Bruce was not driving it.'

Alicia had left the message for Pieter, and shortly after, it rang. Pieter was on the line, somewhere locally. Alicia did not answer the call but allowed it to ring out.

She said, 'We seem to be getting places. I will bet anyone who wants to take it that if you went down to the wharf and looked over that ship, you will find your killers, because I believe Bruce will be leaving as well.'

'I think it is time I went back to my office and rallied the troops,' said Paul.

'Can we come too, Paul?' said Percy and Simon.

'I would like to face up to this Pieter,' said Simon.

Alicia laughed. 'He is only a boy straight out of school, Simon. Not worth your muscle. Bruce is the organiser and has been able to sway Pieter to do what he himself would like to do, but he is too much of a coward and had to get Pieter to do his dirty work. You will see it as soon as you are face to face with them. We do not know Pieter, but we admire his brother Sacha. He is a really good bloke, as the Australians amongst us would say.'

James had been quiet for a while and said, 'I think we have it, ladies and gentlemen. It all makes sense. Thank you, all, for participating in our what-if of the day. Come back on Monday, and we will try it again on another case. You said when you came in, Paul, that you have four cold cases for us?'

'I wish you the best of luck with them. We could not work them out. But then we could not work out the other four cold cases, and you solved them very quickly. Are you coming with me? Percy and Simon, it is time to catch a ship.'

'We will leave your dinners in the oven, Percy and Simon. I will be fast asleep when you come home,' said Alicia cheerily.

'And I will hear the story tomorrow over breakfast as I will be fast asleep beside Alicia.'

'Simon, do not overdo things, you are still recuperating' turning to James and Alicia, Granny said 'I will probably beat you all. It has been a very long day at the office. I need my eight hours sleep.'

Ken looked at Kate and said, 'I think those three make a lot of sense, Kate. Do you agree?

'I am with you, Ken. We will see you all on Monday if all goes well. It is great to have you all back.'

Printed in the United States
By Bookmasters